PENGUIN B[ ]

1519

BITTER HONE[ ]

and other sto[ ]

ALBERTO MORAVIA

Bitter Honeymoon

AND OTHER STORIES

ALBERTO MORAVIA

Penguin Books

IN ASSOCIATION WITH SECKER & WARBURG

Penguin Books Ltd, Harmondsworth, Middlesex
AUSTRALIA: Penguin Books Pty Ltd, 762 Whitehorse Road,
Mitcham, Victoria

—

Cortigiana stanca (*Tired Courtesan*) was first published in 1927, *Inverno di malato*
(*A Sick Boy's Winter*) in 1930, *L'imbroglio* (*The Imbroglio*) in 1937, *La caduta*
(*The Fall*) in 1940, *L'amante infelice* (*The Unfortunate Lover*) in 1943, *Ritorno
al mare* (*Back to the Sea*) in 1945, *L'ufficiale inglese* (*The British Officer*) in 1946,
and *Luna di miele, sole di fiele* (*Bitter Honeymoon*) in 1952
First published in English by Secker & Warburg 1954
Published in Penguin Books 1961

—

A Sick Boy's Winter is translated by Baptista Gilliat Smith, *Bitter Honeymoon* by
Frances Frenaye, and the remainder by Bernard Wall, who made the selec-
tion in consultation with the author

Made and printed in Great Britain
by C. Nicholls & Company Ltd.

CONTENTS

TIRED COURTESAN

Slowly, closing the door behind him with a thrust of the shoulders and keeping his eyes fixed on his mistress, the young man entered the room. On his way through the streets, his imagination had been persistently assailed by a growing desire to conjure up a picture of an overripe Maria Teresa, a Maria Teresa with ponderous breasts, an abundant stomach that quivered on the slackened joints of the groin, and pasty, shapeless thighs – a Maria Teresa on the threshold of old age, whom it would be easy to give up, now that he had no money left to keep her. These visions of a body in decline, added to and touched up to the point of caricature by his complacent imagination, had given him a measure of courage as he walked from street to street with anguished mind and fists deep in his empty pockets.

But now that he was seated on the deep divan in the sitting-room with his mistress on his knee, he perceived that the picture he had deliberately conjured up with a view to their imminent separation melted away when face to face with reality. His induced repugnance for her body, which he had purposely visualized as tired and flabby, was now a thing of the past; and so was his plan for a calm separation – 'Maria Teresa, I've come to tell you . . .'

For today, as on every other day, he was assailed by renewed desire. He looked at her dear head with its hard, fine features and perceived he had been mistaken. There was nothing over-ripe or tired about her. A soft white cloth enfolded her head like a turban. Her oval face beneath it was encrusted with make-up. She was not long out of her bath and had draped her damp body in a huckaback wrap of the kind thrown over the shoulders of exhausted prize-fighters. But on her calm face there was a look of triumph. Seeing her so careless of her own nakedness and any unfavourable impression it might make on him (her wrap had slipped from her shoulders on to her lover's knee, but she had not bothered to replace it; she had merely bent her head to one side and lit a cigarette) – an attitude so far removed from his miserly calculations about middle age and youth (what do the years matter? her shameless indifference seemed to say, what does time matter to a body consecrated by so much payment and admiration?), and so unlike the selfish picture he had tried to form – seeing all this, the young man was invaded by a deep uneasiness. 'This is the last time I shall ever come to see her,' he could not help thinking with regret as he avidly embraced her listless limbs.

Though he did not admit it even to himself, he would have loved her more, a thousand times more, wholeheartedly – albeit with a love confused with compassion (You're old, my poor Maria Teresa, but you still have me) – if he had felt beneath his restless hands a flabbier flesh, a skin more withered and with the bloom no longer on it. All his love would have gone out to a poor ageing woman whom he could have held, though not without disgust, upon his knee and close to his own breast. True, her breasts, which with every breath seemed to be vainly trying to regain the level of the bust from which age had driven them, her powerful and comfortable haunches numbing his knees, her huge opulent back, an ancient desert of flesh, no longer divided by the furrow of the spine – all these reassured him that the woman was past her prime. Marité was finished, he thought as he gazed at her; youth and beauty were finished for her. But when he lifted his eyes from the seated body and caught sight of the hard, firm face under the bright sheen of make-up, he mistrusted his eyes; and the thought of leaving this still desirable woman to other lovers filled him with childish and greedy rage.

'It's time we were going out,' he said at last when, sated and disillusioned, he pushed her away, 'so get dressed.' She rose to her feet at once, folding the wrap round her with a theatrical gesture. 'No. I won't get dressed,' she said after a slight pause. 'Tonight we'll eat at home. . . . Besides, I've . . . well, I've got something to say to you.'

Now she was smiling, seemingly pleased with herself, with

much the same embarrassed and treacherous smile she might have worn were she going to forestall her lover's intentions and be the one to speak the words of dismissal. Troubled in spite of himself, the young man asked her what had happened. She hesitated and then admitted that she was expecting an extremely important telephone call. 'Here it comes,' he couldn't help thinking, as if in mortal fear of being turned away by the mistress he had just been planning to jilt. Who could it be who was going to telephone? he asked after a pause. A man who once loved her very much, answered Maria Teresa, still hesitant. When? Many years ago; but she had met him in the street yesterday and they had recognized each other and talked of the old days, and she had gathered that he had become pretty rich, though whether by inheritance or his own efforts she did not know. But the young man had stopped listening, once more a prey to irrational and melancholy jealousy. So there had once been another Maria Teresa, he thought, a young and modest girl, without that tired smile and the wrap that was always slipping, and other men had made love to her before him.

He heard the door shut and gave a start. The woman had gone out of the room. He spent the next ten minutes without moving or making a sound, racked by agonizing doubts.

She returned carrying the tea things. There was another silence as she set the cups, teapot, and biscuits on the table. The young man could not help smiling, though against his will, for it awakened a perverse love in him to see her paying such minute attention to her every action, no longer a mistress, but a housewife. When she asked him how much sugar he wanted, he suddenly felt a strong desire to hug her. 'Two lumps, darling; two lumps,' he answered nervously. The warmth of the drink thawed the cold that had gripped him. He munched the toast and gulped down the great draughts of boiling tea; and while he ate and drank he kept his eyes on the figure of the woman bending over the steaming teapot. And so, in silence, his jealous uneasiness evaporated like damp from a drenched coat spread out on a stove to dry.

Scarcely had they finished sipping their tea when dusk descended on them. They remained still and silent in the grey twilight, their eyes fixed on the empty cups. Then Maria Teresa got up, lit a lamp and sat down near the telephone from which the voice from her youth would emerge, as from the dark cave of a Sibyl. The young man got up too and took a turn round the room. In a corner there was a cabinet; he absent-mindedly opened a drawer and let an uninterested eye fall on the contents. What he saw was face after face in higgledy-piggledy disorder like a pack of cards when the game is over and accounts have been settled. Suddenly interested, he sat down by the cabinet and pulled out a bunch of the faded photographs. 'Well, well,' he muttered, and looked the woman up and down. 'So many of them . . . my predecessors.'

Without uttering a word or giving any sign that his indiscretion annoyed her, the woman kept her eyes upon him tranquilly and without emotion, and this hurt him like sharp steel probing an anaesthetized wound. She should not be so calm, he thought indignantly; anyone but Maria Teresa would have snatched the photographs away and shut them up again in the cabinet. All those bloodless portraits stared at him with the pinched look of prisoners emerging at long last into the light of day. It had been as pointless to bury them in that cabinet as in memory; now that they had returned to life they must seem to her inseparable from the time, long ago, when they had lain beside her young body. The young man held them all in his ironical hands, the years and the men; and they accused her. Of what? Of being no longer the girl she once was. Witnesses, judge, everyone necessary was present; the trial could begin.

Prisoner, do you recognize this man? When you met him you were eighteen. Your hair was piled on top of your head and puffed out over your uncovered brow. Your starched man's collar chafed your neck and chin; your glorious young bust was held up with whalebone corsets and peeped out rosily beneath the lace cascades of your chemise. Your body curved and bent lithely within the spirals of your skirt, and you had a superb way of running and kicking up your heels, and the roving eye could never venture higher than your boots buttoned half-way up your calves. But amid the flowers and tobacco smoke of the café-concerts and to the illusory and melancholy sound of the can-can, the dancing-girls rhythmically lifted their black-stockinged legs as high as the curls on their foreheads, with red garters and a rustling, swirling foam of lace that could never be too thick or too deep around their thighs. You were eighteen and there wasn't a trace of make-up on your cheeks, which in moments of shyness could blush like a rose; your lips weren't painted, but bright and pouting and claiming attention; your eyes had no salve nor false lashes, but were innocent, and at the slightest weariness were surrounded with a give-away circle. With this man you danced the last waltz and the first tango. And what about this one? And this?

The young man had taken out some of the photographs and was showing them to the woman, pressing for names and dates, for all the world as if they were evidence for the prosecution against a prisoner reluctant to confess any share in guilt. And she, like a prisoner in the dock, craned her neck and fixed her eyes on those forgotten faces, examining the faded features and consenting to name them in a bored petulant voice. B. was an actor and now had a job in the cinema. That other one was a count and had been killed in the war. The next was S., a banker, who had since gone smash and was dead too, she thought. Last of all he pointed to a fat man with heavy eyebrows wearing a dinner jacket. Who on earth was he? A waiter?

For the first time some gleam of emotion broke through her apathy and indifference. He was a magnate from Milan, she said wistfully, and the richest of them all. 'He gave me a villa,' she went on dreamily, 'a lovely villa, with two storeys and a garden.' She looked straight in front of her with fascinated eyes, as if she could make out the structure of her former dwelling, stone by stone. Then, after a moment's silence and as if talking to herself: 'Yes, indeed, I'd be very rich by now if I'd kept everything I've been given.' The young man said nothing, for it seemed to him monstrous that she should have regrets; she had lived a whole life, he was thinking, and all she could do was long for the money she had enjoyed only too well and wish that she had been prudent and miserly. He watched her get up with a murmur of 'How cold it is' and move with a shudder of her whole body to where she could stand with her back to the stove. The trial was over. Prisoner, have you anything to add? You haven't? Then off with you. You're condemned – condemned to grow old, to wrinkles and grey hair, to passion spent and frozen memories. Everything was over really – houses, lovers, parties, dresses, and smiles. Maria Teresa was sinking among the ashes of her past like a ship in the night.

He began another search in the cabinet. There were some Japanese prints whose obscene impassivity made them seem almost ritualistic; some pornographic photographs of the kind sold in seaports and doubtful suburbs of great cities; old picture postcards of the streets and squares of Paris, Berlin, Vienna, and Petersburg, with all the people who a few years later were driven mad, ruined, slaughtered or scattered, photographed in the prime of life strolling along the pavements with their tiny hats, umbrellas, and horse-carriages; finally, there were packets and packets of love-letters tied together with discoloured ribbon, the handwriting still looking pretentious, though the ink had faded and had never since seen the light. The young man merely glanced at all these old things; what he drew out and weighed in the palm of his hand was a tiny revolver of nickelled steel and mother-of-pearl.

'And this,' he asked, 'what's this doing here?'

'It's to defend myself,' she answered as if it were perfectly normal, unhurriedly pushing aside the muzzle of the gun that he had jokingly levelled at her forehead. 'Anyway,' she went on after a moment with self-satisfied resignation, 'I'm sure I'll come to a violent end.' She spoke as if she meant it. Obviously her stale and disillusioned imagination – that of an adventuress – was flattered by the idea of a modern tragedy played out between four walls. It was the only thing left – the detective-story ending. Dawn in a third-class hotel bedroom, furniture thrown all over the place, the unmade bed drenched with blood, fingerprints taken, the air stale with scent, sleep and death, and then the short newspaper story – that would be how she would end.

As she said all this her gaze alternated between the young man and the revolver, her eyes bright and alluring as if she wanted to seduce even death. Then she stopped talking about herself and told the story of a friend of hers who had been killed in mysterious circumstances two years earlier, and finished rather melodramatically, with bowed head, a glance at her own seated body, and a deep sigh. 'That's how I shall end up too.'

But the young man had begun laughing. 'What an absurd idea, Marité,' he exclaimed, and, throwing the revolver back into the cabinet, he sat down beside her and put his arm round her waist. No, he went on, maliciously reassuring, she wouldn't die a violent death; she'd die in her bed of old age and sickness. She wasn't a *femme fatale*, and she shouldn't delude herself into thinking she was. In any case, such women didn't exist any more except on the movies.

As he made these unkind remarks he tried to embrace her, but she pushed him away firmly, barely concealing her aversion. 'Now you're being beastly,' she muttered through clenched teeth. She got up and went to fetch a bottle of cognac and a glass. 'Old and lonely,' he went on repeating. He saw her shrug her shoulders with indifference; and, lifting her eyebrows and lowering her lids to shield her eyes from the smoke of the cigarette stuck to her lower lip, she uncorked the bottle and poured out a drink. It was at this moment that the telephone began to ring.

She took her time putting down the glass and lifting up the receiver, but she asked 'Who is it?' immediately. 'Oh.' Her voice was disappointed. 'His secretary?' Then she listened in silence, looking anxiously and inquiringly around as if seeking a pretext for his explanations. 'You mean I can't speak to him?' She asked at last. 'Not even for a minute, only a minute?' But obviously the person at the other end of the wire had hung up. 'Only for a minute,' she repeated and then dreamily, slowly, put the receiver down and looked straight in front of her.

'Well,' asked the young man, 'have you got what you wanted?' At this question she stared and looked at him curiously, as if seeing him for the first time; but she didn't answer. The liqueur glass wasn't quite empty, she sipped it, examined the bottom and said slowly as she rose to her feet: 'I must go and get the supper.' One following the other, they left the smoky sitting-room.

In the dark passage he took her by the shoulders, drew her to him and kissed her. He thought she responded and returned the kiss, if not with affection, at least with desire, as if she needed comforting and had fallen back on the reaction she knew best. He even thought she was trembling. But when they reached the kitchen he saw that she bent over the stove and lit the flame with her usual hard, reflective face.

This was the first time they had eaten in the flat, and the young man, who had no idea of Maria Teresa's domestic abilities, foresaw a cold supper bought in the shops. So he was astonished to see the woman girding herself to do the cooking. The kitchen looked as if it was never used. There were no stains or cracks on the white-tiled walls; there was no trace of smoke in the chimney and the three iron stoves looked as if they had never been lit; the salt and pepper, the sugar, cinnamon, and saffron could never have been taken from the porcelain containers ranged along the ledge, nor the bronze and aluminium pans from the hooks where they hung gleaming like hats on a hat-stand. The kitchen was virginal and icy. You could see that the house was always deserted at dinner-time, its mistress always out, and no cook or other servants. It was a model kitchen of the kind to be seen in the windows of household furnishing shops; all that was lacking to complete the picture was the tin cook with static profile and fixed, glacial eyes going from one oven to the next with the stiff little steps of an automaton.

However, with perfect composure and precise, expert movements that revealed the ease of experience, Maria Teresa prepared the supper unaided. A clear herb soup, two steaks fried with breadcrumbs, spinach and potatoes, and to end up with a chocolate mousse that she had got ready in the morning and put in the icebox. Seated at the marble-topped table in the middle of the dazzling-white kitchen, the bewildered young man watched her as she busied herself at the stoves, her sleeves rolled up, her face harder and more concentrated than ever. He watched her take a good pinch of salt, throw it carefully into the soup and then try the flavour with the tip of the wooden spoon raised to her parted lips – the lips which a few minutes before in the passage had yielded to his. Every now and again during these practical operations her ill-fastened wrap fell open in front; she was then a naked woman bending over the pans with ladle in one hand and fork in the other, exposing her breasts to the steam from the food while her stomach was tinged by the red of the flame.

The lamp hanging in the middle of the room cast its light on the shining majolica tiles which flashed back its reflection. The room was a cube of white light with the two lovers inside like two well-preserved corpses in a block of mortuary ice. Within these four sides Maria Teresa moved to and fro, while from his seat at the marble-topped table the young man watched her. He was disconcerted, almost shocked. Now and again he lowered his eyes to the lozenge-tiled floor and felt as if on this chessboard he had lost his hard, attractive-faced queen. He was not a postman or a porter, he thought, who could pour out a hearty drink and then drag the cook complete with ladles and apron on to his lap. This was not the woman he loved. But Maria Teresa was already sitting at the table, boasting of her prowess as a housewife.

They ate in silence without looking at one another. In the end he said that to see her cooking you would think that she had never done anything else in her life. 'I have done so many things,' she said tonelessly, keeping her eyes on her plate. The wrap opened again and he could see her breasts quivering with every movement, as if animated by a life of their own.

There was another long silence. 'I told you that that gentleman I was talking to on the telephone,' she began at last, wiping her mouth with the napkin and putting it back on her naked knees, 'used to love me very much . . . As a matter of fact, he was the first . . . I was sixteen . . . ' On hearing this, the young man felt a renewal of the confused jealousy he had experienced earlier, but this time it was mingled with a bitter and melancholy feeling of pity. So it was really true: Maria Teresa had been sixteen; she had really passed through that springtime; she had laughed, wept, danced, and loved and had enjoyed her salad days: now she was silently gathering the breadcrumbs with uncertain fingers and appeared tired.

'He's very rich,' she went on, 'but he refuses me even the little money I ask for.' The young man was looking at her and felt he ought to be moved, but he did not know exactly what misfortune to be moved by. 'Are you so in need of money?' he asked at last, gently. She immediately gave a loud, dry, scornful laugh. 'Am I in need of money? Of course I am . . . desperately.'

'But what for?' he insisted. 'To buy clothes, or to travel?'

He saw her shake her head, rather embarrassed. No; she

needed money to leave the city and retire to the country. She was tired of living in this disordered way with too many people around. She wanted to be alone in a little town – why not the one where she was born? – to live alone in a little house with a few rooms and a garden. As she spoke she bent her head to one side and caressed her naked shoulder with her cheek.

At this point he interrupted her with an incredulous smile. A garden? And flowers too, he supposed. Yes, she answered; flowers too, of course. Why? No reason, said the young man, and, rising to his feet, he began pacing the room. 'But as he isn't willing to give me the money,' she ended up in a high quavering voice, 'I'll have to do without.'

Supper was over. Maria Teresa got up in her turn, collected the plates and tipped them with a clatter into the sink. The young man stood, depressed, watching the woman who, with her usual concentrated look and picking her teeth with her long, sharp finger-nails, was staring without disgust at the jet of water falling on the dirty plates and dislodging the congealed grease and other remains of supper from the fancy dishes.

Later, during the night, he was aware that she had turned over to the side of the bed and curled up as if to go to sleep. So he said he hoped she would sleep well, and got up to go. She had been his for more than two months, and now he had no money left he had no choice but to leave her. But just as he was carefully freeing his limbs from the folds of the sheets he suddenly realized she was crying. She was no longer curled up but flat on her back with her arm over her eyes like a baby. It was too dark to see the tears, but a ray of light played on the big, babyish grimace that contracted the corners of her mouth. She was weeping silently, without sobs, her tears flowing like blood from a mortal wound.

He stared at her; then he bent down, removed her arm from her eyes and asked her what was the matter. Nothing, she answered. There was nothing the matter. She was only thinking of that telephone call. He saw her lean her head on her shoulder with a gesture that seemed mournful and resigned and he heard her repeat with desolate obstinacy: 'Nothing is the matter with me.' Then after a moment she closed her eyes again and said bitterly, as if she had been caught at a street corner holding out her hand to passers-by: 'But it's hard, it's hard when you have to start begging for your living.'

The young man didn't know what to answer. He stared at her face, hard and firm again like a profile on a medallion, at her eyes deliberately shut as if to court sleep, at her white, fat shoulder under the bristly locks of hair on her neck. To see her so still made it seem as if she had never spoken; he doubted the evidence of his ears and eyes; he would have liked to see her make a crying face again and hear her whimpering voice. As he stared at her he felt he was looking at the face of existence itself, which reveals itself and speaks for a moment and then is silent and still again. His contemplation didn't last long. Then, though with an effort, he straightened up, went to the bath-room, dressed, and tiptoed back. 'I'm off, Marité. Good-bye,' he said in a loud voice.

'See you tomorrow,' she answered without opening her eyes.

He left the room and then the flat, descended the stairs and opened the front door. On the threshold he stopped and hesi-tated, listening to a nearby church bell striking in the silence of the deserted neighbourhood. 'Half past ten,' he thought. 'There's still time to look in at a cinema.' The idea appealed to him, and though he didn't know why he took to it with enthu-siasm. He now felt an insatiable longing for the promiscuous darkness of the cinema with its easy adventures and distant landscapes. To hell with Maria Teresa, he thought by way of conclusion; and, with an effort to overcome the uneasiness oppressing him, he shut the front door behind him and set off towards the centre of the city.

A SICK BOY'S WINTER

WHEN it was snowing or raining, and sun treatment impossible, the two invalids had to spend entire days lying side by side in their little room. To pass the time, Brambilla usually amused himself by teasing his room-mate, Girolamo, who was younger than himself. The boy's family had once been well off, but was now impoverished, and Brambilla, a commercial traveller and the son of a foreman builder, had gradually persuaded him during those eight months they were forced to spend together that to come from a bourgeois, or at least non-working-class, background was little less than a disgrace.

'I'm no gentleman,' he would say, sitting up in bed and turning his blue, false eyes on the mortified boy with a look of studied contempt. 'I wasn't brought up all wrapped in cotton-wool . . . When I was fifteen I was already working in the builder's yard with never a penny in my pocket, and my father wasn't a good-for-nothing, either. He owned nothing, but he had his wits about him. When he came to Milan he was only a bricklayer, but now he has a business of his own. My father is a self-made man. What have you got to say to that? Actions are what you need, not words.'

With the upper part of his body uncovered and leaning on one elbow, the boy gazed at the man with his suffering eyes. He was not aware of the game the other was playing and he felt very humiliated.

'But why blame my father for being born rich?' he asked, in a tremulous voice that betrayed his long and weary exasperation.

'It's his own fault,' Brambilla replied with a half-smile of cruel amusement. 'It's his fault. I, too, was born in fairly comfortable circumstances, but I never dreamt of living at my father's expense. You see, *I* work.'

Certain that he was in the wrong, Girolamo could think of nothing to answer, and was silent: but this was not enough to appease Brambilla, who, after mocking the father, went on to make fun of the boy's sister. In the early days Girolamo had been imprudent enough to show his friend a photograph of his sister, a pretty girl barely over twenty. He was proud of his smart elder sister and he imagined that, by showing her picture to Brambilla, he would somehow go up in the man's esteem. But his naïve supposition at once proved mistaken.

'Well?' the commercial traveller would inquire from time to time, 'and how's your little sister? Who is she flirting with now?'

'Oh! But I don't think she does flirt,' Girolamo protested, too timid to contradict the man outright.

The other would burst out laughing.

'Do you expect me to believe that? You go and tell that to somebody else, not to me. Girls like your sister all have lovers.'

A great indignation welled up in the boy. 'My sister hasn't got lovers,' he wanted to shout, but the man seemed so certain of his facts and the boy was so worn down by the atmosphere of humiliation he had endured for the last eighteen months that he even distrusted his own memory. 'Suppose she really has got a lover?' he asked himself.

'Girls like your sister all have them!' Brambilla went on. 'They look prim and proper and put on saintly airs, but as soon as Papa and Mama have their backs turned, off they rush to their lovers, and when they get there . . . As a matter of fact, I am sure your sister is the easiest kind, what with those eyes of hers and that mouth. She's always visiting men in their love-nests!'

'Why do you talk like that about someone you don't know?' Girolamo then protested.

'Why?' Brambilla replied. 'Because it's true. Take me, for example, I'd never marry a girl like your sister, not for anything in the world. Men don't marry girls like your sister.'

Without thinking how absurd these assertions were, Girolamo felt more than ever humiliated by the commercial traveller's contempt, based entirely on theory, yet he played up to him not altogether unconsciously.

'But to make up for all that, you would get my sister's beauty and intelligence.'

'What do I care about that?' Brambilla would break in. 'No! No! Better stick to your own sort.'

The boy put up with these humiliations almost without realizing it, so saturated was he with the depressing atmosphere of the sanatorium. Brambilla combined his cruelty with a sort of cheerful and complacent despotism, to which Girolamo submitted only the more readily because his mind was completely warped by illness and loneliness. Victimized as he was by others, Girolamo actually felt guilty, and was only too willing to identify himself with his oppressors. Thus he would encourage his companion's sarcasm by making remarks that were consciously ingenuous or clumsy. Occasionally he himself would bring up the subject of his family so as to experience the bitter pleasure of having it run down by the salesman: or he would show off the mannerisms of a rich, spoilt boy and even invent far-fetched stories, because he knew they would at once provoke the ready echo of Brambilla's irony. The latter, moreover, never guessed what lay behind these pathetic tricks, and immediately fell for them. Under such favourable circumstances the range of possible torments had become really quite extensive. One of Brambilla's favourite tricks was to provoke the familiarity and disdain of the subordinate staff, male nurses or cleaners, especially that of a sturdy Austrian, Joseph, who was a trained male nurse.

'Well, Joseph, can you believe it?' the salesman would begin. 'Master Girolamo wants me to marry his sister! What do you say to that, Joseph?'

'It all depends, Signor Brambilla,' answered the Austrian square-head with a knowing laugh.

'What's at the back of his mind?' the other went on. 'Perhaps the young lady has got into some sort of trouble? Perhaps she's pregnant, and they want to saddle her on me. Middle-class people are terrible. What do you think, Joseph?'

'Well, Master Girolamo must have his reasons!' sniggered the male nurse, who, if Brambilla had not egged him on, would never have dared to make fun of a patient. 'No one ever gives anything for nothing.'

'But I never said that!' Girolamo protested at this point.

'Get along with you! You do nothing but sing her praises the whole day long. Joseph, you just tell me what you'd say in my place?'

'Well, Signor Brambilla, I'd have plenty to think about.'

'But you've not seen the woman they want me to marry,' Brambilla continued. Then, turning to Girolamo: 'Show Joseph your sister's photograph! Go on. Let's see it!'

'I don't know where it is.'

'Go on! Don't act like an imbecile. You think that because Joseph isn't a bourgeois like yourself, you've got the right to make fun of him. I tell you he's worth a thousand of you.'

'I never thought of despising Joseph!' the boy protested as he reluctantly handed his sister's picture to the nurse. The latter took it with his large, red, coarse hands.

'Well, what do you think of her, Joseph?' Brambilla asked. 'Do you think she deserves a husband like me? Wouldn't you say she was one of those girls . . . Well . . . I don't know if you get my meaning, but the sort you don't marry?'

It was obvious that, despite this kind of encouragement, the nurse was reluctant to assume the insolent attitude towards the boy that would have pleased Brambilla. He looked first at Girolamo, then at the traveller, and finally, overcoming a natural tendency to be respectful, he answered: 'She's a lovely girl, Signor Brambilla, but perhaps you're right; perhaps she isn't the sort you've got to marry.'

Such impertinence was odious to the boy, but for all that it was not without a certain vanity that he pleaded so exaggeratedly for the photograph back. 'Now you've had a look at her, please, Mr Joseph, be so good as to return the photograph to me.'

He knew that by begging in this way he was placing himself and his sister at the mercy of those coarse hands. But he felt this comedy of supplication was a way of revenging himself for the humiliations the two men were inflicting on him, since it was he who was humbling himself of his own accord, and in a way that was even more cruel. The commercial traveller and the male nurse failed to discern to what extent these entreaties were false or frivolous, and interpreted them as the weakness of a delicate and spoiled youth.

'Shall I give it back to him, Signor Brambilla?' the Austrian asked, with a smile.

"Yes. Give it back to me!' Girolamo implored.

'Go on, give it to him!' the commercial traveller broke in. 'We've got no use for his sister. We've got better girls. You can tell him so yourself, Joseph, our girls are better.'

While all this teasing was just a pastime for Brambilla, it plunged Girolamo into an atmosphere of humiliation and suffering that grew gloomier every day. Yet the more he allowed himself to be drawn into it, the more desperately he clung to the game; so much so, that if anyone had asked him if he were unhappy, he would probably have replied that he wasn't. Since he had nothing to compare his life with, and lacked any clear notion of how he would have lived at home among other boys, he could not gauge the wretchedness of his condition. Gradually and almost unconsciously, he had grown accustomed to living in this stifling atmosphere, to enduring endless humiliations and to being deprived of all the attentions that had been lavished on him at home. He thought he was leading a normal life and that he was still the same person he had been eight months before. But the unnaturalness of his present frame of mind manifested itself in sudden fits of exasperation or bursts of tears, especially at night when Brambilla was asleep. Then, weeping beneath the bed-clothes, he would long desperately for his absent mother's caresses; or, in one of those fits of repentance that show that the crime one repents is non-existent, he would beg his sister, under his breath, to forgive him for all the day's cowardly concessions. Finally, worn out, he would slowly disappear into the underground tunnel of a sick man's sleep. But he found no peace in sleep. His subconscious mind teemed with images; sometimes he dreamt he was weeping and falling down on his knees to implore Brambilla's forgiveness for goodness knows what crime, but Brambilla was implacable and would drive him on, despite his frantic struggles, towards some mysterious punishment; in vain he promised to be good, to stoop to any baseness, to be obedient . . . when some dark thing would come between the two of them and the dream. In the middle of the night he would wake up, trembling from head to foot, with his forehead bathed in sweat. Then he would realize that what had awakened him was the heavy thud of a mass of fresh snow as it fell from the sanatorium roof on to the terrace; and he would soon fall asleep again.

At the beginning of January it snowed for several days running. Confined to their room, the two invalids could see the snow outside creeping down at a slight slant, and so slowly that, if you watched it carefully, it became blurred, and the monotonous whirling seemed not so much to be coming down as to be rising from the earth skywards. Behind this thick curtain, those grey and troubled spectres were the pine trees of the forest near by; the great silence that came from outside suggested how thick and widespread the snowfall was. But if for the inhabitants of the large hotels down in the valley the snow was joyful and picturesque and promised virgin snow-runs for the skiers, for the invalids it was rather what a swell is for fishermen – an irritating interruption; it was a delay in recovery. In the room, almost completely filled by the two beds, where the light was lit even in the morning and the night's stale air was never entirely dispersed, the hours dragged on interminably.

When Brambilla was tired of making fun of Girolamo, he usually began telling about his love affairs. Although physically, with his fair hair, his blue, false eyes and his red face, he looked a typical commercial traveller, through some not uncommon illusion, he thought he was an irresistible lady-killer. For Girolamo, who was hardly more than seventeen years old and quite inexperienced in such things, this was a completely new world; he was all ears and entirely gullible. If the salesman had confided to him that he was a princess's lover, Girolamo would undoubtedly have believed him. However, in all probability, Brambilla's stories were by and large true. They were nearly always about some servant girl he had seized by the waist while she was making a bed, or about little dressmakers whom he would invite to dinner, then to the cinema and finally to some hotel, or quite simply about women he had stopped in the street and left after two hours. But what was certainly untrue was the beauty of these women, the passion Brambilla knew how to kindle in them, and the contempt with which he treated them.

But always, Girolamo believed everything; his admiration for his companion grew greater and greater and he envied him those adventures. Brambilla now represented for him the ideal type whom he would make every effort to resemble.

Sometimes during these accounts Joseph would come in straight from the operating theatre, with his sleeves rolled up on his muscular arms, his hands white with plaster, and with the scissors for cutting bandages sticking out of his overall pocket. He would lean against the foot of Brambilla's bed and remain there for ten minutes or a quarter of an hour listening, sometimes laughing foolishly, often putting in a word of his own. One day when Brambilla had finished, the Austrian turned to the boy and said: 'And you, Master Girolamo, when are you going to tell us about your love affairs?'

It would have been very easy for the boy to tell the truth: 'I've never had a single love affair.' But the fear of revealing such lack of experience and of being laughed at by his sarcastic room-mate made him ashamed of telling the truth and made him assume an attitude of mystery that suggested goodness knows what unbridled excesses.

'My love affairs?' he answered blushing with a kind of coquetry. 'My love affairs aren't fit to be heard.'

Leaning on his elbow, Brambilla looked him straight in the eyes: 'Don't be a fool,' he burst out irritably in the end. 'What affairs can you have had? Only with your nurse when you were in swaddling clothes. You're still wet behind the ears. For goodness sake ... and with that face of yours ... that face!'

'Why?' the boy protested feebly. 'Do you think you're the only person to have had love affairs?'

'Who's saying that?' the other retorted. 'For instance, I feel sure Joseph has had even more affairs than I've had. Isn't that so, Joseph? You just tell him what you have to do for some of the women patients,' and Brambilla winked at the male nurse who gave a boorish laugh. 'But not you – you can't be taken seriously like Joseph. When you, with that face of yours, maintain that you have had affairs, you make even a cat laugh. Tell me, Joseph, what affairs can a young fellow like Girolamo have had?'

The nurse, who had hitherto, despite every provocation,

confined himself to making cautious, ironical remarks, could not, on this occasion, resist such an easy bait: 'Mr Brambilla,' he smiled, 'you have forgotten that Master Girolamo has won Miss Polly's heart.'

This joke about Miss Polly was one of Brambilla's favourites. Miss Polly was an English girl, hardly more than fourteen years old, who had an illness of the spine and was a private patient with a room to herself. Girolamo had made her acquaintance through her mother, who, being anxious that her daughter should have some distraction, had thought that Girolamo would make a suitable companion both on account of his age and of his family background. Such was the lack of amusements in the sanatorium that, despite the difference in their ages, Girolamo had ended by enjoying these visits and looking forward, almost anxiously, to the days fixed for their meetings. To leave his room, with whatever difficulty, to pass along the dark corridors, even in his bed, to descend to the first floor in that comfortably slow yet disquieting lift, to make an almost triumphant entry to that other room so much more spacious than his own, where everything, the flowers in their vases, the photographs, the books, the wallpaper, and even the light seemed to him, because of their novelty, festive and exciting . . . all this was for the boy, although he did not admit it to himself, as intense a pleasure as any prisoner experiences on taking his first steps outside the prison walls. But then Brambilla came on the scene and everything changed. A little teasing, a few remarks like 'Master Girolamo is going down to the nursery today!' sufficed to put an end to his innocent pleasure. He became ashamed of his friendship with Polly; he no longer found any pleasure in their games, in their almost childish conversations, and it was only out of consideration for her mother that he did not give up these visits altogether.

Consequently, Joseph's remark could not fail to wound the boy, but, resorting to the arts of defence so recently acquired, he feigned embarrassment and blushed like a girl; and this further humiliation, self-inflicted, seemed to counteract the effect of the one just suffered, and suggested, at the same time, that he had been able to win one heart at least.

But Brambilla, leaning heavily on his left side, gave him one of the ugliest possible looks and seemed completely unconvinced: 'No, not her, Joseph, not even Miss Doodle or whatever she's called. You wait till a real Englishman turns up from England, and you'll see how she'll send him packing; you'll see how Master Girolamo will be sent flying! I tell you, he's no good!'

At that moment the door opened and the maid came in with the supper tray. Joseph remembered that he had to go down to the X-ray room and went out. That evening the subject of the little English girl was not brought up again.

If at that moment anyone had asked the boy what he thought of Brambilla, he would plainly have ended by admitting that he was certainly not a man to model oneself on; if anyone had asked him to say whom he respected most, apart from considerations of affection, his father or Brambilla, the reply would have been obvious. Yet by one of those frequent contradictions between sense and sensibility, despite his contempt, the boy felt a profound attraction for his room-mate of a kind no other person had ever been able to arouse in him. On one occasion it so happened that some friends of Girolamo's family, smart people who had come up to this mountain resort for winter sports, went all the way up to the sanatorium full of smug pleasure in their own kindness and the prospect of doing a good deed, and more than certain of an enthusiastic welcome; instead of this they were received with impatient coldness by Girolamo, who was nervous and evasive, anxious above all to see them go and to return to his salesman, his poky room, and the bitter-sweet torments of those pitiless conversations. Another time his mother, a little woman with a face ruined by make-up and sorrow and with quick jerky movements, a woman so small that it seemed impossible for Girolamo to be her son – which she herself, if with a certain affectation never ceased to marvel at – arrived on Christmas Day. All decked in furs, her arms laden with presents, she struggled to look cheerful though she was scarcely able to hold back her tears at the sight of her son lying there in his bed. Girolamo, who a few months earlier would never have stopped kissing that face and hair and neck, was now ashamed of embracing this upset woman, and felt embarrassed, silent, almost frigid. While his hands mechanically pushed his mother away from him, his eyes never left the commercial traveller's face, in his terror of seeming ridiculous and his painful concern about what he might think of his mother. After three or four days of this uneasy, cold, and sad visit, to Girolamo's great relief, his mother left, and he was able to return to the company of the salesman, who, against all expectation, instead of making fun of his filial love, reproached him for his heartless and in-human treatment of his mother. 'These middle-class children,' he concluded contemptuously, 'have no love even for their parents.' That same night, with one of those reactions that are all the more violent for the intensity of the feelings involved and the length of time they have been repressed, the boy was overwhelmed by such a longing for his mother that the sound of his sobbing kept Brambilla awake. 'Now there'll be no peace even at night,' he shouted from the darkness. Girolamo curled in terror and held his breath beneath the bedclothes, forgetting his sorrow in his fright, and fell asleep in a bitter confusion.

But the attraction the boy felt for Brambilla was accompanied by a burning desire to be worthy of the salesman's esteem, to be numbered, like Joseph, among his friends. The contempt Bram-billa displayed towards Girolamo seemed above all based on the boy's apparent ineptitude and ingenuousness. He must prove to him that he was in fact neither inept nor ingenuous, that on the contrary he was capable of the same prowess that was his com-panion's boast, that he was, in short, no more and no less a man than Joseph. If he did this, he would at once win Bram-billa's esteem, and consequently, so Girolamo naïvely imagined, his friendship. The blatant fact that neither esteem nor friend-ship, but only a cruel game was here in question, entirely escaped the sick boy, who, unlike the other two, had thrown himself heart and soul into the bitter comedy. Convinced that he must somehow disprove his room-mate's sarcasm by facts, Girolamo cast about for a suitable opportunity and the mention of Polly finally gave him an idea: to win Brambilla's esteem and friendship, he would seduce the little English girl.

It was then the depth of winter. Everything seemed to favour his project. First of all the weather: it was alternately snowing and raining: the sky was always covered with a thick layer of low, grey clouds which ruled sun-treatment out and forced the invalids to keep to their rooms. Secondly, Polly's mother had left for England on business some days before, but only after obtaining permission from the head of the sanatorium for Girolamo to go on visiting her daughter while she was away. Girolamo could therefore carry out his design with the certainty of not being discovered or disturbed.

He was pleased he had taken this decision, as it would make him go up in Brambilla's eyes, but at the same time it filled him with a strange agitation. He had never had any experience of a woman, nor so much as thought about such a thing. Although he had a rough idea of how to set about it, he felt so shy that he doubted whether he would be able so much as to face Polly normally and casually, let alone seduce her.

These purely natural preoccupations were accompanied by others of a purely moral order. Both the mother and the daughter had done him nothing but good; they had given him presents for Christmas, and between Girolamo's family and the English lady there had been an exchange of letters full of mutual regard. Girolamo realized that, over and above the fact that this seduction was in itself something wicked, it was doubly so under the circumstances. It flashed through his mind that if he were discovered he would place himself and his family in the most embarrassing position. But his moral scruples were far more readily overcome than his physical ones.

The fact was that Girolamo felt somewhat resentful of the two foreign ladies, mother and daughter, for the following reasons: he had been offended at being placed on a par with a girl of fourteen and jarred by the closed, family atmosphere with its exchange of letters between the parents; worst of all, in this institution where everyone made fun of him, it was mortifying to be treated with pitying and almost maternal affection by Polly's mother.

'She thinks of me as a poor little invalid,' was roughly what he thought, 'a poor little boy, as good as gold, whom you've got to be kind to, give chocolates and books to, and then say to yourself: "How kind I am!" . . . Well, I'm going to show I don't need anybody and that I'm different from her. I am bad,

really very wicked, and so she had better not bother about me.'
On the other hand, he had always suspected that her kindness
had as its sole purpose that of inducing him to visit her little
girl. 'Brambilla's right,' he thought. 'If an Englishman came
here she would stop taking an interest in me.'

Thinking all this made him feel he was very wicked indeed,
vitiated beyond remedy and beyond hope. This very thirst of his
for the pain of fresh humiliations finally decided him to carry
through his decision to seduce the girl.

On the day appointed for Girolamo's usual visit to the first
floor, dawn broke through a bank of thick low clouds which
lent the whole snowy landscape an air of expectancy and deadly
calm. A black darkness as of night still clung to the rooms and
the passages of the sanatorium. In the yellow light of their
electric bulb, immediately after lunch Brambilla and Girolamo
began a game of chess to while away the time.

The chess-board was placed on a chair between the two beds.
Leaning out of their bedclothes, the two invalids set out the
large pieces, the kings, queens, castles, knights, and bishops,
which the hands of innumerable invalids had polished to a shiny
smoothness, like the beads of an endlessly told rosary. Girolamo
usually played better than Brambilla, but on that day his
thoughts were elsewhere. Oppressed by anxiety and an intolerable unease, he took a listless pleasure in twice letting himself be
beaten by a sniggeringly triumphant Brambilla. But under the
sting of well-aimed sarcasm, his competitive instincts were at
last aroused. He began a third game with clenched teeth, this
time throwing himself into the effort of anticipating his opponent's every move, of building up a fool-proof strategy, of
winning at all costs. But all of a sudden he realized he was on
the point of losing again and in a fit of rage he knocked the
board over – an outburst of nerves which elicited a furious
diatribe from Brambilla. Frightened by what he had done, the
boy could not take his eyes off his companion's face, while his
hands alternated between convulsive protest and a pathetic
attempt to rearrange the scattered pieces. Delighted with this
opportunity for fresh sarcasm, Brambilla was even more insulting. At this point there was a knock at the door and Joseph
entered.

'I've got orders to take Master Girolamo down to Miss Polly's,' he announced with military briskness, and, winking to Brambilla, he began wheeling away the sick boy's bed.

'Well, now I'm in for it!' Girolamo thought. The uneasiness that had been temporarily driven under by the excitement of the game now came back on him worse than ever so that he scarcely heard Brambilla calling out: 'Go on then, off to your girl-friend!' Instead, he sank back on the pillows and for a moment closed his eyes. When he opened them again, he was already outside in the corridor.

In the shadowy corridor, with its string of dim bulbs, other white beds, their occupants pale and motionless under bed-clothes so flat that the beds seemed empty, were being wheeled through the gloom by strong women dressed in white. The rubber wheels sounded muffled and troubled as they rolled over the hair-cord carpets. Then came the downward journey in the lift, with its interminable buzz. In the narrow compartment Joseph sat on the foot of the bed like some new species of guardian angel. All this was familiar to the boy, but his nerves were so taut that he now saw it all in a new light: incongruous and terrifying.

But as soon as he had reached the room and the Austrian had left, after wheeling his bed up beside the little girl's, Girolamo's anxiety was dispelled, and he felt almost too calm. The room was fairly large and bathed in a warm, agreeable glow, the lamp casting a pool of light on the two heads on their adjacent pillows. The two beds, Girolamo's all white and the girl's spread with a patchwork coverlet, were touching one another, and this contact, with the unforeseen possibilities it offered for the realization of his project, was most disturbing to Girolamo. He had meanwhile drawn himself up a bit from the bedclothes and even leant his elbows on the other bed. He began now to examine the girl with curiosity as though seeing her for the first time, and asked her in clumsy French what she had been doing during the last few days.

Polly was fourteen and looked no more than her age. Her fair hair was neatly bobbed just below the ears; she had blue eyes and a healthy rosy face which, though somewhat plain, would have been attractive if her long illness had not made it puffy and given her a sleepy and even sly look. She was not at all advanced for her years, either physically or mentally; if anything, unlike Girolamo, she seemed retarded and deadened by illness.

Girolamo looked at her; he did not know how to begin, and tried to imagine how Brambilla would have set about it. Having learnt from the traveller to scorn all sentiment, he thought that to start with 'I love you' – which he'd never said before – would be naïve, and moreover, would get him nowhere. Not that he thought one had to be cynical, but believed in all good faith that the only thing worth doing with a woman was to embark on a series of actions, each more daring than the one before, which ended in complete seduction. So, with the most natural air in the world, he asked his little friend whether she had ever kissed anyone or been kissed.

The girl shook her head. Lying back on her pillow, she looked at the boy with amazement and curiosity. The blankets half covered her plump breasts. Her cheeks went scarlet – perhaps the room was too hot, or she felt embarrassed. Her arm, bared to the elbow, was curled back round her head and her fingers toyed with a little doll that dangled from the bedpost.

'It's very nice,' he said nervously. Big with ambition yet not knowing the moves, this remark struck him as rather feeble. 'Would you like to try?' he added with an effort. Obviously the girl did not understand what he was talking about, and gave him a questioning smile. Then Girolamo leant out of his bed and kissed her on the cheek.

Her blue eyes gazed at him with a kind of terror. 'She's afraid,' Girolamo thought, 'and she thinks I'm mad.' Although disappointed by his first kiss of love, he was determined to go through with his plan and began covering her face with kisses. A moment later he had seized her listless arm and put it round his neck as though inviting her to reciprocate his tenderness. But her arm hung there motionless. Girolamo, discouraged, was about to abandon his project when suddenly there was a rap at the door.

Red in the face, more through exertion than excitement, more annoyed than frightened, Girolamo drew back. But his appearance was certainly far more distraught than he imagined, for swiftly, without warning, the little girl bent over from her bed, loving and self-assured, and stretched out her hand to smooth his hair and tuck him up. Then she lay down again, satisfied, and with an air of innocence called out: 'Come in!'

It was the post. But her action had been so spontaneously feminine and full of complicity that Girolamo felt himself overcome by a strange agitation he had never known before. The girl no longer appeared childish to him. 'She knows more about it than I do,' he thought as she calmly received her mail. The door had scarcely closed when he threw off the blankets and pressed his lips on her motionless mouth.

Throughout, she remained impassive, neither speaking nor moving, and maintained this pose until the very last minute. Because of her attitude and because he had expected much more, Girolamo had little pleasure in his role of seducer, but found consolation in the thought that he, too, had gained at last this indispensable experience and need no longer be ashamed in Brambilla's presence. But a certain awareness of what he was doing, not with a moral, but a simply physical sensation (at one point, for instance, he felt cold in the small of his back and noticed that by bending forward from his bed his body was completely exposed) made him doubt the advantages of this boost in his self-esteem; rather, he was tempted to lose himself, to sink completely into this hopeless world of degeneration: 'It's all perverse and ridiculous!' his thoughts ran, 'but anyway I'm done for . . . What good would it do to turn back now?'

The room was dark and silent; the two twin beds made a large white patch; in the shadow of the walls you could just make out various objects – flowers, photographs, clothes – which gave Girolamo a sense of luxury and intimacy. From time to time he lay back on his bed, looked around him, and listened with pleasure to the noises of the outside world, like the bells of sledges coming or going, and he wished he'd done nothing at all and longed to return to his innocent amusement; but Polly's white face, her embarrassed stillness and her look of expectancy made him realize what foolish hopes these were, and without enthusiasm he returned to his task of seduction.

But in the corridor, as the Austrian was wheeling him back to his room, he was almost proud of his achievement; he recalled

Brambilla and imagined himself describing what had happened, and their laughing together at the little girl's innocence, and of how he could stand up as a man – before the other man. His cheeks burned with excitement; assured of his room-mate's admiration he felt almost happy; he would have liked to talk with the male nurse or to exchange a few words with the maids who were going from room to room with the supper-trays. But this dream was shattered when, in the lift, Joseph, who as usual had sat down at the foot of the bed, said:

'Well, Master Girolamo, now you'll have to change room-mates!'

'Why?'

'Ah, of course, perhaps you didn't know. The doctor visited Mr Brambilla just now and says he's cured . . . and so Mr Brambilla will be leaving us in a week's time.'

The lift droned upwards. Lying still in his bed, the boy looked at Joseph's red and stupid face, and turned over in his mind these two thoughts: 'Brambilla is cured. Brambilla is leaving.' He felt no envy, but a deep shame that his work of seduction had been done in vain. From now on it would be useless to boast about his childish love affair to the salesman. Brambilla was cured; he was going away, and he wouldn't even listen to him. Brambilla was going away, and he would be left in this dreary prison among the other invalids, weighed down by the thought of his wicked action, which now was of no avail. Furthermore, he realized that he had been alone in taking the game seriously, alone in regarding illness and the life of a sanatorium as quite normal; whereas the traveller, most likely, had treated his own illness and all that went with it, friendships, habits, states of mind, enjoyments, as mere transitory things, to be endured because they were for a short time only. Brambilla had just made use of his passionate friendship – that was all – now he was going away, abandoning Girolamo to his ludicrous and abject good faith.

The bed banged against the door-post of the room and shook him out of his bitter reflections. He looked up before him in the little room was the empty space waiting for his bed, the lighted lamp, and Brambilla sitting and watching him with the expression of someone who has important news to announce. 'I

know all about it!' Girolamo wanted to shout, and then to bury
his head under the bedclothes and cry or sleep, but above all to
hear nothing and to see nothing. But out of vanity he decided
to pretend he hadn't heard the news.

'Ha!' Brambilla said as soon as the door was closed, his joyful expression not masking the coarseness of his features. 'D'you
know the song that goes like this:

> 'Goodbye! Goodbye for ever!
> For distant lands I'm leaving
> And never shall return!'

'What do you mean by that?' Girolamo asked.

'It means I'm going away,' the salesman replied. 'The doctor
saw me today and says I'm all right.'

'Marvellous,' Girolamo began, thinking he ought to congratu-
late him, but Brambilla interrupted – 'I've always said there was
nothing much wrong with me . . . and now, my dear Master
Girolamo, I'm off! In a week's time I shall be in Milan, and you
can bet your life that within a couple of days I'll be sitting in
the Cova with a pretty girl.'

'Yes . . . but to begin with you should take it easy,' Girolamo
said, full of good intentions.

'Why "easy"? The doctor said I could do anything I wanted
. . . In any case, d'you think I'd take *your* advice? What an
idea! An invalid telling a fit man what to do and what not to
do!'

Brambilla went on talking. Watching him, Girolamo sensed
bitterly that his inferiority to the salesman was, in yet another
way, as plain as ever. To begin with, it had been his ignorance
of love-making; now it was his illness. The seduction of the
English girl might well have given him the prestige he so
desired, but now, it seemed, he could only find equality and
achieve his aim by getting well. Brambilla's contempt for him
was now so obvious, and his own sense of shame so sharp, that
for the first time since he had entered the sanatorium the boy
saw clearly that his motives and actions were perverse and
vicious. The very fact that he had come to look on illness as a
normal condition, and a state to acquiesce in, seemed additional
proof of his own incurable depravity. There was no doubt about

it – Brambilla was healthy, and he, Girolamo, was ill. Even in Brambilla's dealings with his women there seemed something fresh and natural, whereas in his own case everything in the relationship with Polly appeared sordid and loathsome.

And Girolamo convinced himself that he was hopelessly degenerate. Then, as Brambilla chattered on about Milan and the people he would meet there, Girolamo, with another stroke of self-humiliation – very like that earlier occasion when he shamed himself of his own free will to shield himself from the torture of others – decided that since he was ill and a patient in the sanatorium, he had no reason to be ashamed of his condition; on the contrary, he should demonstrate that it suited him very well, and take the consequences of such behaviour. What these consequences might be, he couldn't say clearly. Perhaps to sink lower and lower with greater and greater consciousness into that darkness which surrounded him now; to achieve the absolute seduction of his little friend, and to suggest above all the confidence and ease of an animal absorbed in its natural element. This decision set his resentment at rest; he felt safeguarded by this full recognition of his weakness and believed himself perfectly free to embark on a series of actions which in other circumstances must have appeared reprehensible.

The following days were perhaps the gloomiest of that winter spent at the sanatorium. The weather kept changing; one moment brilliant sunshine, the next an overcast sky and sudden snowfalls which made sun treatment difficult and delayed their cure. Brambilla, who was beginning to get up, used to go down to the village by sleigh, and bring back tales of women, of big hotels, of luxurious living, and every kind of amusement; he was full of an insolent joy that caused the boy more suffering than all the sarcasms, and Girolamo was aware that his recognition of his own misery and his yielding to it had given him no strength at all.

'It may seem strange to you,' he said to Brambilla, 'but I don't want to get up . . . I'm perfectly happy here at the sanatorium.'

'Well, there's no accounting for tastes,' the salesman replied, 'but I prefer to get about and feel well.'

Almost every day he was taken to the ground floor to visit his friend, and he had a strange desire to do the most shocking things, and because of her childishness and his own evil intentions, this seemed to him an entirely gratuitous perversion not even justified by the need to win Brambilla's esteem. And after each visit he had a dreadful feeling of revulsion. Polly's docility and her attitude of do as you please aroused in him a fierce irritation. 'If I said the word, she'd go back to all those harmless games we used to play with just the same zeal and just the same indifference,' he thought. He wished she had a will of her own; his absolute authority oppressed him. Once he even thought of consulting Brambilla, but he gave up the idea; and so his project of straightening out his relationship with Polly wasn't carried out. He was too curious – or too weak.

These visits lasted two or three hours. When Girolamo went back to his room, he felt feverish and exhausted. His temperature, the most tangible result of his exertions, went up, lasted all day, and was accompanied by a slight pain in his bad knee, which, after having shown signs of improvement earlier on, now seemed to have got worse again. But Girolamo regarded these alarming symptoms with the greatest indifference; he no longed either hoped or desired to get better. He thought that since defeat was inevitable, it had better be a total one. True enough, the idea of death never crossed his mind, but he was aware of the imminence of some vague catastrophe which would sooner or later put an end to a situation there was no escaping from.

The day came for Brambilla to leave. Immediately after lunch the salesman got up and proceeded to wash and dress with minute care. He shaved, dusted his skin with talc, sprinkled it with eau-de-Cologne, and parted his fair, oily hair down the centre. From a small trunk he took out a blue suit, patent leather shoes, a black overcoat with velvet collar and lapels, and a stiff black hat.

It had snowed all the morning; the sky was a dead and dirty white. In the room there was little light; through the uncurtained windows could be seen on the terrace, outlined against the whitish sky, the black figures of two men going backwards and forwards, shovelling away the snow with huge spades. Lying motionless in his untidy bed, his hair hanging down over his hot, pale face, Girolamo watched Brambilla, who, standing in his striped underpants in front of the looking-glass, was trying in the poor light to put on a collar that was too tight; then his eyes wandered back to the men shovelling snow. He was beginning to feel a bit feverish; the muffled thuds of shovelfuls of snow as they fell into the yard filled his mind with whirling images. He thought of the cold, and the deadly stillness and silence outside. He imagined the men resting from their work every now and again and, with little clouds of breath coming from their mouths, leaning on their shovels and idly watching the snowy landscape. He could imagine this, all white, with here and there trees and huts a sodden black, as though carbonized; and the smoke from the chimneys rising up darker than the snow and lighter than the clouds. Suddenly a flight of ravens rose from the valley, their compact and orderly formation making a black and elegant pattern on the sky. The flock came nearer, flying low, now close, now spread out, but always keeping the pattern; the nearer it came, the more numerous they seemed, and at a given moment the sky seemed full of birds, and they were flying so low that you could make out their wings and their pointed tails. Then, from behind a mound, a volley of gun-shots exploded like a bomb in the middle of the flight. The ravens fell like stones on the snow, black patches on the whiteness, unique and individual, with wings outstretched, tails spread out like a fan, or closed tight like a tulip, or lying on their sides or backs with feet in the air. Other black marks, smaller and hardly visible, were made on the snow by the feathers and down, scattered all about by the explosion. This image of the massacre of the ravens haunted Girolamo's mind; he felt an anguished pleasure as he pictured the funereal birds scattered on the snowy slopes under the shattered sky; he tried to think of Polly, but didn't succeed, and, full of bad temper, still watching Brambilla dressing, he returned to his feverish dreams. At that moment there was a knock on the door and Joseph came in.

'He's come to take me down to Polly,' thought Girolamo and, drawing himself up into a sitting position, he looked on his bedside table for mirror and comb to arrange his tousled hair; but he was stopped by a sign from the nurse.

'There'll be no visit today, Master Girolamo,' the Austrian said, sternly and dryly; and then, turning to the commercial traveller, he said:

'The sleigh is ready, Mr Brambilla.'

'Why?' Girolamo asked, seized with great uneasiness by Joseph's icy manner. 'Is Miss Polly feeling ill?'

'Miss Polly was delirious all night,' the nurse replied, with the same stiffness. 'And now she's a little better . . . but you, Master Girolamo, you're not going to be allowed to visit her ever again.'

'They've found out everything,' the boy thought. He could hardly breathe, broke into a cold sweat, and sank back on his pillow as though he were going to faint. Meanwhile the male nurse had bent down and was tying up Brambilla's small trunk, which was near the door. The commercial traveller, fully dressed by now, with his hat and coat on, was supervising the operation with a serious and preoccupied air: 'Why, never again?' the boy asked at last in a faint voice.

'Doctor's orders,' the Austrian said as he straightened himself, red in the face from his exertions. 'The doctor had a long talk this morning with Miss Polly's mother, who arrived last night. Then he sent for me and said, "Joseph, from now on, on no account must Master Girolamo or any other patient leave his room."'

'And didn't he say why?' Girolamo insisted, terrified by Joseph's abrupt manner. 'Did he say anything else?'

The nurse looked scornful: 'You, Master Girolamo, you know the reason better than I do, so why ask so many questions?'

Brambilla, who had finished seeing to his trunk, came up to them: 'What's happened?' he asked. 'Has Master Girolamo been up to his tricks again?'

'Yes; he has,' the Austrian said darkly. 'And of course, as everyone knows, it's the staff who have to bear the consequences . . . as though we could know what the patients do when they're alone together in their rooms.'

Motionless, his eyes shining, the boy gazed at the two men. His cheeks were flushed and he wanted to cry out in anguish.

'Now,' he thought, 'Brambilla will ask for details and he'll make fun of me as usual.' He would not have admitted it, but, to tell the truth, what he longed for above all at that moment was that the salesman should hurl his customary sarcastic and vulgar remarks at him; that kind of interest struck him as a thousand times better than this cold reserve; quaking, he waited for a remark such as: 'Ha! you seduce little girls, do you?' which would have enabled him, a modest satellite, to re-enter, even in an underhand way, that proud orbit. But he was disappointed.

'It's always the same,' Brambilla announced contemptuously, not seeming to want to know more than what he'd already heard. 'These molly-coddled kids are all alike; they think only of themselves. What do they care if others have to suffer the consequences. They don't give a damn . . .'

'But what's Joseph got to do with it?' Girolamo began, almost losing his head on account of their coldness. 'Can't I do what I like?'

Brambilla, who was picking up his newspapers, turned on him.

'Shut up,' he broke in. 'You ought to be ashamed of yourself!' Then, addressing the nurse, 'Well, we can be off now!'

Joseph threw open the door, bent down and lifted the trunk on to his shoulders. 'Another thing,' he said to the boy before going out, 'You won't get off lightly, Master Girolamo. The doctor is furious. You'll find out tomorrow.'

Girolamo now placed his last hopes in the commercial traveller's farewell. The reserve and disapproval of the two men had filled him with such an acute feeling of guilt and had convinced him so completely of his own unworthiness that, at that moment, the least sign of affection from his room-mate would have certainly moved him to tears as a mark of almost super-human kindness. Therefore he watched Brambilla with anxious eyes. 'We've been together almost nine months,' he thought. 'Oughtn't we to embrace?'

But Brambilla, who had finished collecting his things, was already closer to the door than to the bed. 'I don't think I've left anything behind,' he said from the doorway as he passed a searching glance round the room, which, already, was full of twilight. The boy saw him hesitate and then open the door.

'Well, then, goodbye, and all the best,' Girolamo suddenly heard coming from the dusk of the doorway. He wanted to jump up from his bed and say something. But there was no time. The door was already shut.

Meanwhile, night had fallen, and the dark shadows, broken only by the whiteness of the sheets thrown back on Brambilla's bed, filled the room. For a little while the boy remained motionless, listening eagerly to the noises that came from outside. He heard the jingling bells of the sleigh that was carrying the traveller away fade into the frozen night and die away completely; he also heard the door of the neighbouring room bang, and someone talking. At this point a cold shudder, due to the fever, no doubt, ran through his body. Curling himself up, he pulled his rumpled blankets over his ears.

Everything that the nurse had said in that dark and disgusted tone of voice about his little friend now came back to him with an intensity peculiar to all feverish conditions. The thought that Polly had been delirious all night long at first filled him with a wild and bitter remorse. He imagined the little girl as he had seen her so often, white and motionless beneath the low light of the lamp. He seemed to sense a connexion between that fixed look of terror he had so often surprised in her blue eyes and the delirium, followed by the confession and the scandal and her mother's intervention. 'Obviously,' he thought, 'she had an immense respect for me, a kind of admiration, although she never told me so, and it's for this reason that she let me act as I did without making a protest, without even daring to breathe, but then what happened filled her with shame and fear. Later she never stopped thinking about it and, finally, after being delirious all night, as soon as she saw her mother she could no longer restrain herself, and confessed everything in a burst of tears . . .' Thinking this suddenly made him realize that his little friend had ranged herself against him with Brambilla and Joseph, and was justified in doing so. 'I'm alone,' he thought once more. 'Nobody will have anything to do with me ever again.'

The unexpected entry of the maid with the supper-tray made him sit up and turn on the light. The woman was dark, small but sturdy, and not unattractive, though she had an unusual characteristic: her forearms, cheeks, upper lip and even her neck were covered with a growth of dark, downy hair that made one think she must have a tremendously hairy body. She first put the tray down on the table, and then, still without uttering a word, she began to strip Brambilla's bed. Usually, whenever she came into the room, she would chat with the boy and most of all with Brambilla, who was particularly attracted by her hairiness. Girolamo, who had always thought of her as too forward and a little cheap, now resented her ostentatious coldness, which he took for reproach and condemnation. 'She knows everything too,' he thought in despair, 'and she despises me the same as all the others.' Now the whole of his being was bent on obtaining from this woman some small sign of pity or respect. He longed to say something or do something that would have won her over, but he had only to look at that face bent over the heap of linen in the corner of the room to feel himself incapable of so much as opening his mouth.

But, just as she was about to leave, he managed to overcome his shyness. 'Tell me,' he asked with an effort. 'How is Miss Polly?'

The woman, with the linen bundled under her arm, was already by the door.

'What? You – you, of all people,' she burst out violently, 'dare to ask me a question like that? What cheek!' she added with a sarcastic laugh. 'First the fellow does the damage and then, without turning a hair, he asks after her health.'

There was a moment of silence. Girolamo felt even his ears burning.

'Miss Polly's better,' the maid concluded dryly. 'Is there anything else?'

'And the doctor,' Girolamo went on, 'when is he coming to see me?'

'Tomorrow morning – and then you'll have to face the music! Anything else?'

'But why?' insisted Girolamo, who had suddenly turned pale. 'What do you mean . . . face the music?'

The woman gave him a sidelong glance. She herself did not know what she had meant by those words, nor what the doctor would decide the following day, but in her genuine indignation no condemnation seemed strong enough.

'What it means,' she said, 'is that after what you've done, the doctor might send you away. Anything else?'

'Take my supper away,' said the boy in a final attempt to move the woman to pity by refusing his food. 'I can't eat to-night.'

Once more she laughed sarcastically. 'Now, don't go and play the martyr. Eat your food. Anyway, even if you don't eat, it won't make Miss Polly any the better! What more can I do for you?'

'Nothing.'

The door shut. For a moment Girolamo remained in the same position, sitting up in bed. Then, without touching the food on the tray, he curled up again under the blankets with his face turned towards the window. His thoughts were confused; he believed it was all up with him. 'Send me away,' he thought; 'the doctor will send me away'; and although he was convinced that he deserved this punishment, the prospect of it filled him with unspeakable dismay. He knew what a sacrifice his family had made to send him to the sanatorium; and in the intensity of fever he seemed to see, stage by stage, everything that would take place: his departure, the arrival at home, his mother's tears, his father's reproaches; in short, all those reactions so painful and humiliating that such an event would produce in a family like his, a family which already found it difficult to make ends meet. And through certain childish scruples, quite unrelated to reality, he felt he owed them a boundless debt of gratitude.

He was deeply agitated by these thoughts, as though the doctor were already there ordering him to leave, and he began to toss and turn beneath the bedclothes and to shake his head. 'No; not this,' he thought as he writhed. 'Anything but this!' He did not admit it to himself, but what made him suffer most in the face of this bitter prospect was the loss of his parents' esteem and affection. Never having made any distinction between them and the people at the sanatorium, Girolamo was certain that, as soon as they knew the truth, they too would despise him, like everyone else; and with terror he imagined his life at home, ill and despised, a source of endless displeasure and trouble, with little hope of recovery and no hope whatsoever of happiness.

'Anything but this!' he repeated over and over again. 'Anything but this!'

He was very tired and suddenly was overcome by a great desire to sleep, to forget everything, and to sink into oblivion. He put out the light and five minutes later was sound asleep. But at once he began to have confused dreams. He was lying on his iron bedstead in a large, empty room with grey, bare walls. In the middle was a table of carved wood, and leaning against it nonchalantly was a man, still young: his father. They were talking quietly, and his father told him that he no longer had enough money to keep him at the sanatorium. He did not appear irritated and annoyed; he was smiling resignedly. Girolamo agreed with his father; obviously, if there was no more money, it was no longer possible to continue the treatment, but he was thinking, thinking hard, in an effort to find a way out, and suddenly he thought he had found one. 'I'll marry Polly!' he exclaimed. This suggestion met with his father's approval; and now the little English girl must be told the news. Girolamo's father left the table and wheeled his son's bed out of the room. Now they were in the dark corridor of the sanatorium. The father had difficulty in guiding the bed; he was not as skilful as Joseph, and, besides, the black corridor was full of white beds being wheeled in both directions by male and female nurses. Another thing that slowed down their progress was the endless stopping in front of innumerable shops which somehow or other had their blazing and dazzling windows on either side of the corridor. These shops were really magnificent. In the windows that were as deep as caves, displayed in a blaze of light were rare objects of gold and other precious metals, and small trinkets, gorgeous raiments, bronzes and weapons. Girolamo gazed at all these beautiful things. He suddenly thought of giving his future wife a surprise by actually bringing her a complete trousseau – no sooner said than done! The father went into a shop and came out a moment later with a wonderful wedding dress all white and gleaming with a long, billowing veil and a train; from another shop he brought back a wreath of orange blossom, and from yet another more garments. Everything was placed on Girolamo's bed. The wedding dress with all its veils made a splash of almost blinding light in the surrounding darkness. They went on along the corridor and at last reached the lift that was to take them to the first floor. Now they were in it; the lift began to descend. But it seemed to take longer than usual, and the electric buzz sounded louder and more persistent. As Girolamo looked at the bridal gown at the foot of his bed, an absurd anguish oppressed him. 'Stop, stop!' he kept on saying. 'We've got to stop!' But the lift kept on going down, the buzzing grew louder and louder, then became a howl . . . And at this point the dream was shattered and the boy woke up.

The darkness of his room filled his wide-open eyes, but the howling he had heard in the dream went on and on until it seemed to fill each little nook of silence. At first, still very sleepy, he could not understand what it was, then, not far from his room, a noise of footsteps hurrying down the wooden stairs of the sanatorium, as though people were running away, suddenly made him realize what it was: 'It's the siren in the tower, the fire-alarm,' he thought. 'The sanatorium is on fire, and that noise – it's the nurses running away.'

Hurriedly he turned on the light. At that moment with the wailing siren sounding through the air and the clatter of footsteps down the stairs, the isolation of his room appeared terrifying. 'The sanatorium is built almost entirely of wood,' he thought, 'and it'll burn in a flash . . . And there's only one lift, and that can hold only one bed at a time . . . and there are over eighty beds.' While he was working all this out, he was watching the door; the siren sounded louder and the stairs still clattered with footsteps. Suddenly, although he knew very well that, with his leg attached to the pulley, he would not be able to free himself, he began to twist and turn in his bed. The pulley squeaked and the bed groaned. Then, trying another method, he used all his strength to move the bed towards the door; but the bed would not move. 'I shall have to stay here,' he thought at last, dropping back on to his pillow, more in anger than in fear. 'Tied by one foot . . . in this trap, waiting for death . . . ' It seemed to him that this sort of death would be the final injustice after a chain of undeserved misfortunes. Suddenly he was seized with rage against the fate which struck at him while others went scot-free. 'Damn it,' he muttered, looking around, white in the face, trembling and grinding his teeth with a passion to bite and wound and revenge himself for all his suffering now that he was at death's door. 'Damn it. Damn the sanatorium. Damn Polly. Damn the doctors . . .' His eyes fell on the supper-tray and its plates of cold food. He leaned forward and pushed it off the table. There was a crash of broken china. Then he threw down the ink-pot and everything else he could lay his hands on, and did not stop until he was tired out and there was nothing left to destroy.

Then he noticed with astonishment that the wailing of the siren and the clatter on the stairs had stopped, and that neither the crackling of fire, nor flame, nor smoke, nor indeed any of the terrifying signs of conflagration had come to disturb the isolation of his room. Suddenly the truth dawned on him; in all probability a haystack had caught fire, and those people who'd been running down the stairs were not running away, but only hurrying to enjoy the unusual sight of a fire in the snow, in the heart of a winter's night.

He was so relieved that his eyes filled with tears; seeing the broken plates on the floor, he recalled his contortions and curses of a moment ago, and was overcome by a sudden unbearable shame. To have gone so far in that moment of panic as to curse the little girl whom he knew he had wronged appeared to him the clearest sign of the depths to which he'd sunk.

'I deserved to die!' he thought with conviction. Full of remorse and good intentions, he wished he was able to walk so that he might get up at once and go to Polly and ask her forgiveness. For a moment he thought of making a solemn promise to marry her as soon as she was grown up, but obviously this was absurd. He was the lowest of all men and the most evil; and so the idea of being expelled from the sanatorium the next day no longer frightened him, but even gave him a sense of relief. 'I do deserve it!' he thought. Now that the humiliation and contempt which were in store for him seemed desirable, he was pleased to imagine that his punishment would be just, and he believed that, through these new sufferings, he would manage at last to free himself from the black despair that had weighed on him ever since that evening when he kissed Polly for the first time. After that, his mind would be at ease, and he could concentrate on getting well. The belief that the following day he would be punished severely and justly filled him with hope and peace. He shut his eyes, very like a child who, after a fright or a fit of temper, falls asleep in its mother's arms. And he fell asleep.

He was awakened in the morning by a shaft of sunlight, not warm, but extraordinarily clear and bright, slanting through the window and falling on the bed. He opened his eyes, and his first thought was of joy at the fine day. 'What a wonderful blue sky!' he thought, looking at the window. 'At last I can lie in the sun and get well.' And he was beginning to wonder why no one had come to wake him up and put him out on the terrace, when from the room next door he heard the sound of men talking. One voice, loud and confident, was asking questions and giving orders, while the others sounded submissive and deferential. 'The Director!' he guessed at once and the thought petrified him. 'He's already next door, and he'll be here in a minute.'

Every aspect of his awful situation came home to him; the little girl, the scandal already spreading, his imminent dismissal from the sanatorium . . . and for a moment anguish and terror overwhelmed him. 'He'll be here in a minute,' he thought, 'and I haven't washed, or combed my hair. The whole room's in a mess and there's a terrible fug.' He wanted to clear up, but he didn't know where to begin. Then his startled gaze fell on the floor and there, between the two beds, he caught sight of the tray, and the broken plates, and among the fragments, the food, caked on the dark, polished floor. 'To think I'd forgotten . . .' For a moment he hesitated, and then leant forward with the hope of hiding the mess under the bed. The door opened and, followed by his assistant and Joseph, the Director came in. This man who terrified Girolamo, and likewise, though for quite different reasons, the whole of the medical staff from his assistant down to the lowest nurse was fairly typical of a certain kind of modern doctor. He was not so much a man of learning as an expert and calculating manipulator, both of his own gifts and of the immense gullibility of the sick. A good surgeon, if lacking distinction, but above all endowed with a fine intuition of the psychologically expedient, the sight of cowardice in the face of pain together with a real experience of the ignorance and incompetence of doctors had filled him from his early days with the greatest contempt for mankind, and he firmly believed that in order to get on in the world it was essential to have a haughty manner, a harsh, convincing tone, and in fact all those external signs of authority that are generally supposed to conceal equivalent knowledge and skill. The doctor was tall and heavily built, with pale hands sparsely covered with long black hairs, a close-cropped head, cold, penetrating eyes, a hooked nose, and a neat, pointed beard: the appearance of a musketeer or an inquisitor. Add to all this an abrupt and commanding way of walking, talking, and looking, occasional but well-timed acts of good nature and a way of laughing which made his admirers say, 'He's a hard man, of course, but what a kind laugh he has,' and you will have a fairly accurate idea of the man.

As the door opened, Girolamo, who was absorbed in trying to push the remains of his supper under the bed, and was leaning out uncovered to the waist, with his hair almost touching the floor, quickly drew himself up. While keeping his eyes steadily fixed on the Director, who, followed by his assistant and Joseph, was approaching slowly and with almost a look of suspicion, Girolamo straightened his bedclothes and smoothed down his hair as best he could. His heart was thumping and he could hardly breathe for anxiety. Then, remembering the reason for his panic, he calmed down: 'Now he'll tell me I'm going to be sent home,' he thought, and clenched his teeth. 'He's going to tell me I've done something dreadful. I'm ready to obey him, to undergo any punishment, if only he'll hurry up.' Though he felt like calling out, 'Hurry up, please! Do hurry up!' he was just able to restrain himself and, with a flushed face, he watched the doctor and the two men come slowly towards him.

But as if determined to thwart Girolamo, the Director seemed to be in no hurry at all. He came closer, and, when he had reached the bedside, stood still, shaking his head ironically at the sight of the tray and the broken plates on the floor; then, looking straight at the boy, said: 'Well, young man, I've heard some fine tales about you.'

Girolamo went pale. 'This is it now,' he thought and he wanted to cry out with misery.

'But if I have to leave,' he managed to get out at last, tremulously, 'then, oh, Doctor, please send me away as soon as possible.'

The Director gave him a look. 'Leave? Who told you you were going to leave?'

A thick mist clouded Girolamo's eyes.

'Because of what I've done,' he stammered. 'Polly . . . the first floor.'

At last the Director seemed to understand. 'Oh, that,' he exclaimed, going right up to the bed with a sign to the others to follow. 'I'm afraid you're mistaken there, my boy . . . What the patients get up to is none of our business. This is a clinic, not a reformatory. What matters to us is not your soul, but your body, and only a part of that. However, I have given orders that you are not to be taken down to the first floor from now on. As to your leaving us, you will leave when we think fit.' And, signing to the male nurse, he added: 'Pull back those bedclothes!'

The Austrian obeyed. Lying there uncovered, Girolamo shivered. There was too much confusion in his mind for him to think anything. He was annihilated, and felt an acute sense of his utter insignificance. Meanwhile, the doctor was bending over him, carefully fingering his sick knee with those thick, white, stumpy hands of his. As he watched him, Girolamo felt he was no more than a lump of flesh with neither will nor intelligence.

The doctor straightened himself: 'Show me those X-rays,' he said to his assistant.

The latter was holding a sheaf of metallic envelopes. From these he drew out three photographs of Girolamo's knee and handed them to the doctor, who held them up to the light to examine and compare them. The first X-ray showed, against a black background, a whitish patch formed by the rotula and the conjunction of the femur and tibia; it was clouded and deformed. In the second negative this cloudiness was smaller and surrounded by a dark outline; but in the third it was just the same as in the first, if anything, slightly worse. The doctor handed the X-rays back to his assistant and turned to the boy.

'You're no better now than when you first arrived . . . What have you got to say to that?'

'What? How do you mean?' the boy was beginning, but the older man broke in: 'You just concentrate on getting better. If I were you, I wouldn't take my illness so lightly. Now off you go for your sun treatment. Joseph, put him out on the balcony,' and at this, without waiting for Girolamo's reply, the Director and his assistant left the room.

Joseph threw open the windows, gave the boy his sun-glasses and a cloth for his loins, stripped the bedclothes off him, and with his strong arms had the bed out in a moment. The boy suddenly found himself in the open air, curled up naked and self-conscious on the mattress. It was cold, and the cheerful sun-light on the terrace was only just warm enough to stop him shivering. On the dazzling sheets of the other beds brown bodies were already exposed to the sun, and even the scars, boils, and abscesses that here and there disfigured those motionless limbs looked less repellent in the beautiful light of the morning. Some of the patients were reading, others lying back flat as corpses. Others again, at the far end of the terrace, had put on a gramophone, and at intervals he could hear its harsh tones carried by the wind. The day could not have been lovelier: as far as his eye could reach, he saw distant against the hard, clear sky the ring of jagged peaks that crowned the valley; the pine forests sprinkled with fresh snow, and on the glistening slopes the little black shapes of the skiers flashing hither and thither, falling down, picking themselves up, disappearing and reappearing again from behind the white hills. But Girolamo gazed at this festive landscape with eyes full of tears. Nothing had happened. He would not see Brambilla again, nor the little English girl. He was alone; and his recovery seemed a long, long way off.

THE IMBROGLIO

GIANMARIA's shyness was caused by his youth and his fantastically fertile imagination, and it was so deep-rooted, yet accompanied by a furious desire to appear easy and frank, that it often led to a peculiar kind of effrontery that was both imprudent and ineffectual. His obsessive fear of feeling shy would sometimes lead him to plunge headlong into actions which really needed a planned and cautious approach; or cause him to fling himself blindly, as if frightened of his own courage, into absurd, fruitless, or dangerous enterprises from which anyone with self-confidence would have held back. Moreover, his obstinate desire to appear different from what he was, and to force the expression of his own nature, led him into unnecessary actions dictated by abstract and rigid calculations of his own, and these deluded him into thinking that he was providing himself with motives and rules of conduct which in reality were entirely lacking in him. And his oddest characteristic, once he had assumed a role, was that, like certain great actors, he threw himself into these fraudulent and exacting parts to the point of believing in them: indeed, he became sensible of certain feelings that had started as simple make-believe.

This happened in a *pensione* in Rome shortly after his arrival from his native city. Alone and unbefriended, after a week of discouraging solitude he made up his mind finally to escape from his condition at no matter what cost: he would speak to one of the people staying in the same *pensione*. But which one? On reflection it seemed to him that the most suitable would be a girl called Santina whom he saw every day at meal-times in the dining-room. At this time it would not have been easy for him to say whether he really liked the girl; the important thing was to cure himself of his shyness by speaking to her; then, of course, once he had made her acquaintance he would court her, for to do less would be to fail in his duty as a man. But three or four days passed without providing an opportunity for him to put his plan into action; and meanwhile his constant watching of the girl made him think of her less as a means for overcoming his shyness and more as a person; he came to realize that he liked her. Finally, his prolonged indecision induced a state of panic and he could think of nothing but Santina and the necessity of speaking to her. He couldn't sleep. Every time he met her he turned pale and caught his breath. He now realized that it was no longer a matter of getting to know her, but of seducing her; and so, though his timidity remained unchanged, his aspirations grew bolder and bolder. A few more days elapsed during which Gianmaria experienced that ardour peculiar to young men towards an accessible woman, until finally he worked himself up into feeling all the pains and longings of a misunderstood lover. Then, one frenzied evening, he made one of his typically sudden and gratuitous decisions: whatever happened, he would speak to Santina during or after supper, anyway before midnight.

Now that his mind was taken up entirely with his decision, he was more meticulous than usual with his toilet. He had spent the afternoon lying on the hard, tumble-down sofa, studying the dispensations of international law, and chain-smoking, so that the vast and badly-lit room with its thickly-frescoed ceiling and dark furniture, where nothing looked clean and white except the towels hanging by the basin, was filled with a heavy bluish fug, making what was really icy cold look as though it were heated. The moment he heard the hollow, metallic sound of the supper-gong in the passage, he threw aside his law book, but didn't rise from the sofa, for he ate alone and quickly, and he wanted to be the last to reach the dining-room so as not to be the first to leave it. But he was incapable of sitting still for more than a minute. He suddenly got up and went to the mirror.

He began by looking at his face. Though there was nothing irregular or misshapen about it, he was convinced that he was ugly because of the childish and inexpressive immaturity of his features – they were hopelessly adolescent. Emphasizing his youthful look of which he was so ashamed were three things he found especially disagreeable: the dark, tired-looking crow's-feet under his bright black eyes, which for some reason suggested a disordered life; the thickness of the dark brown hair on his forehead – he had vainly tried to smooth it with lotions and greases; and a persistent and unextinguishable crop of pimples on his neck, forehead, and cheeks which were only slightly concealed by the down that was just beginning to grow – and this was the most unbecoming thing of all. He was not handsome, he reflected, as he scrutinized himself carefully, yet – he didn't know why – his face, be it handsome or ugly, attracted him in spite of himself. What lay concealed behind the mysterious brightness of the eyes? Where had he picked up the rather bitter line curving at the corner of the mouth? Was there not some trace of aristocratic pride in the arch – admittedly not very marked – of his thick eyebrows? Such were the questions he asked himself as he examined his reflection. He noticed in addition that by some extraordinary benevolence of Fate, on this day which was so important, his pimples seemed smaller and less visible; there was one under his cheekbone, but it was only just beginning and, though painful, it would not show that evening. When he had finally finished his careful scrutiny, he began to dress. He had only two suits; a grey one for every day and a blue one for evenings. He was wearing the first, and he now took the second from the huge evil-smelling cupboard full of coat-hangers and laid it out carefully on the red bed-cover. Next he took a pair of black shoes, rather worn but still in good condition, from the wardrobe, and from a drawer in the enormous chest the only silk socks he possessed. He undressed hurriedly and gazed at himself for a moment in the huge shadowy mirror; he had not yet managed to get used to his own nakedness and looked at it with the same scandalized and attracted astonishment that he felt for a woman's naked body. Then with a shiver he leapt over the frozen brick floor towards the door and took off the hook, which was as ornate as a candelabra, the only article hanging on it, a white shirt that he had worn once already, but was still clean.

He put on the shirt, socks, and trousers – the latter not without the boyish joy he had felt the first time he put them on. He then went to the wash-stand, which was dominated by two huge water-jugs and two capacious bowls of flowery green china, and washed his hands and face in cold water. He wasted some time searching in the dust and cobwebs for the soap that had slid off the wet marble and skidded over the floor; then he ducked his head into the water, plastered down his wet hair with brilliantine and began combing it carefully. But his hair was too wet and oily and stuck up in sharp, shiny tufts showing his white scalp. Once more he began combing furiously, but by this time the dampness had gone so that his hair no longer held together, but was as unruly as a porcupine's bristles, and he had to dip his head into the bowl all over again. This time he didn't use his brush and comb, but smoothed his hair with his brilliantine-anointed hand and then swathed it in a towel like a turban. With his head thus enveloped, he paced up and down the room, every now and again giving vent to his rage as he struggled to fasten his starched collar. When it was thoroughly crumpled he threw it away and took another, the only one left, and this he fastened almost at once. As he was tying the knot of his tie the unpleasant rumpus of the gong began once more in the passage. It was supper-time.

Unexpectedly he was overcome by the anxious and intolerable uneasiness he knew so well – his shyness; his heart began beating furiously, he caught his breath, and such was his upset state that he opened the door and went out into the corridor with the towel round his head. Luckily, in the doorway, he turned as usual to take a look at himself in the cupboard mirror, where he caught sight of an Indian dignitary with a dark, suspicious-looking face beneath a white turban, and with a single leap he was back in his room. He had escaped by the skin of his teeth. Supposing he had gone wandering round the *pensione* with his head swathed in a towel! For a moment he even forgot Santina in his agitation, and when he finally left his room was relieved to find that the mishap had, if anything, calmed him.

The Pensione Humboldt, once the property of an elderly Englishwoman who had fallen in love with Rome and now managed on behalf of her heirs by a young widow called Nina Lepri, was on the fourth storey of a massive and gloomy mansion with an over-ornamented façade of stuccos, caryatids, balconies, and columns, the whole being distempered in yellow and glazed with dark dust. The *pensione* was exactly like nearly every other *pensione* of medium standing; it had the same old musty furniture, the same doubtful cleanness, the same smell of cooking, the same deep silence, and the same mysterious comings and goings from room to room. But in one particular it not so much differed from as excelled over all its kind – in the number and length of its passages: in this respect the Pensione Humboldt could be called not only exceptional, but unique. Its passages – low, long, narrow, dark, and gloomy, and occasionally interrupted by dingy double-doors – spread out in every direction making the whole apartment seem like a dead and buried labyrinth. And so confusing were these passages that, even a week after his arrival, Gianmaria was as vague about their lay-out as on his first day and wandered along them blindly by guesswork.

On this evening he realized as soon as he had left his room – perhaps it was due to his disturbed state of mind – that he had forgotten the way to the dining-room. All he could remember was that it had a door with green glass panels. So, hesitating a little and sometimes sighing, he negotiated a long stretch of the passage, turned a corner, and at the end caught sight of the bright glass panels he was looking for. 'Here we are,' he thought, and with a jerk to his jacket and a touch to his tie he assumed an air of dignity and went in.

He was unaware that he had entered the wrong room until he had carefully closed the door and turned round to look for his table. What he saw was one of the many rooms in the *pensione,* with the usual painted ceiling and dingy furniture and appearance of dusty age. But here there was a partition across the room with feminine garments hanging higgledy-piggledy from it, and by the partition was the figure of a woman in a very peculiar attitude, and the woman was immediately recognizable as Santina. She was leaning with one shoulder against the partition trying with awkward movements to pull her day-dress over her head. Her head and arms were muffled in the up-turned dress; her body, contracted by the effort of getting free, was clothed in a pale green petticoat trimmed with yellow lace and with shoulder-straps of rose-coloured ribbon. Though utterly taken by surprise, Gianmaria could not resist staying to glance at the body of the girl whose face he knew so well, but which was now hidden.

The body was childish, thin, and graceless, with bony shoulders, flat stomach, and jutting hips. Where the lace of the petticoat ended, half-way down her thighs, lean, badly-shaped legs emerged in dark stockings. Gianmaria, in his amazement and curiosity, found himself particularly noticing the strange contrast between the childlike slimness of her body and the two rounds of the nipples veiled beneath the greenish petticoat, for these were abnormally large, like two great dark crown pieces; also the long, thick, black hair that darkened the armpits of her two thin upraised arms. In the space of a second the body with muffled head and naked shoulders, the partition with the clothes and towels hanging from it, every detail of this strange picture was imprinted for ever on Gianmaria's memory. Then 'Who's that?' shouted a rough and angry voice, rather hoarse and with a strong regional accent. And at the same time the girl's hips and legs made a clumsy and furious movement of impatience and she struck the floor with her heel. 'It's nothing whatever,' Gianmaria muttered as if speaking to himself rather than to the shrouded figure. And then he withdrew into the passage as quickly as he could, closing the tinkling green glass door after him.

The unexpected apparition of Santina's unexpected body had a profound effect on Gianmaria's inexperienced mind. As he retreated along the passage he told himself that were he to fail to make a conquest of this easily available girl he would be good for nothing at all. But his plans to seduce her were not as cynical as might appear at first sight. Gianmaria had the jargon and attitudes of cynicism that he felt to be obligatory, but his real feelings were naïve and, within the limits of his passionate character, respectful; they were really very like the feelings of all those other young men from the provinces who fall in love once and then while away their youth in long and awkward engagements. He thought he had all the cool nerve needed to seduce the girl, but really, after initial advances and successes, he would have been quite unable to check the scruples of his inexperienced mind.

So thinking, he reached the dining-room and, once more

adopting the casual, impassive expression of a self-confident man, he went in, trying to make no noise. But the door stuck and then suddenly gave, making the glass windows in their loosened sockets tinkle like a cluster of bells, so that he was the cynosure of all his fellow guests' eyes. Embarrassed, and unaware that he was making a face as if to say, 'It's nothing. It's only me,' he swayed across the creaking wooden floor and reached his table.

The only difference between the dining-room and the other rooms in the *pensione* was its shape. It was long for its width, almost like a tunnel, and had a high-vaulted ceiling decorated with the usual faded incomprehensible arabesques. Two lamps with white glass shades spread a gloomy light over the tables arranged round the walls. Across one of the ends of the room was a longer table on which piles of plates and cutlery were ranged in a row, and a dozen little baskets tied with red ribbon each containing an apple, a tangerine, and a little dried fruit. This was the table used by the waitresses when they went to and fro to serve the meal; and Nina Lepri the manageress spent her time on her feet between that table and an opening in the wall behind it through which, from time to time, appeared the muscular arm of the cook handing plates of food over from the kitchen. From her place of command behind the cutlery and napkin table, the manageress could observe the whole length of the room down to the green glass door at the bottom, the two rows of tables with the guests sitting at them, and in the distance at the far end Gianmaria, alone, sitting puffing out his chest and facing his plate and his bottle – so exactly opposite her that their glances often met. These glances were indifferent if appraising, for though the manageress had a family relationship with all her clients she gave her confidence to none – indeed, she seemed to want to hold them aloof from her private life. The manageress was tall and rather beautiful – at least, so Gianmaria thought as he watched her, which he did less for preference than because of his position facing her. She was fair-skinned, with a pale, cold face, two large, tranquil eyes, and a long, aquiline nose above a wide, sinuous mouth. Her hair was black and she wore it smoothed over her ears and with a bun at the back of her neck. Her bust and hips were soft and fat, but not beautiful;

yet they had the indefinable and seductive cosiness of delicate amplitude. A lazy composure emanated from her movements and her face. She always dressed in black; and both her physical appearance – still youthful, yet overlaid by middle age – and her composed and reserved manner made her seem the incarnation of the spirit inhabiting the long passages and squalid rooms of the *pensione*.

As Gianmaria entered, the manageress was standing behind the table with a ladle in her hand distributing the soup from a steaming tureen while two waitresses proffered her bowls, one by one. Nearly all the guests were seated already; Gianmaria saw at a glance that the only ones still absent were Santina and her mother. There were not many people at the *pensione*. There was a young provincial married couple with rough red faces, who never spoke yet never stopped smiling; there was an old office clerk, almost blind and quite toothless, who had the distinction of never eating anything except boiled chicken, morning or evening, and of this fact he would frequently boast with all the stupidity of a man preoccupied by his health and calculating the hundreds and even thousands of birds he had devoured in his life. Then there were two elderly English women, grey and gouty, one of whom kept a pet dog in her room and during meals would put the remains of her food on a small dish which she would take, limping and trembling, to her pet; and finally there was a certain Signor Negrini, a man of middle age who ate alone, but seemed to be on terms of friendship with Santina and her mother. All these people conversed with one another in loud voices from their tables, making a running commentary between one mouthful and the next on the quality of the food and the news they had read in the morning papers. After a rapid glance around, Gianmaria began to eat.

Though he would not admit it to himself, he was now cast down at the thought that perhaps Santina and her mother had been invited out to supper. He would have liked to ask Negrini, who was sitting next to him and who, he supposed, knew all there was to know about the two women; but his habitual shyness prevented him from uttering a word. Several times he opened his mouth to say something and then shut it again. At last he thought: 'I'll count ten and then make it a matter of life and death to speak to him.' This decision brought a feeling of liberation, for he felt that by the very fact of taking it he was out of the neutral and undecided zone of shyness. So he began counting slowly, his eyes fixed on the manageress, who was standing there behind her table between two piles of plates (he might have been looking at the picture of a rather distracted yet thoughtful saint placed above an altar between two fantastic candelabra). When he reached 'five' he stopped for a moment and said softly but audibly 'six, seven, eight.' At that moment there was an echoing tinkle at the door and the two women came in.

The girl burst into the room as though in a violent hurry. She greeted the other guests with rapid gestures of head and eyes, and her long evening dress of coarse blue silk rustled behind her. Her mother, who was short, dignified and placid, followed her unhurriedly, looking around from deep faded black eye-sockets. Gianmaria, remembering all too well the half-naked body he had caught sight of in the room with the partition, could not help contrasting it with the head which was now uncovered and visible to his eyes, and he came to the conclusion that the only face that fitted the immature woman's body was indeed the one he was looking at. And he decided, too, that no other mouth could have emitted the hoarse, graceless accents that still rang in his ears. Her hair, which was stiff, curly and black, swept backwards on to her neck as if blown by a nonstop breeze; her rough low forehead had the vague lines that seem to suggest the obstinacy and obtuseness of limited intelligence; her eyes were huge and seemed to jut out even beyond the level of her cheeks under rather swollen eyelids; their expression betokened feeble-mindedness and greed – like those of a drug-addict – and a fatuous falseness caused by a continual surge of ideas of a practical nature. Her protruding cheekbones, her snub nose, her large mouth that often opened in an inscrutable smile over her widely-spaced and uneven teeth, and her tiny chin hardly visible beneath her thick lower lip completed the portrait of this Santina with whom Gianmaria had become so enraptured that he loved not only her few graces, but also her many defects. Her face was all dusted over with powder as white as chalk, her lips were plastered with too much lipstick, and at table she sat in an indirect light that threw her hypocritically swollen eyelids into relief, as also the obtuse lines on her forehead and the impudent dimples in her cheeks; and, while keeping up a show of talking to her mother, she kept her greedy shameless eyes fixed on Gianmaria. As for him, though his decision to make a conquest of Santina had been impelled by no motive other than satisfying a point of honour and his own self-esteem, he felt his mind invaded by the boldest of hopes as he noticed her glances, which were an unexpected novelty of the evening. His heart beat furiously, and his breath came in short gasps; he seemed to see Santina, thin and gawky in her green petticoat, her thin legs in their black stockings, lying on a bed. As he played with his food he began to eye the girl in a way that he imagined to be discreet, but in fact the violence of his glances was noticeable not only to the girl, but also to the other guests and even to the manageress as she stood at the opposite end of the room behind her table.

By this time they had reached the third course and the game of glances between him and the girl was in full swing; indeed, at one moment she smiled at him, a frank, provocative, characteristic smile, while at the same time indicating her mother out of the corner of her eye as if to say. 'I like you looking at me, but take care. My mother is here.' Then the two waitresses changed the plates and Gianmaria saw the manageress take up a large tray from the table and hand it to one of them. It was the cheese tray. It would soon be time for fruit, and then the meal would be over. But the other waitress had a smaller plate on which there seemed to be only one single piece of cheese, and she crossed the room making straight for Gianmaria.

This waitress was a simple country girl with round red cheeks, who was always ready to burst out laughing at the slightest provocation. Perhaps it was her constant inclination to ill-repressed mirth that prevented Gianmaria from suspecting something when he saw her face, as she served him, light up like a lantern with mischievous gaiety that her cotton-gloved hand, held against her mouth, was quite unable to conceal. What should have warned him was the silence that followed the clatter of knives and forks in the dining-room. But he was so taken up by his extraordinary state of excitement and the hundred mad plans he was making that he paid no attention either to the silence or the laughter. The plate contained one slice of yellowish Gruyère; not without difficulty, for the cheese was hard and dry, he cut a piece off, put it on his plate, and began eating, as if with a compunction. Hence it was only after he had chewed for a little while that he became aware of a revolting and loathsome taste in his mouth, a taste different from that of any possible cheese, which first mingled with and then dominated the taste of bread; a taste, in fact, of soap.

So far was he from supposing that the taste had to do with the substance he was chewing that, though he had to spit out his mouthful, he doubted the evidence of his own palate, and began, with feelings of perplexity and nausea, to examine the remaining piece of Gruyère with the end of his knife. Then he heard Santina's voice, clear and distinct. 'Does the cheese taste nice?' she asked in a mischievous tone.

As if the signal had been long-awaited, a great burst of laughter broke from every table. They all laughed – the two newly-weds, politely but with enjoyment; the two English women revealing their teeth among their creases and white curls; the old half-blind office clerk opening his black toothless mouth to its widest extent and flopping back in his chair; Signor Negrini, Santina, and her mother, sympathetically, affectionately. Gianmaria, crimson with embarrassment, his mouth full of froth, still couldn't quite understand. He looked first at the plate, then at the laughing faces, and said: 'Yes, but . . . what has happened? It seems to be soap.'

'What do you mean – soap?' the girl answered knowingly. 'Of course not . . . It's cheese.'

At this point Signor Negrini broke in with the casual authority characteristic of him: 'No. It's soap,' he said. 'But every good joke is short-lived. I don't advise you to eat any more of it or you'll never, never get it out of your mouth.'

But Gianmaria, sickened, was hardly listening, engrossed in spitting out lathery saliva into his handkerchief; and, pouring out a glass of water, he rinsed his mouth. Everybody went on laughing while he spat out soapy water, and all the while he was raging with anger and humiliation. So this, he thought furiously, was why Santina had given him so many glances and smiled at him – so as to make him fall into this stupid trap. He was distracted from his mixed feelings of resentment and humiliation by the peaceful voice of the manageress, who in the meantime had left her place behind the table and come up to him.

'Who played this stupid joke?' she asked. 'I'm terribly sorry, Signor Bargigli, but don't worry. Who played this joke? Edvige, was it you?'

Gianmaria spat out some more soapy saliva and looked up. Red in the face in her struggle between fear and giggles, Edvige the servant began defending herself against the severe and inquisitorial manageress. 'The real fact is that it was Signorina Rinaldi who gave me that cheese, and she said she would take all the responsibility. It isn't my fault.'

Gianmaria saw the manageress's gaze, dark yet composed, turn towards Santina, who confessed in a friendly, good-tempered voice: 'Yes; I gave it to her. We wanted to have a joke, something to laugh about . . . but I'm sure Signor Bargigli isn't offended . . . After all, we all live in the same *pensione*, and it's like being in a family.' As she spoke she turned to Gianmaria and looked at him with an uncharacteristic expression of sweetness and gentleness which drove the rage and humiliation out of the boy's inexperienced heart.

'Of course I'm not offended,' he said, still spitting out soap. 'But what a disgusting taste! What loathsome soap!'

'Of course, soap *is* soap,' observed Signor Negrini. The laughter was now on the decline, and the manageress, seeing how things were, apologized again to Gianmaria, said a few words of reprimand to the servant, who made off still red and giggling, and then re-crossed the room and resumed her place behind her table, tall and dignified and looking down. But Santina did not seem satisfied by Gianmaria's subdued answer, and in a tone of authoritative goodwill she said: 'Come and eat your fruit course with us, to show that you really aren't offended. Mama, make room for Signor Bargigli; he's coming to eat his fruit with us.'

Gianmaria hesitated. He was still blushing and still had the taste of soap in his mouth. Yet he was tempted, and could not resist such a friendly invitation. With head hanging to conceal his confusion, like a schoolboy summoned to the master's desk embarrassed by the mocking looks of his fellows, he got up and went and sat down at the two women's table. Everyone seemed to approve of his behaviour. Signor Negrini applauded: 'Bravo! That's the spirit! That's character!'

Santina's mother might have been about fifty, and the most obvious thing about her was the disproportion between her large, handsome head and her short body, a disproportion which, when she walked, recalled those enormous cardboard heads on top of minute bodies in carnival processions. On her large, flat, flaccid face there were queer blotches of red, white, and pink, as if even constant washing had never been able to remove the clinging traces of former make-up from her saturated skin. Her round black eyes, too, looked as if they had been washed and washed again, yet her sparse eyelids, like her cheeks, retained little black specks, the indelible marks of salve. She gave Gianmaria a cordial welcome, motioned him to a chair and bestowed on him a wide, conventional smile which revealed a few teeth of doubtful whiteness beside others that gleamed with old yellow gold.

'Santina was trying to play a practical joke, the wretched girl,' she said, glancing at her daughter threateningly through her eyeglass. 'I simply can't keep her in order; while she's doing one thing, she's busy thinking up a hundred others. But, as Signor Negrini said, you've got enough character not to take it too badly. Tell me, what you are up to here in Rome, Signor Bargigli? Are you studying?'

'I'm doing my first year of law,' answered Gianmaria shyly, taking a tangerine from the little fruit-basket he had brought from his own table and beginning to peel it.

'So you're to be a lawyer?'

'Well, as a matter of fact, I'm not,' Gianmaria answered awkwardly. 'I'm going to be a diplomat.'

'Ah, diplomacy. A fine career. I've known a number of diplomats. One of my cousins, called Rinaldi like us, was in diplomacy. Have you come across him?'

'No; to tell you the truth, I haven't.'

'Mama,' the daughter interrupted, 'what was the name of that young man we met last year at Ostia? He was a diplomat too. Was it Colleoni?'

'Pierleoni,' her mother corrected her. 'You may have come across him, a tall, dark young man with a Vandyke beard.'

Gianmaria, who was now feeling much more at his ease had to admit regretfully that he did not know the bearded Pierleoni either. But by now the ice had been broken and the mother went on with her fluent and affected small talk, telling him that they were Romans and had only been in that *pensione* a few months, that the food was good, but the rooms were dark and sunless and the beds appalling; indeed, they intended to move to another *pensione* – and so on. Gianmaria swallowed the sections of the tangerine and tried to answer as best he could without removing his eyes from Santina's face. His perturbed desires of a little while ago had now returned, and were being aggravated by the fact that Santina, who never uttered a word, but kept her eyes cast down while she cracked nuts and prised them out of their shells, was all the time pressing his foot with the toe of her shoe. At this contact a swarm of hopes and images began taking shape in his mind. He felt confident of victory, and yet could not believe in his imagination when it represented Santina's thin and ardent body close against his, and her arms around him, under the frozen sheets of one of these huge, creaking *pensione* beds. What disturbed him most of all was the girl's expert double-dealing – her face so impassive and her foot so busy under the table seemed an irresistible, almost devilish, piece of provocation. This, he realized, was the first love-affair of his life, and he felt drunk and distracted as if he had been quaffing heady wine after a long fast.

Then, as if out of a thick fog, he heard a honeyed voice saying, 'Permit me. The name's Negrini,' and placed beneath his eyes he saw a dark, rough, hairy hand with a heavy gold ring with a diamond on the little finger. 'My name's Bargigli,' he quickly answered, rising to his feet and shaking hands. And yet for some reason Negrini's friendliness did not impress him as much as Santina's mother's. This Negrini fellow had a rather dark skin, something between yellow and olive, the colour of people who suffer from their liver, and his eyes were as black as coal with bloodshot whites; his head was round and bald and his features were small and polished. Gianmaria also noticed that his ear was tiny, round and perfectly shaped and finished like a navel – and this last particular filled him with a strong, unreasonable feeling of revulsion. Negrini, with his dark, liverish skin, was wearing a light, coffee-coloured suit, driven by one of those oddities of taste so noticeable in coloured people. He sat down comfortably, drew a long, flat, gold cigarette-case from his back trouser pocket, sprang it open and presented it to the other three at the table. The two women and Gianmaria helped themselves, and then Santina's mother turned to the newcomer and said:

'Count Bargigli has come to Rome to take up diplomacy . . .'

Gianmaria was taken aback. He had unreasonably expected some other kind of compliment from Santina's mother. Negrini, on his side, received this information with indifference or even cold hostility, the boy thought.

'Or rather,' Negrini corrected as he blew smoke through his nostrils and surveyed the room with sated, bored eyes, 'he hopes to go into diplomacy. Whether he will succeed is another matter.'

'What do you mean?' Gianmaria asked, full of hatred for his liverish opponent.

'I mean, my dear Bargigli,' the other answered coldly, 'that bright fellows like you, and of good family, who say as soon as they meet you, "I'm going to be a diplomat," are to be found on every tree. But think how many of them really enter that career, and how many end up as mere clerks in some dismal ministry at six or eight hundred lire a month. That's what I mean.'

Gianmaria stared at Negrini, quite taken aback by such unforeseen unpleasantness. 'But I've not come to Rome to become a clerk,' he said finally. 'I've come to go into diplomacy, and I'll see to it that I do.'

'I wish you luck with all my heart,' said the other sardonically, 'But you do know what you need to be successful, don't you? Or haven't you any idea?'

'What?'

'This,' and Negrini made a highly significant gesture, rubbing the thumb and forefinger of his right hand together. 'Have you got that – money – filthy lucre? Because if you haven't you may as well give up the idea of diplomacy straight away.'

Reddening with indignation and anger, Gianmaria nodded.

'We're rich,' he said, feeling all the while that perhaps he was doing wrong. 'We're landowners; and then we own houses in Florence.'

'In that case,' said Negrini, rising suddenly to his feet and laughing, 'in that case, my dear Count Bargigli, there is nothing more to be said. You have sealed my lips with an irrefutable argument. If you've got the wherewithal, that's everything. I won't say another word.' He repeated, 'I won't say another word,' as, hand in trouser pocket, and puffing smoke through his nose, he walked up and down in front of the table. Santina's mother, who had been silent during the verbal duel between Gianmaria and Negrini, now rose to her feet. Dryly she observed: 'It's obvious, Negrini, you don't know what you're talking about. Any fool knows the Bargiglis are one of the richest families in Arezzo. And now, what about going? Everyone seems to have gone.'

They made their way out of the now deserted dining-room. Santina's mother led the way with Negrini, who kept whispering to her, and then, behind, followed Gianmaria and Santina. But in the doorway Santina, who up till now had not opened her mouth, pulled Gianmaria back and with a furtive glance up the shadowy corridor along which her mother and Negrini were slowly making their way side by side, she whispered in a mysterious and meaningful way: 'Come to my room for a moment. I've got something to give you.'

In his state of emotional upset all Gianmaria could do was to give an affirmative nod. The girl gave him another provocative glance from her protruding and moist pupils, and with a rustle of moving silk she led the way down the corridor. By now her mother and Negrini were out of sight, and from the drawing-room could be heard the stifled rhythm of dance-music over the radio. Still ahead, and now and again turning with a finger to her lips to hush him, she led the way to her room, and with a careful look behind her she gently unlocked the door and pushed Gianmaria forward into the darkness and followed after him.

'If Mother finds out she'll be furious,' she said in a low voice as she switched on the centre light. The room was still in the state in which Gianmaria had already seen it, and he experienced a fleeting feeling of embarrassment as he caught sight of the crumpled stockings and petticoats on the partition. Then he mechanically made his way to the table and picked up a book lying there – a battered volume with a glaring cover, a detective story. Santina, meanwhile, had disappeared behind the partition into the other half of the room.

She returned almost at once with a gentle, penitent expression on her face and holding a gardenia with its stalk wrapped in silver paper. 'I was given a basketful by a tiresome young man who is following me around,' she said in her harsh voice as she eagerly drew close to Gianmaria. 'But I want you to have one because I'm afraid you're still offended about the soap. And I like you, whereas I can't stand that other young man. No. Wait. I'll fix it in your buttonhole.' And without stopping her flow of talk she stood on tiptoe and put the flower through the lapel of Gianmaria's coat. As she was doing this she leant her body against his and a strong smell of sweat and scented skin rose to his nostrils from her thin shoulders. Stunned by the smell and attracted by the vicinity of her body, Gianmaria made one of those half-happy, half-anguished automatic gestures that sometimes make one shout or gesticulate in one's sleep: he lifted his arm and held it tightly round her thin, bony waist, pulling her towards him. While she, under pretext of smelling the flower, had drawn even nearer and nimbly lifted her head and thrown her arms round his neck. They kissed.

'Oh Lord, what have I done now? Mama's coming,' she said as soon as they had separated, pushing him from her and circling the room. 'What have I done? If Mama found out!' She put her hand to her forehead. 'Go quickly,' she said and hustled him from the room. 'Quickly. Leave me,' she repeated in a low voice as she closed the door behind her, and herself went out into the corridor. Gianmaria was thoroughly excited and could not understand why she was so nervous. 'But there's no one here,' he pleaded. 'Let's go back to your room for a minute – only for a minute . . .'

They carried on their whispered argument pressed against each other in the silent, shadowy passage. Then the girl became serious and, holding a finger motionless between her lips, appeared to be reflecting. Finally she said: 'Listen. It's quite

impossible here. Mama may come, and then all would be up
with me. Listen. I'm going out to a dance with Mama and
Negrini now. But . . . but when I come back I'll come and join
you for a minute in your room. Is that all right? But mind you
leave the door ajar so that I can get in without making a noise.
So it's agreed, then?' And before Gianmaria had recovered from
his surprise and delight and had time to answer she had ran off
and disappeared round the passage corner.

If he had been told about it a day earlier, Gianmaria would
never have been able to believe that the suffering caused by a
few hours delay over the possession of a longed-for objective
could be so bitter and unbearable. But as soon as Santina had
disappeared, the thought of the two or three hours that divided
him from the time of her return suddenly assailed him with
such wild impatience that he felt he would never be able to hold
out under the anguish of waiting for so long.

'If I could only stop feeling and thinking and go to sleep and
wake up again at the moment of Santina's entry into the room!'
he thought as he went down the passage. 'But that's only talk.
What can I do to pass the time?' As he walked he made gestures of dismay with his hands, and in this way he reached the
hall, which was already deserted and nocturnal with the coat-
rack empty and the light dim. He was on the point of turning
back to his room when his attention was drawn by a closed
door on which was written the word 'Bureau'. 'Good idea,' he
thought. 'I received my bill today. I'll go and pay it.' He
thought that if he managed to find a lot of little practical things
to dispose of before midnight those few terribly painful hours
would pass more quickly. He drew the bill from his pocket and
knocked on the door.

Immediately from within a sweet and singing voice answered
with a 'Come in' modulated like the song of a cuckoo. He
pushed open the door and went in.

He noticed the room first. It was small and low, a mere hole
with an inclining ceiling, but, unlike the other rooms in the
pensione, it was furnished with a cosiness all its own. The window was shaded by bright curtains; in one corner stood a rose-
upholstered sofa scattered with coloured cushions; there were

armchairs round the fireplace, in which the remaining logs of a wood fire were collapsing into ashes. The manageress was sitting at a writing desk near the fireplace with her back to the door. Gianmaria, his bill in his hand, felt a sense of well-being, yet also a sense of trespassing – as if he were making his way into a private place – as he took two steps across the carpet and, owing to the smallness of the room, found himself beside the woman.

She was sitting on a stool too small for her haunches. Office materials were neatly arranged on the green cloth of the writing desk. At the moment of his entry she was reading a book held open on a black oilcloth portfolio, and a just-lit cigarette was smoking on the rim of the ashtray.

'I've come,' Gianmaria began shyly, 'to pay the bill . . . '

The woman had turned round as he entered, and as he held out the bill she turned even further in his direction, so that he could see the only defect, if so it could be called, in the pale, cold harmony of her face – her large, protruding though nobly-shaped nose.

'But there's no hurry about that,' she said with a smile as she took the paper from him. 'You've only been here a week. Don't stay standing. Take a seat.'

Gianmaria sat awkwardly on the very low sofa. As he felt it give beneath him it passed through his mind that it must be one of those divans that become beds at night by the removal of cushions and coverings. And when he saw the manageress bending her fine head of black hair and checking the figures on the bill with a pencil, he could not help imagining the woman as she would be in an hour or two, her huge white nakedness on the point of getting into bed in her warm room under the inclining roof. Nor did it occur to him to think of his fantasies as anything but the outcome of stray curiosity, in view of the detachment and chastity of the person who inspired them and of himself to whom they occurred.

As soon as she had checked his account, the manageress opened a drawer, took out a stamp and printed the word 'Paid' on the bill. Meanwhile, Gianmaria, watching closely in spite of his imaginings, drew his wallet out of his pocket and extracted a five-hundred lire bank-note which he handed to her. She hastily, furtively, examined it against the light and then opened another drawer and took out a few banknotes and a packet of silver change, which she broke open, counted out the change and handed it to Gianmaria.

'There you are, Signor Bargigli,' she said; 'and here's the bill; but, as I said, there was no need to pay it so soon, you only received the bill this morning.'

Her words were said in such a way as to imply: 'I'm not sending you away. If you want to stay and chat, please do . . . ' or at least that was what Gianmaria supposed. He was not, in fact, very interested in the manageress, but, given the hours that still lay in front of him before Santina's return, he welcomed the veiled invitation to stay. He sat down again with an apology and mentioned his solitude, and then asked the woman whether other arrivals were expected at the *pensione*.

She turned round completely, crossed her strong legs and, putting a tiny handkerchief to her large nose, blew it gently and noiselessly, as if with regret. Then she answered that unfortunately this year was very unlike the one before, during which, thanks to the Jubilee, the *pensione* had been always crowded out.

'And what about you, Signor Bargigli,' she went on, 'do you intend to stay with us for some time?'

An uncontrollable shudder ran through the boy's limbs, for in his mind's eye he had suddenly visualized Santina's sensual face in the act of offering him her lips. But the manageress mistook his shudder of desire for a shiver of cold and, going to the fire-place, knelt down calmly on the carpet, and proceeded, with un-impaired dignity and unchecked flow of talk, to stir the half-extinguished embers and throw a few shavings and twigs on to the flames to revive them. Then she rose.

'And where does your family live, Signor Bargigli?'

'My father's dead. My mother and brothers are in Arezzo.'

'Oh, your father's dead, is he?' She was seated again on her stool. 'I'm sorry for you, but I'm even more sorry for your poor mother, left when still young with the burden of children to look after. Are you the eldest?'

'Yes; I am.'

She looked at him without speaking for a moment, then she said with pathos and a shake of her head: 'None of us can know how sad your mother feels at having you far away from home.'

Gianmaria felt uneasy and didn't know what to answer; but the picture of Santina once more floated in front of his eyes, and instinctively he trembled again. Again the manageress noticed.

'You must be unwell,' she said, and as if the gestures were perfectly normal and natural she got up and laid her delicate, long, cold hand on his forehead. 'Forgive me for letting myself touch your forehead . . . but you're burning hot.'

'I'm burning hot?' Gianmaria repeated, feeling indeed that he was so, at the contrast of her cold hand with the fire within him.

'Yes. At least, that's my opinion,' she said, and she went calmly to her writing-desk, opened one of the drawers and produced a thermometer and started shaking it. When he caught sight of the thermometer Gianmaria felt her maternal solicitude and his imaginary fever to be really absurd, and he rose quickly to his feet.

'No, honestly . . . ' he protested. 'Please don't take my temperature. Perhaps I don't feel very well, but for heaven's sake, not that. Look, I'd better go to bed; a good night's sleep will put me right I know.'

The manageress stood with the thermometer in her hand looking at him, and her black eyes reflected the disappointment she was trying to control.

'As you like,' she said at last. 'Yes; you're quite right to go to bed; indeed, if it's not a nuisance, I'll come along in half an hour and bring you some hot lemonade. That's what you need. And then you'll be able to tell me whether you want anything else.'

Gianmaria retreated awkwardly towards the door. 'Thanks enormously,' he said. 'Yes; that's what I need. Thanks ever so much.' And so, between thanking her and bowing, he at last got outside the warm little room and into the large, cold hall.

'Heavens, what a bore,' he then thought as, worn out, he regained his own room and shut the door with relief. 'She's a good, kind woman of course, but so gushing. For two pins she would have offered to undress me and put me to bed like a child.' He was relieved to be free of her solicitude, though he felt a twinge of regret, for she was really a very nice woman, and now he had left her he didn't know what to do to pass the two hours still remaining before midnight.

He was filled with acute impatience and began walking up and down the room. Then his eye fell on the university curricula scattered over the floor near the sofa and the bitter thought of passing his time studying the dispensations of international law crossed his mind. He collected the papers, stretched himself out on the sofa, and began reading. However, he didn't take in a word, and had to read the same sentence over and over again to see what it meant; Santina's image was continually before his eyes, although he stubbornly went on reading. After about half an hour had passed in this strange form of study, a creaking behind him warned him that the door was opening.

'It's the manageress with the hot lemonade,' he thought crossly, while, with the almost unconscious coquetry of a young man who wants to be helped and made a fuss of, he hurriedly took out a cigarette, lit it without lifting his eyes from his papers, and otherwise did not move. Instead, however, of seeing the tall black figure of the manageress, he felt two hands cover his eyes, and a familiar hoarse voice said : 'Cuckoo. Guess who it is.'

'Santina,' he thought. His pulses throbbed, he threw down his cigarette and jumped to his feet. Santina was standing in front of him with her thin body bent backwards and roaring with laughter.

'You must admit that you didn't expect to see me back so soon, did you, dear?' she said; and then, growing serious, 'But I told Mama that I didn't feel well and got a friend to escort me back; you know, that young man who gave me the gardenias . . . and what a job I had to get rid of him ! He wouldn't believe I felt ill and wanted to force his way in, the little beast.'

But Gianmaria had already stopped listening; he had put his arm round her waist and was forcing her to sit down beside him on the sofa. 'Not so fast,' she urged, giving a frightened glance at the door. Reluctantly she sat down and let him kiss her – a long kiss; from her mouth Gianmaria's lips strayed to her neck, from her neck to her shoulders. Then he began to lower the shoulder-strap of her dress. But at this moment, quite unexpectedly, the girl began to struggle and shake her head, moaning harshly and distractedly.

Finally, she managed to push him away. 'No, no. Better not,' she said in a broken, breathless voice. 'You're not like all the others; you're different. I can feel it. I can feel it. No; I can't, I can't. It's impossible.' Gianmaria drew back and stared at her in complete amazement.

'What do you mean? What's the matter with you? Why?'

'If you knew why, you would never look at me again,' she said, and then buried her face in her hands and shook her head, groaning. 'I can't. I can't.'

'But why? What can't you do?'

'I can't tell you. I can't.'

Suddenly Gianmaria made up his mind and gripped her arms seriously, with a rough jerk. 'Shut up,' he said. 'Tell me what's the matter. What is it you can't tell me?'

'I can't. I can't . . . Leave me. I can't.'

'You're going to answer me properly and at once,' he stated, giving her a harder jerk than before. Then quite suddenly, as if she had awakened from a nightmare and was still dazed and unable to distinguish the real world, she became silent, motionless, and grave, staring long at Gianmaria out of large eyes. 'But if I tell you you'll hate me,' she said at last, still hesitating.

'Don't you worry,' Gianmaria promised, putting his hand on his heart. 'Whatever it is, I won't hate you.'

'But I know you will. You'll hate me.' And she started her groaning again.

'But I've promised you.'

'I know, but even so I feel you'll hate me.'

They were beside each other on the sofa. Santina's dress, which was long and full, covered Gianmaria's left leg in its folds and then spread out on the floor; her feet were on the papers scattered on the ground. Then, just as Gianmaria was laboriously trying to take her in his arms and achieve with kisses and caresses what he had failed to get with roughness, just as his longing lips were on the point of meeting the cold, shrinking ones of the girl, there were two distinct taps on the door. Santina hurriedly pulled herself free and leapt to her feet.

'It's my mother. Now she'll find me and give me a good scolding. It's all up with me,' and she began leaping round the room as if possessed.

But Gianmaria remembered the manageress's promise. 'It isn't your mother,' he assured her softly. 'It's the manageress.'

'What can she want – that horrid, boring woman?'

'Get in here,' Gianmaria ordered, and he flung open the doors of the great empty cupboard. Santina hesitated – she would have liked to protest and make a scene, but this time Gianmaria was adamant. He took her under the armpits, lifted her bodily into the cupboard, and turned the key in the lock. Then he went to the door and opened it. Yes; it was the manageress, and in her hand was a plate on which stood a glass of lemonade.

'I've come to bring you your lemonade,' she said, and without any fuss went and placed the glass on the bedside table. 'Do you need anything else?' she asked, stopping by the bed and looking not at Gianmaria, but all round the room.

Gianmaria followed the slow, calm glance of those eyes and saw that they dwelt with some insistence on the sofa. So he looked there too and perceived that Santina's little pink cloak had been left on the floor on top of the scattered papers. He turned red, thinking What a disaster, not knowing where to look. 'No. I don't need anything, thank you.'

But the manageress showed no sign of having even noticed the cloak.

'Have you enough blankets?' she asked, and, hardly bending, she carefully felt with her hand between the bedcovers as if to count them and measure their thickness.

'Yes; thank you. There are too many, if anything.'

'Good night, then,' she said, and with the same simplicity with which she had come in she passed by the awkward, shamefaced Gianmaria and went out.

No sooner had the door closed than there was a rattle of clothes-hangers and rustling of silk inside the cupboard. Gianmaria ran to open it, but hardly had he turned the key before the doors were suddenly flung open and Santina fell on top of him. He would have liked to take advantage of the incident to kiss her and draw her down on to the bed. But Santina was in a high rage and pushed him away.

'What did that Nosy Parker want in your room?' she asked rudely.

Gianmaria felt flattered by the jealousy in her tone of voice. 'She was only bringing me some lemonade,' he answered pointing to the glass.

'Well, I bet she came to see if you were alone,' said the girl gruffly. She didn't go back to the sofa; after she had walked round the room for a while she sat on the edge of the bed. 'Just to think, here I am in your room and at this hour of the night, and I don't even know your name . . . ' and she began to fiddle with the folds of her dress with downcast eyes.

Gianmaria told her his name, and, encouraged by her new gentleness, tried to kiss her. This time Santina allowed him to, though she made no response to his advances. She looked faint or half-dead, her arms and breast motionless, listless, her mouth half-open, her eyes half-closed. When Gianmaria pulled her one way, she fell on him in another; when he straightened her head, which had fallen backwards, it weakly collapsed on to her chest again; when he tried to put one of her arms round his neck it slid away lifelessly. The only sign of life was that every now and then she groaned and sighed. Yet as soon as he tried again to slip down one of her shoulder-straps, she awoke and pushed him away. 'No, no. It's impossible,' she said again. 'Impossible.' Then she threw herself on one side of the bed, buried her head in her arms, and emitted melancholy breathless sounds, half-cough, half-sob.

By this time Gianmaria's patience was at an end and he felt a strong urge to give her a good smack on her buttocks, which stuck out small and hard from her prostrate position under the wide folds of her dress – like the wire or stuffing of a doll with dislocated limbs. But he restrained himself and tried to lift her up with all the gentle persuasiveness he could muster. His efforts, however, would have been vain had not Santina suddenly changed her position and with a quick movement leapt into a sitting position on the bed. 'Do you know who I am?' she asked him.

'Yes. Santina Rinaldi. Isn't that your name?'

'Yes; that's my name,' she explained, now brutally frank, 'But that woman who's with me isn't my mother and isn't called Rinaldi. She's called Ida Cocanari.'

Their glances met. 'What do you mean?' asked Gianmaria, all at sea.

'I mean,' the girl explained simply, 'that the Cocanari woman is a friend of mine and she and Negrini use me to make money . . . '

'To make money?'

Santina grew restless and agitated again. 'Yes. Don't you get me? To make money. And I can't stand it any longer. I can't stand it any longer, and I don't want to go on doing it.'

'But how do you mean, to make money?'

She looked at him suspiciously for a moment. 'When there's someone like you,' she then explained with a rush, 'or, for instance, a well-to-do man who's alone and getting on in years, I get to know him and make him fall in love with me. Then I say, for example, that I owe some money, that I have to pay a bill, that I need a dress, and then that person gives me the money, and I divide it with the Cocanari woman and Negrini. Of course' – she made a gesture of disdain with her hand – 'of course I don't let them touch a hair of my head, but men are all alike and they're always hoping. Then one fine day we go off to another *pensione* in some other town and begin again. In addition, Negrini is very good at cards and makes a little money like that . . . '

Gianmaria, who was new to this sort of thing, was not so much horrified as simply astounded. 'But that's called cheating,' he said at last.

'It doesn't matter what you call it,' the girl answered with a shrug. And then, as if her confession had wrung out of her all the cynicism of which she was capable, she put her hands in her hair and shook her head in desperation. 'And now they want me to do the same thing with you too,' she began, groaning. 'But I don't want to. I don't want to. You're different from all the others. And then I'm tired, worn out, and I don't want to go on doing horrible things, and I hate them both, anyway. And you're so much better than they are. Oh how miserable I am! How miserable!' Her whole body twitched, and she acted as if she wanted to tear her hair; then, holding her red, unhappy face between the palms of her hands, she looked Gianmaria straight in the eyes. 'And now I've told you all this, you hate me, don't you? You hate me and you were the only person in the world who could have helped me. Oh, how wretched I am!'

She was mistaken. Not only did Gianmaria not hate her, but for the first time in his life he experienced a new feeling – unlike the hate she feared she had inspired, and unlike the physical desire that he had felt for her so far: the strong and unbearable emotion of pity. 'Poor Santina,' he thought as he looked at her. 'Poor Santina, an inexperienced girl and daughter of who knows what poor parents, who has endured who knows what want, and has now been thrust along the path of vice by that Fury, Cocanari, and the worthy Negrini. Poor Santina, astray, off the straight path against her will and her own deep aspirations.' He would have liked to have said these things aloud to her, to have reassured her, given vent to his overflowing emotions. But all he did was to take her hands gently away from her face and answer:

'Of course I don't. Why do you think I should hate you? I not only don't hate you; I am fonder of you than before.'

Santina lowered her eyes like someone confused by an act of outstanding, undeserved kindness, and her mouth made a little pout of contrition. 'But I thought . . . ' she began.

'I don't hate you at all,' Gianmaria went on, deeply moved, his lips grazing the powder on her face. 'And to prove it to you I am ready to change my words into deeds. I am ready to do anything to get you out of the clutches of that woman and that man Negrini, who I must confess I loathed from the moment I set eyes on him. If I can be of any help to set you free and start a new life, you've only to ask me and I'll do anything in my power . . . '

Santina looked up at him with an expression of gratitude and admiration. 'You're so good,' she said. 'I knew you were so good and I could trust you like a brother.' Gianmaria made a bashful gesture as if to say: 'Leave aside my good qualities. Let's talk about you.' She hesitated; then at last she said: 'So I can count on you.'

'Indeed you can, for anything I can do.'

She looked as if she could not believe in her own good luck, gazing straight ahead and every now and then giving a shake of her head. 'Oh, if you only knew,' she said at last; 'if you only knew how good it is to meet someone like you who are so kind, so kind . . . ' Then she grasped his hands and fixed her eyes anxiously on him. 'So if I told you, dear, that you could help me, and told you the way, would you do it?'

Gianmaria gave a fervent nod. 'What I find extraordinary is that you could still doubt it, after all I've said.'

'I can hardly believe it,' said Santina, and then once more there was a long silence. Then from an ancient church nearby, whose apse and bell-tower backed on to the *pensione,* the hour began to chime. Seated side by side on the bed in the squalid and shadowy old room, the boy and girl counted twelve hoarse clangs, then two sharper lighter ones; half past midnight. Santina leapt up from the bed.

'It's late. I ought to be off.' She was nervous.

Gianmaria bent down to pick up the pink cloak and threw it over her shoulders. 'But aren't you going to tell me how I can help you?'

'Tomorrow,' she answered hurriedly. 'Tomorrow. It's too late now. And then I mustn't give them the impression that I'm fond of you, and I mustn't get you into the mess they want.'

'Of course not,' Gianmaria agreed. 'Then I'll see you tomorrow,' and he began to put his arms round her. He immediately felt Santina's hands held out in front of her to fend him off, and as in view of their new and innocent relationship this seemed to him perfectly natural, he changed the direction of his kiss from her mouth to her low and narrow forehead. 'Till tomorrow, dear,' he said as they drew apart.

'Sleep well,' she whispered. And, moving lightly on feet hidden by her long, trailing skirt, she went to the door; she turned back to blow him a kiss on her finger-tips, and then disappeared.

For a long time after Santina had left him Gianmaria stayed sitting on the edge of the bed with dangling legs and downcast eyes. He thought he was pondering deeply and methodically on all that had passed, but his mind was in fact a void – partly because he was so tired and partly because the unexpected and strange turn of events had stunned him. At last he shook himself, undressed, and slid down between the cold sheets of the enormous bed. He fell immediately into heavy sleep and dreamed the following dream:

He seemed to be with the manageress in one of the passages of the *pensione* near the green glass door of the entrance to Santina's room. As his dream began the manageress was making a mysterious sign with her finger for silence and was at the same time slowly unlocking the door. They entered the room on tiptoe and discovered that it was brimful of vases of fibre and manure and dense flowering shrubs which, although the room was dark and large, cast a strange light from their hard, cold electric colours – red, blue, green, yellow, and violet – exactly like flowers in public gardens when the black clouds of a threatening storm lurk thick and low in the sky and a cold, wild wind rises and a pale, oblique light, heralding the false twilight of lightning, lies heavy upon the green flower-beds enamelled with arabesques of many-coloured flowers. But these extraordinary greenhouse blooms attracted Gianmaria's attention for a moment only. His gaze was drawn to two backs in the middle of the room bending over something luminous – the two backs, as he realized at once, of the Cocanari woman and Negrini. The latter, for some reason, possibly to be freer in his movements, had taken off his coat and waistcoat so that above his light-coloured trousers, between the strips of his braces, there stuck out a crumpled shirt of doubtful cleanliness: whereas the Cocanari woman was dressed in black and looked all set to go out, with a feathered hat on her head and a large square handbag dangling from her wrist. Both were bending over that cradle of light and making incomprehensible gestures with their arms. His curiosity aroused, Gianmaria drew closer and then saw that they were smoothing and tucking up the covers of a little white bed in which Santina was lying. The latter was propped up with pillows and the whole of her bust emerged from the bed. She was dressed in a clean nightdress decorated with lace ribbons and rosebuds, she had her arms stretched out over the coverings and, strange to say, despite the shameless bargain on which the two pimps were engaged, she did not look remotely sad – she was smiling contentedly. Indignant and enraged, Gianmaria wanted to drive those two loathsome creatures away from the bed and rescue Santina, but he did not feel strong

enough to face them alone, so he turned back to the manageress
to enlist her help. To his surprise, he discovered that she was no
longer beside him, but sitting at her writing desk in the very
middle of the cases of bright-coloured and dazzling flowers.
She was bending over the oilcloth portfolio, arranging piles and
piles of silver coins in rows. He ran up to her, implored her
passionately to bestir herself, to get up and come and help him,
but it was like talking to the deaf; she did not even lift her
head. At this point in staggered the old clerk with his lifeless,
empty eyes behind his thick glasses and his black, toothless
mouth. Gianmaria suddenly became convinced that he was the
decrepit lover that the pimps wanted to tie up with Santina;
and filled with aggressive indignation he rushed to the girl's
pillow and she immediately threw her arms round his neck.
Meanwhile, at the other end of the bed the two accomplices
were engaged in an incomprehensible discussion with the old
clerk, and as they discussed they lifted the bedclothes and were
bending over Santina's feet. Santina did not seem to notice their
bargaining, but clung ever more passionately to Gianmaria,
who returned her embrace, but did not remove his eyes from
the three who were arguing at the foot of the bed. As the discussion continued he saw them lift up the bedclothes a little higher
and uncover Santina's thin legs beyond her feet; he would have
liked to stretch out his hand and throw down the upturned bedclothes, but he was unable to do so, for he was strangled by
Santina's embrace. He struggled, though not removing his lips
from hers. 'Stop, you swine,' he wanted to shout; the three were
now almost beside him, their stunted shadows extended threateningly over the white bed; he struggled with increased violence, and at last he woke up.

The cold darkness of the room surrounded him; with his
arms he was gripping the pillow and furiously pressing his lips
against it. Though wide awake, he could taste the fleshy flavour
of Santina's lips mingled with the rough, unpleasant flavour of
the linen; there was no doubt about it, he was awake; but on
the pillow the girl's mouth had miraculously flowered. This
strange and disturbing sensation lasted for more than a minute
during which rage and frustration mingled; he kept kissing
and biting the rough fabric of his pillow till his teeth were

numb. Then his mouth became weary and all that was left was the linen soaked with his saliva, and in a cold sweat he sat up and lit the lamp on the bedside table.

The clock by the lamp showed it was three in the morning. 'I've been having a nightmare all night,' he thought as he scratched his ruffled head with both hands. His mouth and throat felt bitter and pasty, he took the lemonade glass from the table and emptied it in one gulp. Then just as he had done when urged by the fantastic impulses of his dream, he got out of bed and in pyjamas and bare feet stole out into the passage.

The brown walls, the red floor carpet, and the grey, bolted doors were dim in the light of the weak, spaced lamps. Shivering, he traversed the whole length of the passage that ended with his room, turned and made straight for the green glass door behind which Santina was sleeping. He had no idea why he was making this nocturnal exploration – possibly it was to prove to himself and to Santina how much he loved her and up to what point he was determined to snatch her from the hands of her two ignoble accomplices. Standing at the door and not unaware of the bizarre absurdity of his position, he pressed his lips against the glass. 'Tomorrow,' he thought. 'I swear to you, Santina, that I will see to it that you won't have to live with Negrini and the Cocanari woman any longer.' He was strangely moved by the idea that the girl was asleep behind those glass panes. He would have liked to hear the tranquil sound of her breathing; he strained his ear, but all he took in was the deep, nocturnal silence in which the *pensione* was immersed. At last, when his whole body was frozen and he began shivering and his teeth began chattering, he went back to his room, slid between the sheets and immediately fell asleep.

The next day was Sunday, and it was cloudy, cold, and windy. Gianmaria got up early to go to his course of pre-military instruction, and spent the whole morning with others of his age-group doing rifle-practice and marching up and down on some ground near the barracks. Though they were on a lower and subconscious plane, thoughts of Santina never left him for a moment even during these exercises. When he at last hurried back to the *pensione*, sweaty, weary, and dishevelled, he hoped to see her in the dining-room. But it was late, and all he found was his own table laid in the long and empty room. His lonely and melancholy lunch was overshadowed by the anxiety of not knowing where Santina was nor when he would be able to see her. He was forlornly cracking the two or three nuts in the fruit-basket when the manageress came into the room and advanced towards him.

'Good afternoon, Signor Bargigli,' she began with calm politeness. 'Did you sleep well after all last night?'

'Marvellously, thanks; marvellously,' Gianmaria answered hurriedly, rising to his feet.

'As I knew you had to go to military training, I had your lunch kept warm,' she went on. She did not ask him to sit down again, and her eyes fixed on him a dark glance. 'Was it warm?'

'Yes; very, thank you.'

The woman's eyes were expressionless, but the rest of her face seemed caressing, protective, and sympathetic, as if trying to say: 'You're just a boy and you touch my heart; I'd like you to feel at home here.' Meanwhile, with her hand she adjusted the knot of the ribbon on the fruit-basket. At last she said: 'I've got a letter for you from Signorina Rinaldi, who went away this morning and asked me to give it to you.' She placed the envelope on the table and left the room as unhurriedly as she had entered.

When he heard the words 'went away' the blood suddenly fled from Gianmaria's cheeks: his face became icy pale and he felt as if he might faint. But the minute the manageress had left the room he seized the envelope and opened it. The letter was short: 'I have had to go out of Rome, but will be back in the afternoon. Be at the Electra Café near here around five, the one on the Lungotevere, and wait for me in the red room. Yours . . .' and there followed a scrawl in which it would have been difficult to decipher the name of Santina Rinaldi.

He was so relieved that he felt he was returning to the open air after being in the underworld; he leapt from the chair on which he had collapsed and improvised a kind of war-dance on the creaking wooden floorboards in the middle of the empty room. Then, still exulting so that he felt he was still dancing, he ran to his room, set the alarm clock for an hour a little earlier than the one Santina had mentioned, lay down without undressing on his bed, and immediately fell into deep sleep. The nervous strain of the day before, his early rise that morning and the fatigue of the military exercises had worn him out, and now that his fears had been banished from his mind he was full of hope and disposed for forgetfulness; thus, unlike the previous night, his sleep was light and restful. At half-past four, before the alarm could rouse him, he reopened his eyes and gazed happily at the room, which was already invaded by the shadows of winter twilight. 'In a little while I'll be seeing Santina,' he thought; and beyond this happy thought his mind did not go. He washed, he combed his hair very carefully, applying a greater quantity of brilliantine than usual, he noted with satisfaction that his pimples were less noticeable than yesterday, he put on a dark suit, he tied his best tie, and at last in a state of mingled agitation and content he left the *pensione*.

He was feeling in such a good mood and so free from doubts about himself and so open to impressions from the world outside that as soon as he got into the street he could not help noticing with delight the dark, stormy brightness of the winter sunset. The streets of tall houses, black with people and dotted with red lights, stretched away into a distance of clear streaks of light shot from the dark rims of the stormy clouds. And rising upward into the cool, darkening sky the trees standing in round holes in the pavements looked like black candlesticks in the cold air, with the pure outline of their leafless branches. Through the bare branches blew the clapping wind, making the shop awnings swell and flop; it lay in wait at street corners for passers-by, caught them unawares, making them run clumsily after their hats, which went spinning away like tops on the edge of their brims. Gianmaria watched one of these hat-chases with amusement, and then entered the café in which Santina had given him the appointment.

He had little difficulty in finding the red room; it was the furthest away both from the bar with its continuous inflow of callers, its crash of glasses and change, and from the orchestra composed of women sitting on a kind of dais and tuning up before beginning to play. When one of the musicians saw

Gianmaria come in, she bent over to a companion and whispered something in her ear, smiling. Gianmaria noticed the smile and was pleased; all this, he felt, was a good omen.

He didn't have long to wait in the depths of the deserted red room. Less than ten minutes had passed, and the orchestra had only just embarked on the great march from *Aida* when Santina made her appearance. Her hands were hidden in the pockets of a bright overcoat, she had a little hat balanced on the back of her head which left her forehead uncovered, and she walked slackly with chest back and stomach out. There was a deceptively desperate look in her usually stupid eyes, and the corners of her badly-painted mouth curved in a bitter and resolute line. Without a word or any response to Gianmaria's greeting she sat down, took a cigarette, lit it, and said 'A brandy' to the waiter; then bent her head down, her cigarette between her lips and the smoke in her eyes, and, gently pummelling her knees with her gloveless, frost-reddened hands, seemed to be lost in sad meditation. Some minutes of silence thus passed. Then: 'What's the matter?' Gianmaria ventured to say. 'Why are you so sad?'

Santina wrenched the cigarette from her lips. 'What's the matter' she said violently. 'The matter is I can't go on . . . That's what's the matter. The matter is I'm sick of this life and of life itself. The matter is that if I died at this very moment I'd die happy.'

'You looked on things differently last night,' Gianmaria pointed out.

She shrugged her shoulders. 'Last night was last night,' she answered. 'But no, I see I'll never be able to get away from this life, never; I see that all efforts are useless, that I'll never, never have the spunk to leave that couple, even if I could think of a way.' She shook her head with bitter conviction, put the cigarette back between her lips and began once more gazing in front of her. There was another silence; from the adjoining room the instruments of the orchestra could be heard tuning up, and from time to time the coffee urn emitted a long snort.

'But last night,' Gianmaria insisted gently, 'you told me that if I helped you, you could get free from them. Do you mean you've forgotten that?'

'One says so many things,' she muttered. Then she turned and looked at him. 'No; I haven't forgotten,' she said, 'but what help can you give, in fact? You're only a boy, and, certain things I can't possibly ask of you. And then how long have we known each other? Hardly a day.'

Gianmaria made a gesture of protest. 'Time doesn't come into it; one can get to know someone better in a single day than in ten years, and as for me being a boy' – he could not help blushing – 'I hardly think age enters in either. My help can be just as good as anyone else's.'

Suddenly the girl began to rave just as on the previous evening. 'But no, but no,' she reiterated, groaning. 'There are some things I can't ask of you. I can't. I feel it. I can't . . . And even if I did you couldn't give them to me, you couldn't. I feel it. You couldn't.'

This wounding of Gianmaria's self-esteem made him feel he was capable of any kind of sacrifice; if Santina had asked him to marry her, he would have accepted enthusiastically. 'Only put me to the test,' he said. 'If you don't put me to the test, but just go on saying, "I can't," you'll never get anywhere.'

'But I know. I know. You can't.'

'Then try to tell me why.'

Again she looked at him attentively, sideways, with the appraising look of a cook bringing a cake from the oven and judging by her eye whether it is just right. 'Have you three thousand?' she then asked shortly and dryly.

Gianmaria's eyes widened. 'Three thousand what?'

'Three thousand what?' she repeated sarcastically. 'Three thousand lire, of course. And now you see I was right. You can't. I knew you wouldn't be able to help me, and all I can do is to go on with this hellish life. But luckily I've an infallible way of cutting it short . . . '

She was right. Gianmaria did not possess three thousand lire. Embarrassed, irritated, but at the same time incapable of thinking of anything else now that his self-esteem was at stake, he wanted to gain time while he thought how he could raise the sum. 'What way?' he asked.

Santina laughed bitterly. 'Oh, a very simple economical way, a nice little bottle of veronal. Tonight, before I go to bed, I'm going to drink the whole lot, and tomorrow, as they say, my sufferings will be over . . . ' After saying this, and as if to drive home her resolution with a gesture, she took the glass of cognac and swallowed it in one gulp. 'And now,' she added, half rising, 'what about leaving?'

But Gianmaria held her back by her arm. 'Wait a minute,' he said in a brotherly but firm voice, forcing her to sit down again. 'Where do you keep that bottle?'

Santina gave him a treacherous look. 'At home.'

But Gianmaria's eyes were intent on the bag Santina was clasping under her arm. 'Hand me your bag,' he ordered.

She hedged. 'No. What's it to do with you?'

'Give me that bag.'

'No. I won't.'

'Yes. You will.'

They had a brief struggle, Gianmaria trying to seize the bag and Santina trying to hold it. In the end the girl had the worst of it and, letting go, she sank back into her chair, humiliated.

'You're beastly,' she said slowly, drawling her words. 'You've hurt my wrists.' But Gianmaria was not listening. He had opened the bag and among her powder compact and lipstick and other trinkets he had found the bottle of veronal. 'In the meantime,' he began, half severely, half facetiously, 'this veronal will do excellently to water this plant, and perhaps it will go to sleep and begin to snore,' and he uncorked the bottle and poured the liquid over the earth in a great green vase containing a palm that stood behind the armchair.

Santina watched his actions with a contemptuous, almost ironical air. 'If you suppose you impress me that way . . . ' was all she said. 'As if I couldn't buy another one at the chemist's at the corner.'

'Next,' Gianmaria went on without paying any attention to her, 'you'll now kindly tell me what you need those three thousand lire for, and if they really are necessary we'll see to getting them for you.' He was lying – he did not possess the money and he knew of no way of getting it.

Santina looked at him doubtfully. 'Can I be frank with you? I don't know why, but I feel embarrassed . . . '

'But why feel embarrassed? Why? And with me . . . ' Gian-maria bent over affectionately and took her hands.

She seemed reassured. 'I have to tell you,' she began timidly and reluctantly, without looking up, 'that I have a mother – not the woman with whom I'm staying, but a real mother.'

'I see.'

'And my mother's very poor,' she went on after a moment, her voice filled with emotion.

'I understand.'

'And in addition she's ill, very ill . . . ' She looked up and gazed at Gianmaria questioningly. Then all of a sudden she began talking easily and fluently. 'And as she's ill and has no money,' she went on, 'and as I receive half the money I make in the way I've told you, I send this money for her to be nursed in a sanatorium near Trieste. Now you see why I have to stay with Negrini and the Cocanari woman, for if I were alone, even if I found a good job, I could never make enough to provide for Mother's cure as well as for myself. But if I could find three thousand lire, as I've also got some money put aside, I would at least have a breathing space – say, for a year or so – and be able to leave Negrini and the Cocanari woman and look for a job. But if I failed to find one, I couldn't possibly drive my poor Mama out of the sanatorium – she's so ill she wouldn't survive a month – and so I have made the best of things hoping for better times. But now I've lost all hope and I just can't carry on, and that's why I wanted to kill myself.'

'I must take care not to let her see my feelings,' Gianmaria thought, but his eyes were swimming with tears; such self-sacri-fice seemed to him almost superhuman; and it was with diffi-culty that he stopped himself from falling on his knees in the middle of the room before such a saint.

'But what illness has your mother got?' he asked at last.

She touched her chest with a look of apprehension and afflic-tion. 'She's tubercular. She coughs and spits blood.'

Gianmaria was busy thinking things over. He knew that he had only two thousand lire of his own. Where could he find the other thousand? Whom could he ask? He could not ask his family; they were too far away and would delay sending it and would want explanations, and when they received them they would almost certainly refuse. So to whom could he go? 'Couldn't you manage with less?' he broke in.

He saw her shake her head. 'No, alas! We really need three thousand. But don't bother.' She then became appealing: 'Why should I bother you? I'll find my own way out ... or I'll fail to – and as far as you're concerned it will be all the same, so don't bother.'

These were just the words needed to confirm Gianmaria in his philanthropic obstinacy. 'Wait,' he answered. He now began running over in his mind the tiny list of people he knew in Rome, nearly all relatives, old people or anyway his seniors, with whom he had not yet put in an appearance. One after another these people filed through his mind, and all of them for one reason or another seemed to him incapable of affording the help he needed. What he needed was to find someone who would agree to loan him the money without telling his family or asking for explanations. He would then see to repaying the debt either by recourse to his mother or by saving on his daily expenditure, small and great. His reflections took place under Santina's brooding eyes, in which poorly dissimulated hope was vainly attempting to adopt the disguise of affliction.

'Uncle Mattia,' he suddenly said to himself. 'Why didn't I think of him sooner?'

Uncle Mattia was a brother of his father, a man of around fifty and in all probability rich; a bachelor who lived alone in a house at no great distance from the *pensione*. Gianmaria hardly knew him; all he knew was that he had led a very fast life and then, as the result of a mysterious illness – no one knew whether it was of nervous origin or caused by something else – he had completely retired, rarely went out of the house, and only saw a few intimates. Gianmaria would have been unable to explain why it was precisely Uncle Mattia who was destined to give him the money; he had a presentiment that he would give it, and that was enough.

'When do you need the money?' he asked the girl in a businesslike way.

A greedy smile of temptation and delight vainly tried to keep back, but finally lifted the corners of Santina's wide mouth and produced a dimple of joy in her thin powdery cheeks. 'It must be when *you* think best, mustn't it? When you have it.'

'That won't do,' Gianmaria corrected her, for he wanted her admiration. 'Say exactly when you need it.'

'But I don't know,' she answered, still affecting embarrassment. 'This evening, tomorrow morning. . . . '

'This evening,' Gianmaria said resolutely. 'Then it's agreed. You'll have it this evening. And now let's go.' And still with the air of a man who is master of himself, of others, and of circumstances, he rose and threw a coin on the table.

'But why such a hurry? Couldn't we stay a little while?' the girl protested, for it was her turn to be disconcerted by his sudden decision. Gianmaria answered that if he was to find the money before evening he must be quick; and this time Santina had no answer to make, but followed him silently out of the café.

But when they were in the street the girl took his arm and led him towards a dark and deserted patch of gardens stretching along the river embankment.

'How can I ever repay you for all your kindness to me?' she murmured softly as she walked along by his side in the woody and misty shadows among the bare flower-beds, the black, leafless trees and the damp benches. 'Just in one day you've done more for me than any other person during my whole life. Oh it really does one good to meet people occasionally who are good like you.'

This talk about gratitude, and her praise, made Gianmaria slightly uncomfortable, for, though he was capable of behaving generously, he did not like to hear it commented on. In addition, he would have preferred kisses to words – kisses of the kind she had given him in the beginning. 'Give me a kiss,' he asked her, stopping suddenly and taking her by the arm.

Santina looked at him in surprise and then began to struggle and rave. 'There you are. You too want something in exchange for your money,' she said, pushing him away. 'You're just like the others. Even you don't respect me.'

Gianmaria bit his lip. 'She's right,' he reflected, 'I play the man of virtue, the benefactor, and then I try to get my kindness repaid exactly like all the others.' Disappointed and angry with himself, he let the girl go and with his elbows propped on the balustrade, he leant over and gazed at the river. Santina at once came close beside him. 'I say, I hope you're not offended with me. Are you?' she whispered to him, breathless, anxious, and as she spoke she took his hand and passed it behind her back so that Gianmaria's arm was round her waist. 'You see, at the moment I don't feel like it, but later, when I'm free of Negrini and the Cocanari woman and have found a job and am sure of being able to pay for Mama, then I'll be yours – because I like you, you know. Don't think I don't like you. And we'll rent a nice little room and I'll come and join you every day and we'll make love, and I'll be yours only and no one else's.' Santina spoke in the darkness, holding herself close to him, and her voice was quick, hoarse, and insinuating. 'What a strange mixture of innocence and corruption, vulgarity and delicacy,' Gianmaria thought as he listened to her. And his plan to help in her redemption was stronger than ever. Then he saw her turn her gaze towards the Tiber and stare at the flowing water. In that stretch of river, which was especially dark, all they could see at the bottom of the tall, slanting embankment was a dark and scintillating movement. 'And yet,' she philosophized in a low voice, 'think how much easier it would be if I threw myself over this wall and let myself be carried away by the tide . . . the next day you'd read in the paper: "The body of an unknown girl was discovered in the vicinity of Ponte Garibaldi." It would make an impression on you for a minute and then you'd forget about it. Don't you think it would be much simpler?'

Gianmaria shook his head. 'No; it wouldn't be simpler,' he answered. 'And then, what would be the point of it? Living is so wonderful.' As he said this he felt he'd never said anything truer or more heartfelt. 'Yes; life is wonderful,' he repeated happily, pressing his thigh against Santina's, which was hard and bony. 'Let's be off,' he added; then: 'It's time for me to be going.'

They left the little gardens and reached the point where the bridge began, and there they separated. Santina took the direction of the *pensione*; Gianmaria made his way across the bridge to the other side of the river where his uncle lived.

Two ancient cariatyds with muscular arms folded over their heads holding up a marble balcony – their Herculean torsos blackened with dust and lined by dark runnels caused by the rain – guarded the main door through which Gianmaria made his way ten minutes after he had left Santina. Beyond the main door he could distinguish a narrow courtyard covered by some dark vegetation. Here a fountain lay concealed, and the splash of its falling jet was limpidly amplified by the frozen echo of the stone roof of the main entrance. Here the stairway to the upper storeys rose with wide steps laid with a red carpet. Gianmaria mounted the first flight, crossed a landing without doors on which two dusty earthenware statues stood and watched from within twin niches, mounted a second flight which was rather narrower and steeper, crossed a windowed corridor looking out over the courtyard, and at last rang at a little door which had no name-plate.

The door was opened by a middle-aged manservant without livery, but wearing a stiff collar, a white tie and dark grey clothes, very much like a verger. On hearing Gianmaria's name, he ushered him in with a sad, resigned air, and with a bored mutter of 'I'll go and see if the Count is at home,' disappeared, closing a white-lacquered door behind him. Yet Gianmaria was not kept waiting long; after a moment the same manservant reappeared, threw both the portals wide open and told him to follow. Thus they crossed half a dozen rooms hung with red material and furnished uniformly with black mortuary furniture encrusted with bone ornaments, and lined with pictures kept behind glass and framed, too, in black. At last they reached a bright round room like a small temple with a white boxed ceiling and a circle of Doric pillars, and between the pillars busts of the ancients on pedestals. A square marble table resting on two winged bronze sphinxes stood in the middle of this room at the exact point where the temple altar would have been. By the table two people were sitting: Gianmaria's uncle and an old lady dressed in mourning with long black veils falling from a Mary Queen of Scots coif, black gloves, and a black ribbon round her wrinkled neck.

Gianmaria's uncle had the appearance and manners of a boy on whom fifty years had suddenly fallen without the transitional

periods of youth and middle age with their provision of grey
hair, lines, afflictions, incurable and ill-repressed melancholias
and complexes. He was tall and thin and wore a grey suit with
a close-cut coat, a bright tie, and a flower in his buttonhole, and
he had a querulous, gentle face which had remained fresh despite his years, with artless blue eyes and a small, upturned
nose. As soon as he caught sight of his nephew he made a great
gesture of astonishment with both his hands and rose to his feet.

'What, what, what!' he began, and each time he said, 'What'
in his rather shrill voice the ceiling returned a clear echo.
'What! Just imagine seeing him! Just imagine!' and at the
same time he tried to fix the monocle hanging on the end of a
black ribbon from the lapel of his coat in his eye-socket, but
whether out of clumsiness or affectation, he couldn't manage it
at once; but when finally it was embedded between his eyebrow
and his cheekbone, he introduced Gianmaria to the old lady, a
princess with a Roman family name and an English Christian
name.

'This,' he said in an affected voice, pointing at Gianmaria,
'this, my dear Edith, is – just imagine – the eldest son of my
poor brother who died two years ago, as you know. On his
mother's side he is related to the Laurenti – you know, the
Laurenti of Lucca, for my sister-in-law was born a Savelli, but
not the Savellis of Ancona; those of Siena, of course, I mean –
the principal branch, to which Laura Savelli also belongs, the
one who married Luigi Carpegna last winter . . .'

He made all these genealogical explanations in a hurry and
in a minor key, treating them as a parenthesis which, though
of slight importance, were necessary to the main argument. But
the old lady was not listening to him; she turned her freckled
and drawn face in its frame of thick, very white hair on Gianmaria, and, fixing him with her hard grey eyes, gave him her
hand to kiss. 'Well, well, well,' his uncle repeated, plainly veil-
ing a reproof beneath his facetiousness. 'And to what do I owe
the unexpected honour of a visit from you? Without a warning,
without a telephone call, without a word, you descend on me
out of the blue. Excellent, excellent. You see, Edith,' he added,
turning to the old lady, 'you see what boys of the young generation are like . . . they don't know the meaning of the word

"respect" or good manners. All that's over and done with, old customs that have had their day. Could you imagine me when I was his age turning up unexpectedly in the house of an uncle I hardly knew, an uncle with whom I had hardly had any relationship? It would have been unthinkable – but times have changed. Excellent! What would you like – a cup of tea and a cake?'

But the old lady did not seem to have the same opinion of Gianmaria's upbringing. 'You were quite right,' she said with a smile. 'There's no need to stand on ceremony with uncles. What's more, Mattia, it shows that he's frank and open and not a little hypocrite, as I'm sure you were at his age.'

These words gave rise to a huge laugh from Uncle Mattia. 'It doesn't matter. It doesn't matter,' he said. 'Indeed you must always behave like this, especially now you see the Princess approves. Well then,' he added with a dart of malevolent irony, 'are they all well at Arezzo, your mother and your little brothers and sisters?'

'Yes; they're all very well,' answered Gianmaria, who was seated by now.

'Fine. Excellent. And what are you up to? Studying at school and going to football matches?'

'I'm at the University,' Gianmaria answered, blushing. 'I'm studying for diplomacy. I haven't been to any football matches yet.'

'And where are you staying? Where are you living?'

'At the Pensione Humboldt.'

'At the Pensione Humboldt,' his uncle repeated with rather exaggerated bewilderment. 'I must admit I've never heard of this Pensione Humboldt. Edith, do you know the Pensione Humboldt?'

The kindly old woman once more came to Gianmaria's rescue. 'Stop, Mattia. Don't be so unkind,' she said. 'Can't you see the poor boy is on pins and needles? I'm quite sure the Pensione Humboldt is an excellent *pensione*."

'Very well. Then in that case let's all go and stay at the Pensione Humboldt – you, too, Edith.' There was a moment of silence. 'But as for you, my dear fellow,' his uncle went on, replacing his monocle in his eye-socket and staring at Gianmaria, 'you haven't yet told me the reason for your delightful and un-expected visit, for a motive there must surely be. Don't say you've come out of affection for me ...'

'It's true I did come for a reason,' he admitted with acute embarrassment, 'but – I'm sorry – I can't tell you just straight off like that. I'd need a private talk with you.'

'You see what a good psychologist I am, Edith,' said Uncle Mattia, turning in triumph to his friend; and then to Gian-maria: 'But why do you want to talk to me alone? You can easily say it all in front of the Princess: she is my *alter ego*: we are two souls in a single body, or rather' – he corrected him-self with an apology – 'two bodies with a single soul.'

Gianmaria looked in consternation first at his uncle and then at the old lady. The latter rose from her chair. 'Mattia, if you want to have a talk, I'll be off,' she began. 'The poor boy is quite intimidated by my presence.'

'Not at all. Not at all,' his uncle broke in firmly, and he made her sit down again. 'You won't move, and he will speak in your presence. What's all this? As if I could have secrets from you!'

Gianmaria hesitated, and then his repugnance was overcome by the thought that the old lady was on his side, and that far from doing him harm her presence might be all to his advan-tage.

'Very well,' he began reluctantly. 'This is what it is.' And now he spoke hurriedly – too hurriedly – as he told his lie, with none of the hesitations and pauses usual in a description of something that has really happened. 'Last night I was with several friends, and we began gambling ...'

'What at?' his uncle broke in with an expression of curiosity on his capricious face.

'At poker,' Gianmaria said at once, 'and I – well, I lost a lot of money, a thousand lire, and now, as I've got to pay within twenty-four hours and I haven't got the money myself, I came to beg you to lend it to me. Then I'll write home and get them to send it.' He stopped, with an uncomfortable feeling that he had expressed himself badly and unconvincingly. The old lady was looking at him, half-puzzled, half-amused, while his uncle studied him solemnly through his monocle. Then suddenly his uncle began laughing and brought his hand down on the table.

'What a wonderful story! Poker, a thousand lire, twenty-four hours to pay, the wealthy uncle who immediately provides the money to save the family honour! What a wonderful story – just like the novelettes of twenty years ago; and I was labouring under the delusion that you were a modern young man, a sport, what they call up-to-date and resourceful; and that you were intelligent.'

The old lady also laughed, though it was not clear whether she was incredulous like his uncle or merely amused. As for Gianmaria, he blushed to the roots of his hair and wished he had never opened his mouth.

'Don't you believe me?' he stammered at last.

His uncle was still laughing. 'Of course I don't believe you. You should look at yourself in the mirror. You haven't got the face of the boy who lost a thousand lire at poker. Has he, Edith?'

The old woman shook her head. 'No. He looks like someone who throws money away on something else,' she said with mischievous indiscretion; and she caressed Gianmaria with her hard, grey eyes, just as the manageress of the *pensione* did whenever she spoke to him.

'It would be far better to say,' went on his uncle, 'that you need a thousand lire – heaven knows why, and I don't want to know – rather than invent all this rubbish. Oh, this modern generation! I really thought it was more outspoken.'

Gianmaria wanted to pin him down. 'Well then, yes. I need a thousand lire,' he said firmly. 'I'm in urgent need of the money. Can you lend it to me?'

He saw his uncle make a gesture of refusal. 'But of course I can't lend it. A thousand lire! If I had a thousand lire, I'd be what here in Rome they call a man of property. A thousand lire in these hard times! Where could I get the money? That's the problem. And then today is Sunday and the banks are shut.'

'So you can't lend it to me.' The tears caught in Gianmaria's voice.

'I've told you I can't. But,' and his uncle turned to the old lady with a facetious air, 'you can ask the Princess. She has a soft spot for you already and she may have the money in her purse . . .'

At these words something almost like hope dawned in Gianmaria's eyes, and when the old lady saw this she was very put out. 'You must be mad, Mattia,' she protested quickly. 'The poor boy. Of course I would give him the money if I had it. But as you say, a thousand lire in these hard times . . . ' She finished the phrase with an expressive gesture of her hands through the black veils that fell from her head.

'It's obvious he isn't going to give me anything,' Gianmaria decided, 'and if I stay I shall only be made a fool of.' This thought was enough to restore the complete calm which his uncle's sarcasm and his own frenzy of frustration had almost made him lose. He rose to his feet quickly. 'Do please excuse me, uncle,' he began.

'Oh, not at all, not at all,' his uncle said as he too got up.

'Do please excuse me,' Gianmaria insisted. And he bent to kiss the hand that the old lady held out to him.

'You must come and call on me,' she said. 'I'm at No. 7, Piazza Campitelli. And don't think your uncle is unkind; he's merely given to teasing. And then it may well be that by refusing you this money he has prevented you from doing something quite idiotic. I'm prepared to bet it has something to do with a woman.'

'It was wrong of you not to say so,' pointed out his uncle, flippant to the last, 'for in that case – I'd have refused just the same.' But he looked very relieved at his nephew's departure, and accompanied him no further than the second room. There, popping out from heaven knows where, the drooping manservant in the grey suit reappeared. Overcome with rage and burning humiliation, Gianmaria made his way quickly to the vestibule, put on his coat with feverish haste, and went out into the corridor.

'And now how shall I have the face to meet Santina and say, "I'm very sorry but I haven't been able to raise the money"?' This was what Gianmaria was thinking as he made his way through the streets towards the *pensione*. He felt that, quite apart from looking like a vain boaster, he would be guilty of a grave fault – that of cruelly letting down the poor girl who had trusted him and looked to him for salvation. Though these bitter thoughts drove the picture of his uncle's ungracious reception of him from his mind, they increased his feelings of remorse about Santina. So that, as he neared the *pensione,* he was feeling not so much angry as deeply humiliated and ashamed. And in addition he was feeling exhausted by the trials and varied events of that unlucky Sunday; he was feeling worn out, unnerved, lost, and young, after the earlier exultation that had made him delude himself into thinking he was a man, confident and self-assured. Then came the last straw, unimportant in itself, but decisive because of its timing, at the moment when his hysteria and wretchedness were at their worst: at the very moment when he entered the hall of the *pensione* the deep metallic clang of the supper-gong broke out.

He had always hated that absurd noise, for it seemed calculated to raise the alarm for heaven knew what calamity rather than announce a modest meal in a family boarding-house. Coming at that moment the booming of the gong not only ripped his raw nerves to pieces, but brought the dining-room vividly before his mind, where, besides the other guests, Negrini, the Cocanari woman, and Santina would be. Worse, Negrini would address him from his table with his swindler's unction and cordiality, the Cocanari woman would smile at him and ogle him with eyes cauterized with mascara, and there might even be some new joke like the one with the soap. And then, worst of all, behind all the goings-on poor Santina would be looking at him questioningly, full of hope and anxiety. These thoughts chased each other through his head as the gong was borne along the passages by a maid, who seemed to hit it with relish. It grew louder and louder, reached the climax of booming and then died away with two or three final bangs. As soon as silence returned, he made a swift decision: to avoid seeing Negrini, the Cocanari woman, Santina and the others he would have his supper brought to his room just for this once.

He thought of informing a maid, but then his eyes fell on the word 'Bureau' on the architrave above the manageress's door, and it seemed to him that the quickest and simplest plan would be to tell her. He went up to the door and knocked. But on this occasion, before the sound of the gently modulated 'Come in', there was a rather long-drawn-out noise of jumbled clothes being moved and of naked footsteps on the floor. Then he heard the melodious voice, pushed open the door, and went in. The manageress was standing by the fireplace, in which a lively fire was blazing. Instead of her usual black dress, she was wearing a long pink house-coat trimmed with white fur. From the way she held her coat across her flank, from her disordered hair, from the slight and girlish glow on her usually pallid cheeks, and from certain intimate articles of clothing that she had not had time to hide, but had left lying on the sofa, Gianmaria realized that she was in the middle of dressing. He also noticed – it seemed, though he could not have said why, an important discovery – that as she stood upright in her long house-coat looking a trifle ruffled and unprepared and lacking her usual distant calm, she was really very beautiful. Then 'I'm so sorry,' he said, embarrassed, 'but I just wanted to say that this evening I shan't be having supper in the dining-room, but in my bedroom.'

The woman had not yet recovered her composure, the blush had not entirely disappeared and now and again a deep breath of emotion swelled her large, soft bosom. To gain time, she looked at Gianmaria in silence and shook her head.

'Why do you want to eat in your room?' she said at last. 'Is it because you don't feel well?'

Gianmaria was beset by an absurd and boyish longing to confide. 'I feel very well,' he answered, and the tears caught in his throat, 'but I'm in a bad temper and I don't want to see anyone.'

'A bad temper?' the manageress repeated softly, looking at him. 'Is it because you've had no news from home?'

'No. Because of something else,' Gianmaria answered curtly; but, strange to say, he did not feel the slightest inclination to leave the warm, cosy little room. 'Because of money,' he added, without thinking.

'Because of money?' she asked solicitously. 'When you paid the bill last night, did it leave you short? Would you like the money back? You can pay at the end of next week.'

Gianmaria wondered what he had better do. He felt extremely agitated. Should he confide the whole business to a woman he hardly knew? He found himself saying: 'Oh, if it were only that, it would be nothing. Unfortunately, it's a much larger sum.'

The manageress suddenly became pressing, almost eager. 'Tell me how much you need,' she said, 'and if I can, if I have it, I shall willingly lend it to you.'

Again Gianmaria asked himself what he had better do; but a strange, uncontrollable emotion caught in his throat and he felt himself carried on to confide in the woman as if she were an indulgent mother. 'I need,' he said in a strangled voice, gazing straight into her motionless black eyes, 'a thousand lire.'

She remained silent, looking at him with a kind of apprehension, Gianmaria thought – the sum was obviously too large. 'You're very kind,' he went on, blushing, 'but you can't possibly lend me that amount, and so . . . ' and he made a convulsive gesture with his hands as if to say : 'So don't let's bother about it.' Still she did not speak, and seemed upset. Then, like a sleep-walker, she took a step forward and lifted an arm towards Gianmaria. The boy suddenly felt the caress of that light cold hand on his hair and cheeks. 'Would it really please you,' she asked at last, without pausing in her gentle caresses, 'if I lent you the money?'

Her pale face was blushing slightly and she gave him a characteristic look that was almost a supplication; then she swiftly withdrew her hand as though it had been burnt and let it fall back again to her side. That caress had finally disclosed to Gianmaria the cause of the manageress's strange behaviour towards him. 'She's in love with me,' he thought. He did not know whether to be pleased or to respond to her feelings; but with one of those canny and self-interested flights of lucidity peculiar to adolescents, the only thing he knew for certain was that the woman's feeling for him had come at a lucky moment and would be useful, for it was obvious that he only needed to persevere and he would get the money he wanted. 'Yes; I would be very pleased,' he answered, somewhat aghast at his own boldness, yet unable to help looking the woman straight in the eyes in a way that was both commanding and flattering, 'because I really do need it.'

Without a word, she turned her back on him, went to the writing-desk, opened a drawer, and began to search. But all of a sudden she was brought to a halt by an unexpected doubt obviously inspired by her many years' experience as a manageress. Standing motionless, her hands in the drawer, she asked, half-turning: 'But are you quite sure that you'll be able to pay the money back?'

When he heard these words a deep blush rushed to Gianmaria's cheeks. 'She doesn't trust me,' he thought, and was assailed by feelings of resentment and wounded pride and by a desire to give the manageress an unquestionable guarantee of his own honesty. His anger and confusion made him hesitate a moment and then: 'Wait a second,' he said. 'I'll be back immediately,' and before the woman had time to recover from her surprise he had left the room.

He ran along the passages to his room; there, his heart full of aggressive anger, he took his suitcase from under the bed, pulled out the papers that filled it and found a black leather box. It contained some cuff-links and studs of onyx and brilliants that had belonged to his father. He ran wildly to the manageress's room, dashed in in a frenzy without knocking and threw the case on to the writing-desk. 'These,' he said, 'are certainly worth three thousand lire, possibly even four. Take them, and then when I get the money back you can return them to me.'

He was panting, dishevelled, furious, and his young face was alive with glowing cheeks and black sparkling eyes. Instead of protesting, the woman gazed at him and gave him an amused and affectionate smile. 'Why are you so headstrong?' she asked calmly, taking her time and offering him the banknote she had taken from the drawer during his absence. 'I only said what I did for something to say. Here's the money, and take your cufflinks. I can trust you without all this . . .'

Oblivious of what he was doing, Gianmaria swiftly pocketed the note, but refused to take back the case. 'No, no. Keep it. You can give it back to me when I get the money. As for supper, I've changed my mind. I'll have it in the dining-room after all. Thanks; and good evening.' As he uttered or rather stammered these jerky phrases he turned on his heel and left the room.

In the passage he drew his pocket-book from his pocket, took out his two other thousand-lire notes, folded them together with the one from the manageress and put them in his trouser pocket. Then, with a confident step, he went to the dining-room door and entered.

The guests were already half-way through supper. 'Good evening. Good evening,' Negrini said immediately and very cordially, but Gianmaria merely answered with a curt nod and went straight to his table. The Cocanari woman also greeted him with a wide and brilliant smile of her dark mouth full of gold teeth, but Gianmaria pretended not to see her. Instead, he fixed his eyes on Santina, and the minute she looked up at him, he cast her a meaning look as if to say, 'I've got the money.' He noticed that she made a discreet sign that she had understood and, satisfied, he began eating.

That evening the manageress failed to put in an appearance. In any case, all Gianmaria's thoughts were for Santina; he ate methodically and slowly, as if every mouthful was remarkably enjoyable, and thus he was able to watch the guests leaving the dining-room one by one; last of all Negrini and the two women got up to go; then, rising in his turn, he approached the three of them.

'What were you doing this morning that made you vanish?' the Cocanari woman asked, offering a plump hand bedecked with valueless rings. 'Were you invited out somewhere?'

'I had my pre-military training,' Gianmaria answered evasively. By now they were in the passage, and just as on the previous day the Cocanari woman and Negrini walked a few steps ahead of Santina and himself. Gianmaria pulled the notes from his pocket and thrust them, folded into four, into the girl's hand. 'There's the three thousand lire,' he whispered. 'Now I'm off to my room, and I'll wait for you there.'

As the girl took the notes she gave his hand a strong squeeze as if to seal their understanding. 'Thanks,' she whispered. She was wearing a grey costume almost like a man's; under her open jacket she had on a little white silk shirt, and her small, pointed breasts could be seen moving freely beneath the light material. 'Give me a kiss,' Gianmaria murmured, ill at ease, as he saw Negrini and the Cocanari woman disappearing behind the corner of the passage. And he tried to embrace her. But the girl pushed him away. 'Not here. Later, in your room,' she whispered. Then she ran away on quick, light feet and disappeared.

Gianmaria felt downcast and vaguely frustrated, but went to his room and took out a book and a packet of cigarettes, then, stretching full-length on the sofa, he began awaiting Santina's arrival. He waited for a long time, reading without understanding a single word, throwing away cigarettes as soon as he had lighted them, listening greedily for sounds from outside, going every now and then to the door to spy along the deserted passage, counting the chimes from the nearby belfry every time it rang. He waited a long time – so long that after he had passed through the phases of impatience, fury and despair and had thought out a thousand hypotheses to account for Santina's incomprehensible non-appearance, he was overcome by a painful, stupified, sleepy state of mind that drove out every other feeling. He seemed to have entered upon a period without end and without light, in which waiting and being disappointed were natural and inevitable. Periodically he would murmur: 'Santina, why don't you come? I am here, waiting for you.' His confused feeling of waking-sleep was like that of a traveller by train at night who does not know whether he is asleep or awake, but every now and again – at halts when he hears the solitary and funereal voice of a railwayman shouting out the name of the station – opens his eyes and tries to peer at the place they have reached, the carriage bathed in darkness and the travellers sprawling on pillows, white handkerchiefs wrapped round the men's collars and the women's eyes tightly shut; and, unable to shake off his torpor, slides back into uneasy sleep the moment the train moves on again, with the quick and regular throb of the tireless wheels on the everlasting rails beating time. At last, in the middle of the night, without knowing what he was doing, Gianmaria got up from the sofa, went over to the bed, undressed mechanically and slipped between the sheets. After a short while he fell into deep slumber.

He was awakened late in the morning by a gentle and musical voice which seemed more dreamt than heard, and by the contact of a shy yet insistent hand on his cheek and neck. 'It must be Santina,' he thought at once without opening his eyes.

Still with this impression, he opened them wide and leapt into a sitting position in his bed. Then in the scattered darkness shot through by a thousand threads of light filtering through the cracks of the shutters he saw, standing by his pillow in a dressing-gown, not Santinas, but the manageress.

'I hope I didn't wake you up too early,' she said softly. 'It's ten o'clock.'

'Oh no,' said Gianmaria with embarrassment. 'I was awake,' and his hands ran down to button up his pyjama top over his naked chest.

With simple, familiar gestures she turned on the weak yellow light of the lamp on the bedside table and then sat down sideways on the edge of the bed. 'It's rather bold of me to come into your room in this way, I know,' she began in a calm voice, gazing at her hands with a kind of cold attention, 'and I wouldn't have done so if an extraordinary thing hadn't happened. You know Signorina Rinaldi? Well, during the night she ran away.'

Gianmaria opened his eyes wide with amazement.

'She ran away,' the manageress repeated, and her voice had just a trace of quiet satisfaction. 'She appears to have made off in a car with a dark young man with whom she often used to go out. She ran away with all the jewels of that woman she was staying with and all the money and valuables of their gentleman friend, that Negrini.'

Gianmaria, his two hands rubbing his eyes, still felt he was dreaming. 'But what . . . '

'It seems that that woman wasn't her mother, but a common kept woman called . . . wait . . . Cocanari, and Negrini was their associate,' the manageress went on coolly and slowly. 'They got together to take in and defraud people. I learnt all this because I found the Cocanari woman weeping and saying that Rinaldi was a thankless creature, and Negrini was shrieking like someone out of his mind. Obviously the Rinaldi girl had done to them what they taught her to do to others. Besides a lot of money, she stole Negrini's cigarette case, his watch, his tie-pin and several other things, and all the Cocanari woman's rings. But what aroused my suspicions about the sort of people they were was that, in spite of the theft, they didn't want to inform the police. Obviously they're afraid that if the Rinaldi girl were arrested all their misdeeds would come to light. In any case, I told them to pack and be out of the *pensione* before midday.'

The manageress told her story with great coolness, but she kept looking at Gianmaria in a queer way, at once grave and inquisitoral. Then she stopped talking and looked at him as if she expected some comment.

As a matter of fact, Gianmaria had no idea what to say. He was less aware of feelings of disappointment and sorrow than of a great iciness in the place where the evening before he had experienced so many warm and generous emotions for Santina. He suddenly felt he had grown up, and now his dark and confused passion for Santina had smashed to pieces and been brushed away, leaving a sense of icy emptiness. He could now see clearly the full significance of his experience, but was unable to think beyond the point of realizing his mistake. His abstract contemplation of his own situation was interrupted by the voice of the manageress. 'The Rinaldi girl has run away,' she said softly with her eyes on him, 'and besides taking the belongings of her accomplices, she also made off with the thousand lire that I lent you yesterday. Didn't she?'

Gianmaria was unable to speak and felt a great longing to hide his face under the sheet. He nodded and lowered his blushing and confused face.

'Yes. But,' he managed to add, 'don't imagine you won't get your money back.'

'What does my money matter?' the woman answered in a tone of bitter and melancholy reproof. At this Gianmaria raised his eyes and saw that she was shaking her head slowly in deprecation, as if to say: 'Why are you being so insensitive? Why do you refuse to understand me?' and at the same time she placed a black object, the case of cuff-links he had left with her the evening before, on the bedside table. He also noticed that she had moved much nearer on the bed and that her powerful, erect bust was almost touching his arm. Then, suddenly, like a fire smouldering under the ashes, which all of a sudden leaps to life and shoots up lively flames, he felt beneath the weight and opacity of his disillusion a violent feeling of attraction towards the gentle, temperate, and loyal woman beside him. It seemed as if he had loved her always, from the day he had first caught sight of her, even during the moments of his greatest exultation about Santina – indeed, at those moments above all, for then he had unknowingly felt her, so pale and calm, to be the natural counterweight to the vulgar and twisted girl. With this in mind, he put out his hand and with the same gentle gesture that she had had for him the evening before, he began caressing her cheek with his fingers. He saw her emotion beneath his light caress and every now and then she closed her eyes with desire for pleasure, as if the better to savour the sweetness that she had longed for so much and had now at last attained. Then, resting with her hands on either side of Gianmaria's body and without opening her tightly shut eyelids, her face white, she permitted her dress to be opened over her naked breasts, bent over him, and offered him her lips.

THE FALL

TANCREDI's illness had lasted a couple of months, and as soon as he was able to get up his parents decided to send him to the seaside. No sooner had they found a villa near a beach than they started making the usual preparations for departure. But the boy felt uneasy when he saw the unseasonable suitcases, the clothes that had not had time to get impregnated with the pungent smell of camphor. The idea of this premature holiday disturbed some hidden sense of order within him, and the interruption of his studies weighed on him, even though he felt unfit to go on with them; it was all a leap in the dark. In other words, he was unable to appreciate that his childhood was over and that he was on the threshold of his turbid and troubled adolescence. When he had taken to his bed his hair had been curly and he himself wilful and capricious; when he got up his hair was cropped and smooth, his neck scrawny, and he was listless and delicate, a victim of obsessions. At one time he hadn't known the meaning of revulsion, fear, or remorse; now there were a hundred reasons for revulsion, fear had caught up with him and didn't give him a moment's respite, and he was beset by remorse, though, try as he might, he couldn't conceive what he was guilty of. Despite these changes, in his mother's eye he was still the same Tancredi, and throughout the journey she treated him as a child – and this made him grind his teeth with shame. When they reached the sea, his mother, who liked playing cards and had found some other people who shared her tastes, put him in charge of Veronica, the maid, whose task it was to keep an eye on him and accompany him to the beach. At first Veronica did this regularly, but after a while she became slack and in the end ceased entirely to bother about him. Tancredi was left alone and completely free.

The villa, the last on that strip of coast, was a massive,

three-storeyed building of the beginning of the century, with sloping roof of slate, round attic skylights, oblong windows, and balconies, bulges, and balustrades. A green-and-red decoration representing a tangle of water-lilies writhing like serpents covered the whole façade, the stalks beginning at ground-level, twisting round the windows and bursting into bloom under the roof. The villa belonged to an antique dealer, a friend of Tancredi's family, who had loaned it to them in return for good turns they had done him in the past; and it contained all his ugliest, most spurious, and unsellable possessions, serving him as a kind of storehouse.

There were rooms on the ground floor containing four wardrobes, one for each wall; there were others with whole battle-lines of tables, great and small; yet others were crammed with cabinets, brackets, and minor knick-knacks. In the overcrowded living-rooms on the second floor there were mirrors of all sizes with over-ornate frames and green reflections. In the bedrooms there were two, three or even four beds ranged side by side, as in a hospital. The lobbies and passages were cluttered up with marble torsos, chests, and pieces of armour; on the walls were huge blackening seventeenth-century pictures; by the staircase hung a series of pale tapestries with a whole population of soft and flowery figures. Everything was dark, dank, creaking, and shadowy. The feeling of the sea never penetrated, nor the radiant light of the coast; for the antique dealer had put some of his pieces of stained glass into the windows, for want of a better place. A musty, tomb-like smell of old wood, mould, and mice hovered in those air-tight rooms, and the furniture with its strange arbitrary arrangement seemed to rebuff human intrusion with surly self-sufficiency. For Tancredi's mother the house was uncomfortable – impossible to keep it clean, impossible to move about without knocking into something – and, as she was always saying, not without complacency, it was a great responsibility living in such a museum, for it would be a disaster if anything got broken. But for Tancredi, given his inclinations, it was worse than uncomfortable; it was terrifying: though not without that background of delicious anguish that fear inspires when it ceases to be an abnormal state and becomes the rule. How this terror had taken root he wouldn't have been able to explain; perhaps it was the terror of death which had come with his illness and survived his recovery; perhaps it was caused by his break from childhood and by the feeling that his strength was not equal to the demands made on it by his new condition. He had a kind of chronic apprehension or feeling of foreboding; as if everything concealed a trap; and he was oppressed by a mystery that he was powerless to solve. This state of mind might possibly have diminished had they taken up residence elsewhere, but the dark house full of furniture seemed made to aggravate his morbid and melancholy states of mind. As always happens in such cases, Tancredi was attracted by everything that helped to keep him immersed in the terror-charged atmosphere. Moreover, he was deeply aware that the atmosphere pervaded not only the whole villa, but the neighbouring enclosure – and beyond that it faded away and evaporated. Soon he came to prefer the house and the enclosure to the silly bathing hut with its crooked sunshade facing the sea, and the sand that you could trickle through your fingers hour after hour.

Little by little he took possession of his domain. He was especially attracted by the attic rooms on the top floor. They were like cells, and their whitewashed ceilings and rough, paved floors suggested tragic, forgotten loves whose secrets had remained locked up with the dust and decay. The antique dealer's huge black pictures, most of them unframed, covered the walls from floor to ceiling, and the figures depicted in violent attitudes among clouds and darkness seemed out-of-place in those low-ceilinged cells. Tancredi unrolled the mattresses and lay flat on his back with his legs in the air for hours on end, letting his imagination run riot – gazing dreamily at the tonsured St Antonys kneeling at the feet of dusky Madonnas, at the rapacious Judiths sitting on the decapitated torsos of Holofernes, at the big-bellied Dianas whose beds, curtains, cushions, and even the divine rain of coins, had been blacked out by the patina of time, so that it was impossible to see what they were waiting for as they lay there in voluptuous attitudes. Tancredi was even more fascinated by what was lacking in the pictures than by what they were intended to signify; the cold faces, the disproportionate limbs, and the false postures. It did not matter to him whether the subjects were sacred or profane so long as he could abandon himself to his imaginings and invent haunting terrors in which he gradually came to believe.

Now, one day, while he was lying on his back, his attention was held by a huge picture hanging on the wall facing him, for it seemed to be almost a reflection of himself. It was probably a copy of a Caravaggio and represented St Paul's fall on the way to Damascus. A bright, smoky shaft of light like the trail of a thunderbolt lit up the saint's naked and emaciated body and hurled him backwards, blinded, legs in air, arms outstretched. All the rest of the picture was in darkness, though it was still just possible to discern the saddle, the mane, the horse's head, and a calm, beardless attendant in a turban – things that seemed to belong to a different world, a reign of peace. Tancredi found this picture astonishing, as though he were seeing it for the first time, and he liked it particularly perhaps because he was lying in the same position as the figure in the picture and thus felt better able to probe its inner meaning. Head down, feet in air, he began thinking, with the dizzy sensation of falling over backwards into an abyss – the lightning in his eyes. But after the event came perfect faith, so that the world which had been simple was now double, for the lightning had laid bare the soul hidden beneath appearances. This was what Tancredi was thinking or, rather, working out in some dim way deep down inside him, when, suddenly, he felt something hard in his pocket and remembered that the day before he had made a much-longed-for catapult with a fork of pinewood and a piece of bicycle tyre, and with the speed of a child his thoughts and wishes suddenly changed their direction – he experienced an irresistible desire to go to the enclosure near the villa and try out his new toy. No sooner thought than done: he leapt from the bed, giddy, flung down the stairs and went out at the back door of the villa. But as soon as he was out of doors the heavy, sultry air undermined his confidence, and it was with slow, uneasy footsteps that he made his way towards the gap in the wall through which he passed every day into the neighbouring enclosure. On reaching the gap, he had to make his way through brambles that he had already trodden down and pushed aside on previous occasions, but this time a bramble caught his arm and pinned him back – and this, in view of his habit of endowing

objects with intelligence, seemed to him a bad omen. 'Don't
you want me to get through?' he murmured as he unhooked
the thorns one by one from his sleeve. 'Tell me, why don't you
want me to get through?' The wall was much higher on the
other side than on the garden side. Tancredi sat on the top,
swung himself round, stuck out his legs and, resting his chest
on the wall, slid down.

The wall bounded the enclosure on three sides; the side opposite Tancredi's villa was bounded by the smooth white end of a
mansion, a slice of house without any windows, so that the
enclosure was quite hidden from view unless someone happened
to look out of the upper windows of the villa – which wasn't
often. The whole extent of the sunk enclosure was rough with
mounds and pitted with holes and littered with tins and every
kind of crumbling refuse: in one corner a tree of medium size
stretched its branches over the wall into the road; tangled shrubs
such as are to be found near the sea grew in patches in the
sandy soil. That day the sky, overcast and dark and presaging a
storm, withheld all light from the sand and stubble, and the
acrid smell from still-fresh heaps of refuse lay heavy in the
motionless air.

As he entered the enclosure Tancredi underwent his usual
transformation. His movements became circumspect, he walked
on tiptoe, looking from side to side in terror. It was partly a
game; but his nervous wariness – and the bramble that had held
him back by the arm – warned him that the game was a façade
and what was real were the traps, though he had no idea where
they lay concealed. He looked up at the sky and saw that, passing over him obliquely, was a dark cloud with a smoky fringe
– beginning over the pinewood and slanting gradually upward
till it reached its greatest height over the sea, like a badly-raised
theatre curtain, so that the whole sky looked lopsided. In the
silence his foot struck noisily on a tin can; with a kick, he
booted it away. Then, with deliberation though without enthu-
siasm, he took up a heap of sharp stones that he had collected
the day before and went to sit on a mound not far from the
wall: here, with the missiles between his legs, he began to
practise with the catapult. The target was a food tin balanced
on the top of the wall. Every time he hit the tin and it fell on

the further side of the wall, Tancredi methodically put another in its place. It was not easy to hit the tins with their rounded, run-away surfaces, but as the stones hit the target Tancredi little by little warmed up to the game he had started so half-heartedly. Then, unexpectedly, at the moment of raising his eyes to take aim after bending down for a stone, he saw a big cat pass cautiously along the ridge of the wall just behind the tin, its blue-greyness standing out against the thicker darker grey of the sky. 'I'll aim at that,' he thought. This was pure showing-off, because he was sure he would not hit it, nor did he want to; he did not even pull the catapult back to its full extent, and he let fly almost gently. As if there was a tenuous nerve attached to the missile and communicating its every vibration to him, he distinctly felt that the stone had hit, not the target, but something soft and living that could only be the cat. In terror he got up from the mound and approached cautiously. The blow seemed to have stunned the cat; it stood there motionless with its astonished face turned in his direction. But on looking more carefully he saw that only one of its eyes sent forth its green rays in wide-open surprise; the other was extinguished and in its place a little bleeding cross deep set in the fur seemed to heighten the glassiness of the eye that remained open; a round convex piece of glass, living and sensitive, had been smashed to pieces.

When he saw this he was speechless with terror. He was less frightened by the clot of blood in the grey fur than by the animal's stillness, as it stood as if turned to stone, and by the gaze of the one eye. His fear was not so much that the beast might spring at him as that it might attach itself to him with a vindictive loyalty – the horror of this was already on him. The cat's expression was one of surprise rather than of hatred, and in the surprise a singular affection seemed already present, as if with the catapult shot that had blinded it in one eye the cat recognized an unbreakable bond between Tancredi and itself. There followed a hollow clap of thunder from the oblique cloud crossing the sky; and with a shout of 'Get off! Get off!' Tancredi waved his arms at the cat. He saw it draw back with an almost pained expression as if to say, 'What harm have I done you that you should chase me away?' and, in a frenzy of terror, he bent down to pick up a stone. But when he stood up again there was only the tin on the wall that had served him as target; the cat had disappeared.

Trembling all over, he threw down the catapult in disgust and made for the gap in the wall. The fading light was grey and gloomy; he noticed, when he had vaulted the wall, that under the leafy trees it was almost dark. Midges were buzzing in the already rain-laden shadows. A smell of washed plates and dead fires came up from the thick, black grating of the kitchen. Tancredi knew that at this time of day the cat usually sat in the corner of the fireplace under the chimney, and as he was about to go into the kitchen he was seized by the craven fear of meeting it. He was convinced for some reason that the beast would never leave his heels from now onwards, that to get rid of it he would have to kill it, and that even after he had killed it the persecution would persist, for there would remain the remorse for an act which he already foresaw would be drawn-out and horrible. However, he screwed up his courage, pulled himself together, and, after trying to pierce the darkness, charged blindly across the kitchen and fumbled at the door leading from that room to the dining-room. The cat was waiting for him in the passage; he felt its fur against his naked legs. The confined space made it more unbearable, and with a shudder and scream he fled into the dining-room.

Here it was no less dark and deserted. By now he had lost his nerve completely, and though there was no sign of the cat he couldn't stop shaking. He picked his way cautiously out of the dining-room and hurried across the entrance hall, trembling in every limb as if his body were trying to run away from him, like a horse from a rider who has lost control; he felt frantically for the light switch, flicked it on and looked around. The cat was the first thing he saw; it was between the legs of an armchair, facing him.

It fixed him with its one green eye, staring and terrified now and quite unlike the shy affection of its first advances. His heart beating wildly, Tancredi retreated, backing upstairs on the stair carpet. Immediately the cat came out from its refuge and followed him, deliberately lifting its face up to him. Still backing up the stairs, Tancredi reached the landing, where there stood a table strewn with ancient weapons: one of these – a pistol or a dagger – he intended to seize and hurl at the cat. The cat continued to climb towards him, fixing him with something that looked like hope. Tancredi's hand fumbled on the table behind him. He clutched a pistol and hurled it blindly. There was a sharp crash followed by the tinkle of broken glass: the pistol had hit the dining-room door. Panic-stricken, Tancredi turned on his heels and fled.

He ran up the two flights of stairs to the third floor landing. A dusky light filtered in from the two windows at the end of the passage and fell on the red brickwork floor. In this halo of grey light Tancredi saw the cat turning round watchfully with its back up, its fur raised. He gave a leap and reached a doorway. With his fingers on the handle, he watched the animal's movements. It did not seem to be aware of his presence, but in the dim light was turning round and round with arched back and tail erect. It might have been looking at its reflection in the floor, for all of a sudden it leapt aside as if in play with its own image. It was then that it first caught sight of Tancredi and made for him with a calm and trusting trot. Tancredi, who had kept his eyes on it all this time, hurriedly entered the room and very slowly, without making a sound, closed the door.

The room in which he found himself was the same as all the others on the third floor. It was almost entirely filled with a great walnut bed whose grey striped mattress looked comforting in the twilight under the low ceiling. On the bedside table stood a candlestick of bright blue glass, but the walls, strangely enough, were bare. Tancredi sat down on the edge of the bed and listened to the furtive nibbling and scurrying of the rats in the space between ceiling and roof. After a moment he felt reassured, and was just going to lie down in his usual way when the deep silence was broken by a strange sound. It was the noise of low chatting voices, engaged in urgent discussion; and it seemed to come from the next room, whose door appeared to be ajar. For a while Tancredi listened, motionless, to the whispering which had an inhuman, improbable quality in the silence of the attic, as if the pieces of antique furniture were talking rather than two people. Suddenly one of the voices was raised, revealing itself as not only human, but that of a man. His curiosity aroused, Tancredi got up and went to take a look through the crack in the door.

At first he saw only a little room in all respects similar to the one he was in; then on the far wall he recognized the picture of the fall of St Paul looking gloomier and eerier than ever. The bed on which his fancy had run riot a few hours earlier as he lay staring at the picture was empty, and he could not conceive where the low voices had come from. The voices had now stopped, and yet the room looked alive and inhabited as if the dark enclosed atmosphere had retained an imprint of the presences so recently within it. What prevented Tancredi from entering the room was a very precise sensation that he would be violating an intimacy that was private and in some way clandestine, and as he watched he had a feeling he had never experienced before – of committing a shameless indiscretion. While he was still looking there began a long, dry, melancholy creaking such as is made when unoiled hinges are being slowly turned by the cautious shutting of a door. There was no doubt about it – at that very moment someone was leaving the room with the least possible noise, but the door with its long high creak was betraying him. Then there was silence again. Suddenly, as if precautious were no longer necessary, the person remaining in the room dropped on to the bed, with a groaning of springs and a creaking of wood. And Tancredi saw two legs stretching along the mattress towards the bottom of the bed; naked and shining white and as if weighed down with languor and the desire for repose. Veronica's legs, Tancredi thought involuntarily, remembering the white face, blue eyes, and fair hair of his mother's maid. The legs, long, slender and slightly convex at the knees, couldn't keep still, though their movements were heavy, weary and voluptuous. The attic window beyond the bed began now to be spattered with dark drops of rain. The legs stopped moving. Tancredi was overcome with a growing and intolerable sense of shameful prying; his cheeks burned and he drew away from the door and sat on his own bed.

He didn't know what to make of what he had seen, but experienced an acute sense of ambiguity and doubt. There was nothing odd about it at first sight. But why should Veronica go to sleep in a room that wasn't hers? And what was all the chattering and the man's voice? But when he embarked on these questions he again experienced the acute sense of shame that had beset him while he was peeping, and in disgust he tried to think of something else.

He got up from the bed and went to sit on the floor in the embrasure of the window; there, feeling utterly safe and happy, he began watching the rain streaking down the window. The little room was almost dark by now, but he thought that the cat might well be waiting for him outside in the passage, whereas in here under the low ceiling and against that big bed he felt secure. Crouched, with his lips against his knees, he watched the rain falling for a long time. When he began dozing he got up automatically and lay on the bed. The mattress, though hard and flat, felt soft after the tiles. He lay on his back and stared at the ceiling listening to the swishing of the rain and the rats scurrying in the rafters. At last his eyelids grew heavy and he fell asleep.

For a while he slumbered dreamlessly and when he reawakened he found himself in darkness. It was already nightfall, but by his reckoning still too early for supper; so he did not stir from the bed. From some point in the ceiling, above his head almost, there came a persistent noise, the stubborn gnawing of a rodent ferociously at work on dry, hard wood. The noise had a rhythm, first loud, then soft, then almost silent – 'It's gone,' thought Tancredi – then loud again and fiercer than ever. After he had lain in wait a little while he felt something falling on top of him – something like a piece of plaster. Convulsed with fear, he groped for the lamp on the bedside table, lit it and looked.

It was as he thought: some plaster had fallen and there was a black hole in the middle of the ceiling. It was small and jagged, but its flaky edges suggested that some vast den lay beyond, so that if the plaster fell Heaven knew what tunnels might not be disclosed. He gazed; and then suddenly something appeared in the hole, something dark, soft and swollen, and with a swift motion there glared the red and raging eye of a rat. A split second – then the hole became black and empty again; but it was enough for Tancredi. He leapt trembling from the bed and ran headlong to call Veronica from the next room. She was no longer on the bed, but sitting on a stool busy sewing.

'Veronica,' he said, his voice throbbing with unspeakable joy. 'Veronica, there's a rat up there . . . '

She looked at him without a word and then put down her work and followed him, or, to be more precise, preceded him into the room.

'Up there,' said Tancredi, staying by the door and pointing to the ceiling.

The maid looked at the hole and still without a word went back to her room and returned armed with a broom. Tancredi watched her get on to the bed and, holding the broom by the brush end, begin to explore the hole with the handle. Heartened by her calmness, Tancredi advanced several steps into the room. The broom-handle went in and out, rubbing with a dull sound against the sides of the hole.

'There. I can feel it,' she said almost with delight. 'Yes; it really is a rat.' But the broom fell from her hands and down fell something large and dark; she fell headlong back on to the bed, her legs open, grasping her loins with her hands, pulling her clothes round her thighs and shouting:

'It jumped on top of me! I've got it on top of me.'

She struggled and her naked legs emerged from her clothes. Tancredi saw that they really were the legs that he had seen lying languidly twitching on the mattress. But amid this display of whiteness there was no rat to be seen, and this gave rise to the suspicion that it must have hidden under a chair, unless it had got under the woman's clothes – and how could it? Tancredi was so terrified that the infuriated rat would bite his legs that he leapt on to a chair.

The woman was still struggling: Tancredi, distraught, jumped from the first chair to another without touching the ground. Breathless, his heart beating frantically, he tried to reach the door and call for help; but it was dark, and this time he really did wake up, trembling and sweating all over – not on the chair as in his dream, nor on the bed where he was when he went to sleep, but in an unknown part of the room. Though he realized that the business of the rat had all been a dream, a frenzied terror was still upon him and he tried wildly to get out of the room or to find a light. But the room seemed to have changed its shape; his outstretched arms met with unforeseen walls and unfamiliar corners; he seemed to be not in the villa at all, but many feet underground, shut up in a tomb. At last the door burst open, the wavering light of a candle broke through the darkness, and while he was turning distractedly two shadows were cast upon the ceiling.

'But he's here,' said his mother's voice with relief. 'I've been looking for you for an hour . . . What on earth made you hide up here in the dark?'

Trembling and weeping, Tancredi ran blindly to the refuge of the two women.

'He must have been frightened by the storm,' said Veronica, stroking his hair. 'He's trembling all over . . . Come. There's nothing to cry about.'

'The rat,' Tancredi couldn't help stammering. 'The rat . . .'

'What rat?' asked his mother without interest. 'If only you wouldn't go and hide as you're always doing.'

'The rat,' Tancredi said again, and meanwhile, still entangled in the atmosphere of his dream, he couldn't help pressing his shoulder against the maid's belly as if to make really sure that the rat hadn't taken refuge there. He noticed her legs, too, despite his terror, and they seemed strange. There was no doubt but that they were the legs he had seen in the adjoining room; but how different they looked. They had then seemed languid and nervously sensitive; now they seemed tall, strong, muscular, like two chiselled pillars of virtue. In the grip of these disturbed sensations, he let himself be consoled a little by the two women; and, drying his eyes mechanically, he followed them out of the room.

It emerged, as they were going downstairs, that a fuse had blown in the storm, and the house had been plunged in darkness.

'Stop crying,' said his mother, walking downstairs with the composure of a woman of the world, preceded by the maid with the candle, 'and go and get your tools. . . . We need your help.'

Here it must be mentioned that Tancredi was very clever with electricity and all mechanical things, and it had long been the custom to seek him out when simple breakdowns occurred that did not require a mechanic.

'Yes mother,' he said obediently.

'We were looking for you all over the house,' the maid admonished him in an unusually affectionate tone of voice. 'What a thoughtless boy you are.'

But Tancredi imagined that she was intending a reference to the scene he had espied through the door, with an obvious desire that he shouldn't tell his mother; and filled with a feeling of deep complicity, he said nothing.

When they reached the ground floor Tancredi went to fetch his tools from the nook where he kept them, and said he was ready. The fuse-box was under the stairs above a cupboard, on top of which all sorts of junk was stored, as if it was an attic. Veronica went to look for a step-ladder, set it against the wall, and held it steady with one hand while she manipulated a candle with the other. Tancredi's mother steadied the ladder on the other side and she too held a candlestick above her head. Between these two guardian angels, Tancredi mounted to the top rung holding a third candle that he was going to fix on the top of the cupboard. When he reached the top of the ladder he tilted the candle for some of the grease to drop and then as best he could fixed the candle on a dusty corner of the cupboard. The flickering light revealed a whole heap of odds and ends – a bronze lamp, innumerable curtain rings, dust-clotted bottles of every size, a legless armchair with the stuffing bulging out from the torn cover. As soon as he had fixed the candle, Tancredi bent down and asked his mother to pass him the screwdriver and two other small tools he had placed on a chair. His mother handed them up to him; but in the moment of straightening up to unfasten some of the screws, Tancredi heard a rustle. He turned and saw – Heaven knows how it had got there – the grey cat advancing on him between the pieces of junk; it had one cautious paw upraised, one wide staring eye, and its violet-coloured lip was drawn back above its teeth. When he saw it panic gripped him, and a fearful anger. 'This time I'll kill it,' he thought, and aimed the screwdriver at the beast. But at that moment there was a dry snap, a flash shot from the fusebox and, blinded, with a cry of dismay he fell headlong back between the two women. The candles went out; in the darkness he felt himself being carried by his feet and shoulders like a dead man to the dining-room. He just heard his mother's voice saying to Veronica: 'In here.' But the blood was already ebbing from his temples, fleeing from his body, and while around him the light returned, an icy blackness robbed him of his last fraction of strength, and he closed his eyes.

Two days later, in the summer-house overlooking the sea, his mother was telling her friends:

'For a moment I was afraid he was hurt . . . but he didn't have a scratch – he merely fainted. The over-excitement . . . I must admit that for a moment I was quite alarmed. The queerest thing was that afterwards we found out that the flash had been caused by the house cat. The poor creature had somehow got itself tangled up with the wire. . . . We found it electrocuted. It seems to have got the shock instead of Tancredi. Anyway, I've strictly forbidden him ever to go near the electricity again. Boys are so reckless.'

'I couldn't agree more,' said one of her friends.

'You shuffle,' said his mother.

And the game began.

THE UNFORTUNATE LOVER

After he had quarrelled and broken with his mistress, Sandro could no longer endure the city in which they had been living together, so he left for an island not far from the coast. It was June and not yet too hot, and as the bathing season began only in July he knew that he would not find many visitors on the island. Everything went well on the day of his arrival. For the sake of greater solitude, he did not go to a hotel, but to furnished rooms let out by a woman. These rooms were arranged side by side and opened out on to a wide balcony enclosed by a colonnade – and this was all that had survived of an ancient convent. Three sides of the original cloister had disappeared and the row of rooms backed on to the precipitous cliff of the island. The rooms looked out over a shady, well-stocked garden, then a slope scattered with white villas, prickly pears, and olive trees, and then the far-away sea, calm and sparkling like glass in the indentations of the rocky coast.

At the time of his arrival all the rooms except the one next to Sandro's were untenanted; and the first time he went out on to the wide balcony he immediately saw the occupant of that one. It was a young and beautiful girl with magnificent fair hair and a face that bore a close resemblance to a little pig. She greeted Sandro and he returned her greeting. She asked him whether he bathed, and he answered that he did so sometimes, and then he went back into his room. From that day onwards he was unable to go out on to the terrace even for a moment without the shutters of the next room bursting open and the girl coming out to talk to him. She was obstinate and not put off by Sandro's brusque replies. She talked to him with both hands resting on the balustrade, her deep-set and inexpressive little eyes falling alternately on the sea and on him. In the end Sandro took care not to appear beneath the colonnade.

He began leading a very regular life. Early every morning he went down to the sea, undressed, and lay on the beach until the sun grew hot enough to allow of bathing. Then he waded into the water, gazing at his white feet shimmering against the rough pebbles. The water would mount slowly and with delicious eagerness, first to his stomach, then to his chest, and then up to his chin. As soon as he felt his feet were off the ground, with a thrust he swam out round the rocks or from point to point along the coast. He noticed that he never thought of anything when swimming, and he liked that. Sometimes he lay on his back with arms outstretched and closed his eyes, letting the slight pull of the current bear him over the calm sea to a chance landing. He would stay a long time like this in the water, his eyes shut, his ears caressed by the waves; then reopen his eyes and in the powerful light see the great red rock of the island weighing down on him out of the blazing sky. Bathing was the pleasantest event of the day, for it distracted him almost completely. After his swim he would climb up to the village again, eat alone in an inn, then go back to his room and try to get a couple of hours' sleep. As long as he had something definite to do, such as swimming or eating or sunbathing, he was fairly successful at keeping his mind off his mistress and the pain of his separation from her. But during the languid and empty hours of the afternoon he was attacked by the bitterness of boredom and wild desire, as if in expectation of something that he knew would never come to pass. By the evening, and after his unavailing efforts to distract himself, he had reached the end of his tether and was in a frenzy.

Two weeks of this life had already passed when he received a postcard of greeting from his mistress from somewhere not far away. The postcard gave her address and was obviously an invitation to begin a correspondence. Sandro wrote a rather longer card and two days later received a note telling him about her health, the weather, and other similar matters. Encouraged, he now sent off an eight-page letter in which he asked to see her even if only for a day. He knew from his experience of her character that she was incapable of love except out of contrariness. And as it turned out, he received no answer. Two more weeks passed and Sandro had given up hope; and then he received a telegram announcing that she was arriving the following day.

The next morning he awoke with a start, afraid that he had overslept. But on looking at his watch he saw that he had still more than an hour before the arrival of the boat. He went out on to the terrace to examine the sea; it was calm, there was no danger of a storm preventing the boat from reaching the jetty. As usual, his next-door neighbour immediately appeared on the terrace and very hurriedly, as though she was afraid he might escape her, told him that it was a fine day. Sandro answered that the day couldn't be finer and went back to his room. In his mind's eye he still pictured the girl standing upright facing the sea, her hands on the balustrade and a silly disconcerted expression on her face.

He finished dressing and made his way unhurriedly down to the square. The early morning had that peculiar, fresh, clear light that in places such as this seems to come less from the sky than the sea. The square was deserted and the tables at the two or three cafés were empty. A few local inhabitants were squatting on the steps of the church enjoying the early sun. The shopkeepers were opening their shops, pulling up the blinds. Occasionally a half-naked woman, an early-riser, with sun-glasses on her nose and a large canvas bag under her arm, would hurriedly cross the square and make for the short-cut down to the sea. For a while Sandro paced up and down the square and then he went to the belvedere.

From up there he could see the whole stretch of the sea, smooth and calm with a few lazy and scattered white tracks – the great wandering crystal serpents of the currents, drifting deadly this way and that. The boat which must contain his mistress was already visible in the narrow channel separating the island from the hills of the mainland. It was moving slowly, leaving a long bright wake on the transparent and luminous sea. Now and again sky and sea seemed to turn to vapour and mingled together and then the boat seemed to be sailing in an undefined zone that was no longer water and not yet air. Sandro lowered his gaze to the precipice beneath the belvedere. The black rails of the funicular descended on their solid bed and disappeared in the green of the hillside: soon the red box-car, bringing up his mistress, would emerge slowly from among the branches and leaves of the lush vines. He left the belvedere and went and sat down in a café, placing himself so that he could keep an eye on the exit of the funicular.

He was pleased to observe that he was feeling calm and clear-headed. After some time a trickle of people began to arrive, their town clothes noticeable in a place where everyone wore sandals and linen trousers. But the first car to come up emptied with no sign of his mistress. In a sudden fit of impatience, he got up from the café and took his place near the entrance to the funicular.

He waited for some ten minutes telling himself that there were no grounds for fear, that his mistress had wired that she was coming, and that she must therefore have come. The second car arrived and the passengers got out one after another, and his mistress still failed to make an appearance. Sandro went to buy a packet of cigarettes and waited for the third car. He smoked the cigarettes half-way down, or perhaps two-thirds, and then threw them away.

Now came the third car. As he had observed from the belvedere, the boat was not very crowded. This time only three or four passengers got out – no more – and a crowd of hotel porters. His mistress was not there.

Mechanically, not knowing what to do, and stunned by his disappointment as if by sunstroke, he set out along the road leading to the jetty. Half-way down he spotted a horse-drawn victoria coming towards him. The driver had to go to the very edge of the road to avoid a lorry loaded with vegetables stationed in front of a shop. Then Sandro saw his mistress.

He waited until the victoria was on a level with him and then called out her name in a clear voice. She turned, and he could see that she was exactly the same. Severely, and as if their meeting displeased her, she said, 'There you are,' and ordered the driver to stop.

'I was waiting for you at the funicular,' Sandro said, walking towards her carriage, but not getting in.

'So I imagined,' she answered in a cross tone of voice. 'But there was such a crowd. . . . I preferred to take a carriage.'

They measured one another with their eyes.

'Why are you standing there?' she asked in her usual hard yet flattering voice; 'why don't you get in? I shall have to go to the hotel first.'

Sandro got in and the horse started up at a trot.

'I've booked a room for you,' he said as he sat down.

'Thanks,' she answered absently. She looked around with satisfied curiosity, then said, 'It's not a bad place, you know.'

'It's famous,' answered Sandro, smiling; but he immediately regretted his phrase – it sounded stupid – and added, 'Are you staying long?'

'I don't know,' she answered in an undecided voice. 'It depends.'

Sandro regretted this question too, for it occurred to him that she might think that her stay on the island mattered to him. And he concluded: 'If you like it, you'll stay . . . otherwise you'll go away?'

'Exactly,' she said with a hard laugh. 'You're being original today.'

Sandro bit his lips till they bled and said nothing more until they reached the square. In the square they got out and Sandro asked the driver how much he wanted. The driver asked for thirty lire. Sandro knew that the proper charge was half as much and answered unthinkingly, 'It's a great deal.'

'Come along. . . . What a long discussion,' she said, glancing around and feigning embarrassment. Sandro bit his lips and paid.

They crossed the square, passed under a narrow archway and began climbing a little street embedded between the tall and serried white houses. Sandro carried the suitcase and his mistress kept a step ahead of him, looking at every object with her characteristic expression of mingled satisfaction and surprise. Every now and again she stopped to gaze up at the summit of the island and contemplate its peculiar architectural formation. Amid the terraces and escarpments far above their heads the blue sky was resplendent. The path twisted, turned into a flight of steps, entered a dark passage-way, and then went on mounting. After the houses came long white walls sprouting greenery, and on top of the walls, tangled with the plants, were half-naked girls and infants who watched them as they passed.

'It really is a pretty place,' she said emphatically. 'Like a dream.'

She talked like this, Sandro thought, because she was not very intelligent and so expressed herself in terms of clichés. But for all that her conventional expressions had far more weight than his more penetrating and subtle ones.

He tried to say something on her level and answered, 'Yes, a dream . . . but a dream for two.'

She appeared not to hear and asked: 'Is there still far to go?'

'We're there,' said Sandro.

He put down the suitcase, took the big iron key from his pocket and inserted it into the keyhole of the old decayed greenish door of the former convent. They entered the dark, cool corridor. 'What thick walls,' she said, glancing at the lantern-holds embedded in the thickness of the vault.

'It was a convent,' Sandro said. He went to the end of the corridor, opened the door and added, 'I booked you a room next door to mine . . . but meanwhile you can come in here.' Without answering, she went straight to the looking-glass hanging over the wash-basin. Sandro sat on the edge of the bed with his eyes on her. He could see her grave and attentive in the mirror. He was glad to watch her now, for on the way up he had not even dared to glance at her for fear of revealing his real feelings. She had large, almond-shaped eyes of a bright, almost furious blue that seemed to consume her forehead beneath her fair, curly hair. The slightness of her forehead and her huge eyes made one think of some animal. And her sharp, chiselled nose, her thin cheeks that seemed to find their outlet in her wide, full mouth, confirmed this impression of animality. It was a face that suggested to one's mind the muzzle of a goat, a tame goat, mad and a trifle obscene. She was thin and ardent, with a long, sensitive neck, bony shoulders, and a very slim waist; but her lips were rounded, and beneath her flanks her thin, listless legs emerged from her wide skirt with an air of dancing, mischievous joy; one expected to see them, with her big feet shod in narrow sandals, uplifted to beat time in a satyr's dance. There was no doubt about her fear of looking tired after the journey; but when she looked at her face she must have been satisfied, for all of a sudden she gave it an oblique glance over her shoulder and began to hum. It was the only tune she knew by heart, and Sandro knew it well for he had often heard her singing it when they were in love. She used to sing it with picturesque irony, parodying the clumsy and provocative gestures and the awkward voices of low music-hall artists. For a moment she went on humming and looking at herself in the mirror; then she turned, put her hands on her hips and intoned the song in a loud voice, shaking her haunches and throwing her feet about in the narrow space between the bed and the wash-basin. As she faced Sandro she kept her eyes down, but whenever she turned her back on him she turned her face so as to give him a look over her shoulder. Her large, red mouth was wide open and he could see the motion of her thick, swift tongue as she sang. She realized that her coquetry was irresistible; indeed, when she came within range Sandro could not resist trying to seize her. She immediately stopped singing and shimmying and said, 'We must be serious.'

'Do you want to see your room?' asked Sandro, angry. She nodded, and Sandro led the way out on to the terrace. Immediately the neighbouring shutters opened and the fair girl appeared. She was just on the point of speaking, and already had her mouth open, when she caught sight of the other woman. Hurriedly she took a bathing costume that had been spread out on the railing and retired to her own room.

'Who is that?' his mistress asked.

'I don't know.'

'Come off it. You know perfectly well. I bet you've already spoken with her, if not worse. . . .' Her tone was mocking and had no trace of jealousy.

'No, no,' Sandro said, laughing, flattered by the thought that she could suspect him of disloyalty to her. Then, realizing that he had made the usual mistake of betraying his feelings, he became grave again.

'This is your room.'

It was a room exactly like Sandro's. The woman sat on the bed and said, 'But I don't yet know whether I'll be staying the night or going off this afternoon.'

'Do whatever you want,' said Sandro in a fury.

She glanced at him and went up to him gaily, provocatively, and stroked his face.

'Are you cross?'

'No,' Sandro said and tried to put his arm round her waist. But she immediately drew away.

'It's too early . . . At least give me time to get used . . . Anyway, I'm really not sure that I'll stay.'

'What about having a bathe?'

'Let's.'

She deposited her suitcase on the bed, took out all her toilet things, and arranged them one by one on the washing shelf. Then she took a canvas bag, into which she put her bathing costume, her rubber cap, a handkerchief, and a bottle of suntan oil, and said she was ready. They set out. Sandro walked a little behind her because he wanted to look at her without her noticing. But when they reached the square she calmly said, 'Let's walk side by side . . . I can't endure having you behind with your eyes fixed on me . . .'

'I wasn't looking at you,' said Sandro.

'Rubbish.'

They crossed the square and took the short-cut down to the sea. For some way the path twisted through bushy gardens whose trees only occasionally permitted a glimpse of blackened fronts of old villas in Moorish or Pompeian style. This was the oldest district on the island, Sandro explained, and those villas all dated back some fifty years. Then the path disappeared between two great rocks, and then they could see the sea at the bottom of a declivity scattered with enormous crags. The short-cut zigzagged down between these crags. Its white-washed parapet gave it the appearance of a grey hem, white-edged, that had fallen from the sky and gently deposited itself between the rocks.

'Where's the bathing place?' Sandro's mistress asked, stopping and looking over the edge.

'Down there,' Sandro said, pointing to some far-away green huts ranged between the rocks along the water's edge at the bottom of the perpendicular island wall.

They began slowly descending the steep little cement road; then she increased her pace, quicker and quicker, and began running headlong, turning back laughingly now and again to glance at Sandro. They were breathless when they arrived and they made their way in silence along the earth footpath between the yellow, dry grass in the sun that burnt their ears. Now the sea was near and was visibly calm. Gently, foamlessly, the water flowed irregularly over the stones of the shore, unrolling slowly like a carpet. The sucking ebb, fresh and sonorous, was audible on the rocks.

As they reached the sea they saw that there were only a few people there, occasional bathers, spread face downwards on the beach, a towel under their heads, or else standing on the shore so that the languid fluctuations of the placid sea could flow over their feet. Sandro led his mistress to the bathing hut; she said she would undress immediately, and locked the door. She emerged shortly afterwards in a rust-coloured bathing-suit, pulling it up round her thighs and glancing about through her sun-glasses. In his turn, Sandro went into the hut, hastily undressed and, leaving his trousers on the floor, emerged in his trunks. But she was nowhere to be seen on the terrace. Instead, as though Sandro had never existed, she was on her way down the steps that led from the bathing-huts to the beach.

He ran after her, and they walked side by side along the narrow beach consisting exclusively of big stones. The stones burnt the soles of Sandro's feet so that he had to perform a kind of dance; whereas his mistress proceeded safely in her rubber-soled slippers. She looked for a quiet nook and as soon as she was seated handed Sandro the bottle of sun-tan oil.

'Rub it on me.'

Sandro took the bottle, uncorked it, poured a little oil into the palm of his hand, and began rubbing it on the woman's back. Her back was slim and as she bent forward he could feel her spine under the skin, which the oil made shiny and brown. When he had finished her back she spread the oil on her arms and front; then she laid a towel on the rocks, reclined on her front, undid her shoulder straps and pulled them down. In this position he could see her slight, pale breasts crushed between her armpits and the ground. Her body, which skipped around gracelessly when she moved, revealed its harmony now that she was lying still. Her back had wide shoulders and grew narrower down to the slim waist. Her haunches were the only part of her that was fleshy and rounded. Her legs were straight from thigh to heel, but they were well-jointed and had no blemish. Her thighs displayed a slackening of the skin below her bathing suit; this was the only evidence which recalled that she was no longer young.

Sandro was also lying on his stomach, though he found the position uncomfortable. Approaching his face to hers, he asked: 'What are you thinking about?'

'Nothing.' She made no movement, her face was concealed behind her huge, dark glasses, her elbows were on the rocks and her head dug into her shoulders. Her hands hung languidly in front of her. They were fleshless, hard, nervous, with slim fingers separated and oddly folded and outstretched as if deformed. A big, heavy ring with her family crest on the stone hung loosely around her thin forefinger. Sandro was tempted by her hands, and the heat of the sun burning his back seemed like temptation too. At last he stretched out a hand and seized hers. She did not move.

'Your sweet hand,' he said, breathing deeply.

The woman said nothing, but a slight quiver of the nostrils warned Sandro that she was annoyed. Her sharp nostrils always quivered like that, suggesting a dog that was going to bite. He had a feeling of panic and hurriedly sought for a more rational reason for seizing her hand.

'Where does this ring come from?'

'You must have seen it a thousand times,' she said drily. And with a rough gesture she pulled the ring off her finger and dropped it on the rocks.

'You're right. I've seen it before,' said Sandro, returning it.

Someone walked past them, but all they could see was the long feet, soft and white, put down, then contracting and curling up on the burning stones.

'I didn't expect to see you again,' began Sandro after a pause. 'I'd made up my mind that if you wrote to me I wouldn't even answer.'

She made no reply.

'You've treated me abominably,' Sandro went on, with the

confused feeling that he was saying the very thing he ought to avoid, 'and I know why it happened.'

'Why?'

'Because I let on too soon that I was in love with you . . . and told you too often.'

She got her bag, opened it, took out her case and lit a cigarette. Then she offered the case to Sandro, who refused.

'I'm sleepy,' she said. 'Let me sleep for a bit.' She lay her head between her arms and closed her eyes.

'How can you manage to sleep and smoke at the same time?' asked Sandro, trying to make his voice cheerful and self-possessed.

'I'll smoke for a while and then go to sleep,' she murmured, the cigarette between her lips.

'It's impossible to do both?'

'Why do you talk so much?' she asked rudely. 'It's so pleasant in the sun if there's silence.'

Sandro bit his lip and gazed around. By now the tiny beach was becoming crowded. Men and women lay on the burning rocks, some on their stomachs, some on their backs, as motionless as the dead. On the terrace of the bathing establishment which stretched among the rocks like a ship's deck one could see the naked backs of a row of bathers on the railing laughing and chatting with others lying in the deck-chairs.

'I'm going to take a dip,' he announced, getting up.

She said nothing. Sandro, disgruntled, walked away over the burning rocks. He passed beneath the bathing establishment and went in the direction of a rock which jutted into the sea like a promontory, thereby forming a little inlet where bathers were close-pressed as waves at the height of the season. High up on this rock was a cement diving platform. Sandro disliked diving and wasn't good at it, but he hoped that once he had left his mistress she would stop dozing and watch him. He would then spring from the high platform and when she saw him perform this deed of valour she might feel some revival of her love for him.

He scrambled over the rock, which was all holes and sharp points that cut his feet. The rock was white with salt and at the bottom of the holes between one hump and another lay green stagnant pools full of refuse and old paper. So, stepping from hump to hump, Sandro reached the platform. He mounted it and stood upright, thinking that his body must make a fine picture against the background of the sky. Then he looked down. Some four yards below him the green water with its bluish and white reflections rippled and shimmered, sparkling in the sun. It looked a long way away and made him feel dizzy. He wondered whether he should call his mistress's attention to the dive he was about to make, and decided against doing so. But at the last moment an unknown impulse made him wave his arms and shout her name. He couldn't see where she was or whether she was looking. He shut his eyes, clasped his hands above his head and cast himself in head first.

His fall seemed long and clumsy, like that of a rock or any other heavy shapeless object. Then his head pierced the water and the rest of his body followed. He opened his eyes in a dense green light, struggled to free himself and felt himself rising again. It seemed to him that he had travelled a long way, but as he emerged from the water he noticed that he was still beneath the rock from which he had jumped. With trepidation and exultation, he struck out for the shore.

He found his mistress beside a basketful of sea-urchins and an untidy-haired boy who was crouching beside her and opening the sea-urchins with a knife and squeezing drops of lemon on them.

'Did you see me?' he asked, panting as he climbed towards her over the burning stones. 'I dived from the top platform . . .'

'You did do a belly-flop!' she observed. The boy offered her a sea-urchin, split open and flavoured; she cautiously took the black husk with its bristling spikes between two fingers and fastidiously ate the deep orange sediment with a spoon.

'Shall we go out in a boat?' Sandro proposed, for despite her caustic comments he still felt much heartened by his heroic dive.

'Let's.'

Sandro ran to the water's edge and slapped his hands to summon the bathing attendant. He and the attendant pushed the boat into the sea. Then they each offered an arm to help his mistress in. She chose the attendant's arm and with a quick jump went to sit in the stern. Sandro leapt nimbly after her, took up the oars and with a few pulls drew the boat out of the inlet. For a short while he rowed energetically, pulling towards the open sea. He wanted to round a promontory formed by a single upright sharp cliff. He knew that behind that rock there were no bathers or bathing beaches, nothing but the sea and the rocks. Meanwhile the woman sat in the stern with her back to him, looking at the steep cliffs of the island.

The promontory was further away than appeared at first sight. As they came below the cliff they saw that it was entirely surrounded by rocky banks, half-submerged and thick with sea-weed, over which the sea flowed to and fro, covering and uncovering them with the movement of the ebb. Sandro gave these banks a wide berth and reached the other side of the promontory. Here they found an inlet much narrower than where the bathing establishments were. The escarpments of the island looked like a castle at this point, with towers, balconies and walls, and beneath the precipitous cliffs the calm water sparkled hazily in the sun, darkened by the seaweed beneath its surface and filled with majestic solitude. In the depths of the cove, backed by the wall of the island, there was a little white pebbly beach. Sandro turned the boat towards this beach. The boat spun over the water and the prow hit the gravel. Then he leapt ashore and offered his hand to his mistress, who also got out.

'Why have we come here?' she asked, looking around.

'Because – ' Sandro said in a choked voice. 'Well, so as to be more alone.'

She looked at him attentively and then asked, 'What time is it?'

Sandro glanced at his wrist-watch and told her the time.

'It's late,' she said. 'We'll have to go back . . . We'll have to eat early, because I have to catch the steamer.'

As she said this she made a determined move and stumbled over the rocks towards the boat. Sandro hurried after her and just as she was putting her hand on the prow of the boat he threw an arm round her waist. She turned round with a questioning look. Without a word, Sandro put his lips against hers and kissed her. At first, as if by instinct, she returned his kiss; then Sandro felt her trying to withdraw and pull her lips away.

Whereupon he put his hand behind her neck and held her head, which she was trying to free.

In the end they drew apart. Hastily, with her eyes downcast, she leapt into the boat, threw herself on the oars, and began unevenly pulling out to sea. Seeing her intention, Sandro leapt into the boat after her, snatched the oars from her hands and gave her a push that made her fall back into the stern.

'We must go back,' she said in a dry, panting voice. 'I've already told you often enough that this behaviour doesn't work with me . . . If at first I may have thought of staying here tonight . . . now I've decided . . . You couldn't have found a better way of making me leave.'

'Liar. You'd already made up your mind to go . . . From the minute you arrived, you've done nothing but talk about leaving.'

'Yes. I know. But perhaps I might have stayed. But as it is, it's finished.'

'Yet you returned my kiss at one moment,' he said with rancour.

'It's not true. You held my head and I couldn't get free.'

A long silence followed. The woman had a far-away look and remained stiff and outraged while Sandro rowed. He kept close to the walls of the island. On the red rock at water level every slight backwash of the sea revealed the dripping beard of the brown-and-green seaweed under a white line of dried salt. Every time the water ebbed the sea made a pleasant gentle cluck against the rock that sounded like a kiss. Beyond the sun sparkled brightly on every ripple.

'All right. You're going,' Sandro said suddenly with an effort. 'But there's no need to stay in a bad temper for the couple of hours we've still got together. At one time you used to enjoy bathing from a boat. Let's let bygones be bygones. You have your swim, and then I'll take you ashore.'

Her glance showed him she was tempted.

'All right . . . provided you don't try on anything else.'

'But it was I who made the suggestion.'

Sandro stopped the boat and the woman stood up in the stern. She put on her rubber bathing-cap, pushing in the unruly curls. Then she tied it under her chin and looked at the sea. When her head was enclosed in the bathing-cap she looked warlike, with her protuberant lips and irritated, almond eyes. She stepped to the edge, lifted her arms, and joined her hands above her head.

'Please don't jerk the boat.'

She bent her legs slightly as though to try out their strength and leapt. She fell faultlessly, head first, body following, and Sandro's last view of her was of her brown thighs – the rather slackened thighs of a woman approaching middle age – tightly pressed together, penetrating the water amid white foam. In the translucent water he saw her turn and swim away like a green and bubbling shadow. Then, as though thrust up by a spring, her head holed the surface of the sea at some distance from the boat. She was a good diver and swimmer and could stay a long time under water.

Sandro watched her shaking her head and swimming with spirit and energy, yet unhurriedly, towards the boat. When she reached it she gripped the edge with both hands and said, puffing a little, 'It's cold.'

'Do you want to dive again?' asked Sandro.

'No.'

'Then I will.'

He crossed the oars inside the boat, mounted the poop and, without bothering to take precautions, for he had lost all hope of being admired by now, he plunged in head first. He fell badly, obliquely, and felt a pain in his side. He quickly broke the surface and blew his nose, looking around to get his bearings.

'What a belly-flop!' she said unmoved.

'I know,' Sandro answered. 'But I don't care.'

'If you don't take trouble you'll never learn.'

Sandro felt tempted to swim out to the open sea and leave her thoroughly in the lurch; she would possibly get into the boat and hurry after him. But instead he found himself to his surprise swimming towards her. When he reached her side he too caught hold of the boat. As he trod water to keep afloat his legs touched hers and gradually their legs became friendlily entangled.

'If I wanted,' he said, looking at her, 'I could take you by the shoulders and hold you under the water until you drowned . . . No one could come to your rescue.'

Returning his gaze she answered: 'Don't be funny . . . I can't endure being funny in the sea.'

'You call it being funny, do you?'

His mistress made no reply, and Sandro, gripping the edge of the boat, leapt in and sat down between the oars.

'Listen,' she said. 'I'm going to swim slowly towards the bathing-huts . . . You follow me in the boat.'

'All right.'

She left the boat and began to swim towards the promontory. In that dark lonely inlet, shadowed by the rocks, her slow, vigorous strokes sent a sparkle of light below and around her, as when a school of fish swarms just beneath the surface of the water. She swam well and evenly, without crabbing a single stroke. Sandro grasped the oars and began rowing slowly. He felt at last that what she did no longer really mattered to him. He would keep his word, take her to lunch at a good inn and do everything he had to do, and then would accompany her to the funicular. Absorbed in these thoughts, he rowed on, dawdling. By now the sun had tired him; he bent down, took the cigarette case from his mistress's bag, and lit a cigarette. She was a good way away, and looked tiny and lost beneath the high cliffs; yet the whole place, with its rock castles and lonely ebb and flow seemed like a theatre backcloth for her swim. Then Sandro saw her stop and wave an arm as if to summon him. He began rowing briskly and a few pulls brought him alongside her.

'I've had enough,' she said as she gripped the boat. 'I haven't got the stamina I used to have. I must be getting old. Help me . . . '

Sandro dropped the oars and gripped her under the armpits. She struggled into the boat, took off her bathing-cap and shook out her flattened hair. Her muscles were still tense and quivering under the skin of her slim body, and the water did not stick to her skin, but divided into great, scattered drops.

'As a matter of fact, it's quite lovely here,' she said after a pause, glancing at the deserted inlet glistening beneath the high walls.

'Why don't you stay?' Sandro asked, and as soon as he had said the words he was astonished at himself. 'You could stay the night, bathe again tomorrow and leave in the afternoon.'

He was afraid that she would say no and thought, 'If she answers grumpily I'll unhook an oar and crack her over the head.' But quite unexpectedly and to his great surprise, she beckoned and said, 'Come here.'

Sandro obeyed and went and sat beside her. She immediately turned, took his face between the palms of her hands, and kissed him on the mouth. Sandro had a fleeting glimpse of the tallest of the cliffs above their heads and then closed his eyes. For the first time for ages he experienced the savour of her mouth, the intoxicating wine of time gone by, so like herself, and he almost fainted at its sweetness. The moment he had so longed for had come at last.

When they broke apart he asked, as if in anger, 'Why did you do that?'

'Just because,' she answered, smiling at him, 'I suddenly felt a strong desire to do so.'

Sandro said nothing, but took up the oars again. He was in a state of great gladness, yet great fear; gladness owing to the hope of renewing his much-regretted relations with his mistress, and fear lest he should take a false step and make a mistake that would once and for all jeopardize the rebirth of their love. It was like hunting some swift, nervous, evasive creature, such as a firefly or moth or bird, with the knowledge that the slightest sound would cause the prey to vanish. He must not make any more mistakes, he thought again; his behaviour must be perfect. His mind concentrated on this subject, he went on rowing.

Meanwhile they had rounded the promontory and the row of bathing huts lining the inlet amongst the irregular rocks was again in sight. The beach was crawling with people. Many bathers were to be seen in the water, some in groups, some alone. A few white pedal-boats were scattered over the open water.

'So you really want to leave today?' asked Sandro.

'I'll see . . . how I feel after lunch.'

Sandro started rowing again and his mistress turned and fixed her gaze on the horizon. Sandro would have preferred not to look at her, but his eyes were inevitably drawn to where she was sitting. She had crossed her thin, muscular legs and was smoking thoughtfully. Out of the blue and as if following a train of thought of her own she said: 'I don't like the room you found me. . . . There's no running water.'

'I thought you were only staying for one day,' Sandro said, delighted, 'but if you stayed longer you could go to a hotel; there are plenty.'

'And are there good walks?' She loved walking; that and swimming, were her favourite pastimes.

'As many as you like.'

They had by now entered the inlet and were among the bathers laughing and splashing in the shallow water. Sandro took the boat ashore and the attendant ran up and helped them to get out. It was already late. Many of the bathers were getting out of the water, which had a hot, used look under the blazing sun; others, already dressed, were slowly making their way up the steep steps from the huts to the road. Sandro dressed first; then his mistress went into the hut. After a short while she emerged dressed, with her bag in one hand and the dripping costume in the other.

'Why not leave it here?' suggested Sandro, pointing to the costume. 'The attendant will look after it.'

'And if I leave?'

'Do just what you wish,' said Sandro and began climbing the steps, turning his back on her. That was the right method, he thought – give her no importance, don't go pressing her and bothering her. When they were in the cab, with a horse which took its time up the steep road, he felt almost certain that his mistress would stay and that their love affair would begin all over again. The cab mounted slowly between luxuriant gardens and shady trees. His mistress talked to the driver, asking for information about the villas they espied through the clumps of trees, and the driver, half turning, answered in dialect. It was extremely hot and no trace of tension and ill-humour remained. She was wearing an aquamarine dress, and against that colour her warm, brown arms were lovely to look at.

At one point Sandro began wondering whether or not he should take her arm. He remembered that in the early days they were together every time he took hold of her arm she squeezed his hand tightly against her side and gave him long, silent glances with loving eyes.

The driver stopped talking and now they had reached the level he put the horse to a trot.

'How marvellous to have you here,' Sandro said, taking her arm.

She didn't answer, but straightened her sun-glasses with her free hand, frowning.

'Elena,' Sandro whispered.

'You haven't changed,' she said, not with ill-will, but as if making an undeniable observation.

'What do you mean?'

'This is neither the time nor the place for emotions.'

A carriage drawn by a white horse that was younger and stronger than theirs drew level and overtook them. In it were sitting a man and a woman. They were holding hands, and the woman's head was resting on her companion's shoulder.

Sandro pointed to the carriage as it drew ahead and said, 'The time and place are all right for *them*.'

She shrugged her shoulders and said no more. Their carriage now began bowling along between village houses, over large, detached flagstones. People scattered in front of them as they went noisily forward. The driver cracked his whip and the cracks made a cool echo against the houses.

They got out in the square. As Sandro was paying the driver, the woman purposefully went to the little funicular station.

'It looks as if I'll have to spend the night here,' she said as they made their way together across the square.

'Do you want to go to a hotel?' Sandro asked crossly.

'Don't be stupid.'

From the square they mounted a stairway leading to a covered gallery that ran like a corridor through the village behind the row of houses facing the sea. The gallery was completely white-washed – with round white roofing, crooked white walls, white pillars – and it looked exactly like a tunnel dug through a solid block of salt or marble. Now and again one of the arcades opened and then, in the bright light, they could discern the sea sparkling and blue as far as the horizon.

'I know a restaurant with a pergola overlooking the sea,' Sandro said.

'I just want to eat. I don't care where. I'm dropping with hunger.'

The terrace under the early green leaves and grape clusters of the pergola was deserted, except for a couple of middle-aged foreigners lunching in a corner.

'There's some first-class wine here,' said Sandro, sitting down contentedly. He knew his mistress liked drinking and became more affectionate when a little tight.

'This is another lovely place,' she said, gazing at the sea through the flower vases on the terrace parapet.

'I told you so. Once you come here you never want to go away.' He felt desirous of making some display of cheerfulness and self-possession. 'I'll go and see what they've got in the kitchen,' he went on and, without waiting for an answer, got up from the table.

The kitchen had a window with wide-open shutters, giving on to the terrace, and he stood at the window and looked in. The short, plump proprietress was working the bellows for the stoves. Under the blackened hood of the fireplace stood a variety of earthenware pots, frying-pans, and saucepans. On a marble-topped table were heaps of fruit, bunches of greenstuff, and fishes of all shapes and sizes.

'What have you got to eat?'

'We've *polpi*,'[1] the woman answered in a sing-song voice without looking round. 'We've potato pie, *melanzane*,[2] peppers, and meat-balls . . . The meat-balls are very good.' She lifted the lid off a saucepan to show them.

'Give me two portions of *melanzane*,' said Sandro. He wanted to give his mistress a surprise and take the dishes himself. The woman uncovered another saucepan and with only two ladlefuls filled two plates to the brim. Sandro took the plates through the window, asked for two sticks of bread, which he put under his arms, and went back to the table.

'What is it?'

'*Melanzane*. . . . It's very nourishing.'

There was a pause.

---

[1] A species of small polypus, eaten fried.   [2] Egg plant.

'Now she's going to say she doesn't like it,' Sandro thought. He felt a fool and thoroughly dissatisfied by his idea of going to get the plates from the kitchen. But to his great surprise, after tasting a little fastidiously on the end of her fork, she said, 'It's very nice,' and began eating with a will.

One of the little girls came and put a full flask of wine on the table. The bottle was big-bellied and of rough, thick glass made to look like the film of moisture on an iced vessel when it comes into contact with the warm air, and it had an orange-ade label on it. Sandro poured out the wine in the glasses and drank; it was light and cool and welcomely thirst-quenching in the burning heat.

'It's good, isn't it?' he asked, putting his glass back on the table.

'Yes; very good,' she said with feeling.

After the *melanzane* they ate *polpi,* followed by a tomato salad. Sandro imagined he was pressing her to drink, but it was really himself who was drinking. Drunkenness removed his timidity and the fear of losing his mistress. He almost began to feel that she didn't matter to him in the slightest; and yet he realized at the same time that he had never before cared so much about her and her love. The meal over, they sat facing one another in silence. His mistress opened her handbag, took out her powder compact, and began touching up her face. Her face looked cold and hostile. Sandro suddenly felt afraid she might feel bored and, remembering that in the old days she used to enjoy his funny stories, he said with a smile: 'I'd like to tell you a story . . . but I don't know whether you'd like to hear it.'

'Go ahead.'

'A certain lady had a lover . . .' Sandro hated funny stories, but he knew she liked them, and he put plenty of gusto into the telling. When he came to the end she laughed in a provocative and flattering way; and with this encouragement he told a second, much spicier, one. She laughed again, this time with real abandon, holding one hand on her chest and shutting her eyes. At this Sandro told a third story, but this one was so spicy that she laughed with reserve, as if afraid of being compromised; yet there was more complicity in her guarded laugh than in the unbridled laughter of before. 'Now I'll show you a trick,' said Sandro. He got up from his place and sat down beside her; and showed her the trick, one with matchsticks. This trick, too, had an obscene meaning and she made him repeat it twice over so as to learn it. 'It's very easy,' she said, surprised. They were now side by side and the terrace was deserted, for the foreigners had paid and gone.

'Do you love me?' Sandro suddenly asked, and, bending forward, he brushed her neck with his lips. He could feel her neck trembling and stiffening beneath his lips, and he thought it was a shiver of pleasure. She made no response. Her face was bowed towards the table and she held her cigarette between her fingers.

Heartened, Sandro took her by the arm, high, near the armpit, and squeezed. Then she turned on him in unexpected fury, her eyes flaming with dogged resentment, and gave his hand a blow.

'Don't touch me. Please don't touch me.'

So violent was her behaviour and her eyes so lit up with fury that Sandro was dumbfounded. His hand was smarting from the large signet ring on her finger. He got up, went round the table and sat down in his original place.

'All right. I won't touch you,' he said. 'But as for you, you're incapable of love.' He was racking his brains for something unpleasant to say.

'I can't bear to have hands touching me.'

'Your heart has become arid . . . You're no longer young . . . You'll never be able to love again . . . Worse, you have never been in love.'

She suddenly blushed all over her face – with her a sign of mortification and pain. Sandro was astonished to see her blue eyes fill with tears.

'Let's go away,' she said, getting up.

Sandro called the proprietress and paid. All the time this was taking place she stood beside him, her face turned obstinately towards the sea. It was perfectly plain that her eyes were full of tears and that she couldn't see the sea, sky or anything else. The minute Sandro finished paying she set out hurriedly, leaving the restaurant ahead of him.

The streets were sun-drenched and deserted, the shutters of all the houses tightly closed, and in one of the cafés a loud-speaker was bellowing to empty tables. They crossed the square and began climbing the path to the convent.

For a while they walked in silence, and then Sandro said: 'Had I known it would upset you so much I wouldn't have said that.'

She answered at once, without looking at him: 'It doesn't matter. I'm nervous, that's all,' and Sandro's heart rose again. There was no undertone of hatred in her voice.

When they reached the convent, Sandro felt in his pocket for the key and she waited meekly for the door to open with the air of a woman who has already given her consent and knows that once indoors there will be no alternative but to make love. Yes, Sandro thought, they would now go to the bedroom, they would have a long embrace and they would relax on the bed together. He felt a pungently pleasant sensation of security and impatience, exactly as in the days of their first happy meetings.

When he had closed the door and they were in the corridor, he said, 'This house may have many disadvantages, but it's extremely quiet . . . it's ideal for resting.'

'I'll go and sleep at once,' she said. 'I feel very tired.'

They entered the room and Sandro shut the door. She went straight to the wash-basin mirror and looked at herself carefully, lifting her lips back from her teeth.

Sandro would have liked to keep well away from her, but – he had no idea why – he suddenly found himself standing just behind her.

'Are you furious with me?' he asked.

'No,' she said absently, still looking into the mirror.

'I thought you hated me.'

She went on looking at herself and made no answer. Through the open window the glistening sea stretched as far as the eye could reach. From the garden below in the silence of the sun came the crowing of a cock. 'Now I'll go to sleep,' she said decidedly, and went and lay down on the bed.

'What do you want me to do?' Sandro asked, standing in the middle of the room. 'If you like, I'll go . . . but if it's all the same to you, I'll stay.'

'It's all right. Stay.' She was lying on her back with one arm shielding her eyes. Her other hand went to her dress, which had slipped up above her knees as she was getting on to the bed, and pulled it down.

He ought not to take advantage of her unwilling invitation, Sandro thought, but should retire to the room next door. She would fall asleep, it might well be true that her nerves were a bit frayed after her journey, and once she had slept all would go well. But however convinced he was of the wisdom of these plans, he was unable to put them into practice. Instead, he drew near the bed and, taking care to make no noise or disturb the mattress, he sat down beside his mistress. She neither spoke nor moved. Her arm over her eyes, she seemed to be drowsing. Still taking care to be as quiet as possible, Sandro drew up his legs and lay down. It was nice to go to sleep side by side.

The woman took a deep breath that sounded like a sigh and made a half-turn towards the wall. But Sandro was already feeling incapable of staying stretched out motionless beside the woman he loved. He drew himself up into a sitting position on his elbow, and, bending over her, he gazed at her.

She made no movement. Probably she was asleep and had not noticed him. For some while Sandro gazed at the arm which covered the woman's face and at the small part of her face that was still visible. Her arm was tough and strong, almost a man's arm, but her wrist was slim, and she had delicate blue veins under the skin. Her eyes were covered by her arm and the only part of her face that showed was her lips, red and full and as if offering themselves. Sandro hesitated for a moment, and then he slowly bent down and put his lips gently towards hers. He did not touch her lips, but could feel the breath from her nostrils and smell the scent of her lipstick. He fully realized that, by behaving in this way, he was making yet another of the mistakes he had sworn to avoid; but he was unable to resist. He now bent over and put his lips against hers. He remembered occasions when their kisses in the torpor of the afternoon used to stretch on lazily and develop into silent and ardent embraces.

But scarcely had their lips met than she leapt up to a sitting position with a look of exasperation.

'So that's it. One can't have a moment's peace.'

'I was looking at you and I couldn't help kissing you.'

'But I want to go to sleep . . . I'm tired . . . So please leave me alone.'

'But I love you.'

'Can you possibly think I don't know it? You've told me often enough.'

'I want to tell you as often as I like.'

'And I want to be left in peace. Can you understand?'

By now they were both shouting, face to face. Sandro lifted his hand and slapped the woman on the cheek.

It was the first time he had hit her; and probably the first time in her life that she had ever been hit; she had always maintained that her lovers revered her. Sandro saw her eyes open wide with anger and astonishment.

'Now I'm going. . . . What a fool I was to come.'

She lifted her feet off the bed and began making for the door. Sandro forestalled her, shut the door, and put the key in his pocket. Then, with a violent push, he threw her on to the bed. She fell in a sitting posture and cracked her head hard against the wall.

'Please understand that you won't stir from here.'

'Help!' she shouted in a loud voice.

Sandro glanced at the wide-open window, thinking that someone might overhear their quarrel. So he went to the window and closed it. But the shutters closed together with the window and plunged the room into darkness. 'Help!' he heard her shout again in the gloom. Her voice was now terrified, and it was obvious she was afraid that Sandro wanted to kill her.

This idea infuriated him, and he threw himself on the bed and seized her by the throat. 'You'll stay here. Do you understand?' He squeezed the thin, nervous neck tightly, but as soon as she began gesticulating and coughing in her suffocation he let go. Not really knowing what to do next, he went to the window and flung it open again. She was kneeling on the bed and clinging with one hand to the bedstead; the other she held to her throat in a fit of coughing. 'Get out!' said Sandro opening the door. 'Go away, if that's what you want! I'm not stopping you.'

Still coughing, she eyed him incredulously, and Sandro had a moment's hope that she would realize that she would not be in the slightest danger if she stayed. Then he saw her looking longingly towards the open door and realized that she was only hesitating to leave for fear of being held back again. 'Get out!' he repeated in agony. This time she did not wait for a second invitation, but leapt off the bed and disappeared into the corridor. Sandro heard her going into the next room and locking the door.

'Now,' he thought, sitting down on the bed before the still open door, 'she'll pack and rush to catch the boat.' He hoped it was not true, but the noise from the next room – a noise of hurried footsteps and moving furniture – confirmed his supposition. He kept wondering whether he ought to go and beg her forgiveness; but each time the thought occurred he dismissed it, for he knew it would be useless. At last he heard the subdued creaking of the door of the next room being very slowly unlocked; his mistress was going, and making use of every subterfuge to conceal the fact from him. Her precautions seemed like an act of final and irremediable hostility and renewed his pain. He would have liked to tell her that she was free to leave openly and he would not move a finger to detain her; but he remained where he was. He heard her tiptoeing over the brick paving of the corridor. The front door closed so gently that for a moment he wondered whether he had misheard. Then he looked out of his room and saw the door of the next room wide open and the empty corridor and the general desertedness.

He went back to his own room and, without thinking began sadly to smooth the crumpled bedcovers. Then he went out on to the terrace.

Between the tall red cliffs topped with vegetation, the sea was dazzling in the sunlight. In the stillness of the garden even the hens were silent. All that could be heard was the buzzing of the insects taking advantage of the dog hours, nestling in the burnt grass and in the cracks of the arid earth. Sandro rested his hands on the balustrade and gazed at the sea. The shutters of the nearby room burst open and the fair girl appeared on the terrace.

She set her short, podgy hands on the balustrade and began

gazing at the sea too, out of her little inexpressive eyes. She really had magnificent fair hair, Sandro thought, but her rounded body looked ridiculous in her brief doll's skirt. He noticed that, far from wilting under his gaze, she betrayed her awareness of it by large and provocative quivers through her muscular thighs and loins, like a horse under his master's touch. Her beautiful body formed a warm, dark shadow beneath her transparent dress.

For a while she continued to gaze at the sea with all her flanks and leg muscles quivering; then she turned to Sandro and asked:

'Aren't you going bathing?'

'I bathed this morning.'

'I go in the afternoon as well.'

'This afternoon I'll be going.'

'Do you know — ?' and she named a locality on the island. 'I always bathe there. I'll be setting out soon.'

'We can go there together, then,' Sandro said.

She looked at him questioningly, as though she had not understood.

'You're going to bathe with me?'

'Yes.'

'I'll go and get ready,' she said, delighted, and she disappeared back into her room. 'I'll be ready in a minute,' she added, appearing for a moment at the window, and then disappeared again.

'All right,' Sandro answered. Hands on the balustrade, he resumed his gazing at the sea. At that moment the church clock in the village began striking. Sandro counted the strokes, thinking of the steamer that would be leaving. It was three o'clock in the afternoon. He re-entered his room and went and sat on the bed.

BACK TO THE SEA

THE landscape was flat, with wide meadows scattered with soft white daisies. On the horizon the pine wood bounded the meadows with a long, unbroken wall of solid and motionless greenery. The car made its way slowly and as though reluctantly, jolting over the holes in the unpaved road. Through the windscreen Lorenzo could see the mass of the pine wood coming to meet him, as if it were moving – melancholy, mysterious, hostile. Lorenzo had planned this outing as a way of making things up with his wife. But now, faced by her solid silence, he felt overcome yet again with timidity. However, as they approached the pines he said: 'Here is the pine wood.'

His wife made no reply. He lifted his hand and adjusted the mirror over the windscreen. When they started out he had tilted it towards her, and during the drive he had done nothing but watch her. She had sat firm and erect, her gloved hand on the door, her coat folded on her knees, her white linen shirt open as far as her breast. Her slender neck rose up from the shirt like a graceful stem. Over her sunburnt face and red mouth her freckles and the soft down on her lips threw a veil of shadowy sensuality. But her eyes, small and black, gazed obstinately ahead, and the upward sweep of her hair from her forehead gave her whole appearance an aggressive, hard look. She had something simian about her, Lorenzo thought; manifest not so much in her features as in her sad, decrepit, and innocent expression, like that of some small monkeys. And like a monkey she put up a pretence of offended dignity which he knew she was quite incapable of.

Now that they were approaching the pine wood it appeared less dense than before, with red trunks leaning this way and that as if they were just about to fall against each other. The car left the road and took to a stretch of bare, soft ground over which the wheels bounded gently. The pine wood was deserted; here and there in the shade stood an uninhabited chalet with closed shutters. Then the wood brightened, the air became white and trembling: the sea.

Lorenzo would have liked to announce the sea as he had announced the wood – but his wife's silence seemed even more determined, and she wouldn't be able to resist the temptation of snubbing him – the sight of the sea caused him such genuine delight. So he remained silent and drove over the bare soil. The car stopped, and for a moment they sat motionless in the shadow of the low hood. They couldn't see the sea properly yet, but they could hear it now the engine was switched off, with its varied and diffused murmur in which each wave seemed to have a different tone. 'Shall we get out?' he suggested at last.

His wife opened the door and put out her legs, hindered by the narrowness of her skirt. Lorenzo followed and shut the door. Immediately they felt the sea wind, strong and warm and fierce, lifting clouds of sand and dust from the rough ground.

'Shall we go down to the sea?'

'Yes; of course.'

They set out across the clearing. The bombardments had ruined much of the promenade; here and there there were wide gaps in the cement paving. There were still a few pillars standing; others had been thrown down and were gradually being covered with sand blown in long tongues as far as the middle of the clearing. When they looked in the direction of the beach they saw that it was criss-crossed all over with barbed-wire entanglements. The wind blew under the barbed wire, smoothing out the sand. The thorny threads of steel, wrapped in a white and furious cloud of dust, stretched away into the distance.

They found a way marked out by poles through the barbed wire to the sea. Lorenzo let his wife go ahead and followed at some distance behind. He did this so as to watch her at his leisure, as he had done earlier in the mirror of the car. After he had managed this manoeuvre, he reflected that perhaps the most pathetic thing about all his misfortunes was his tardy and unforeseen passion for his wife. He had not loved her at first; he had married in a hurry in the interests of his political career.

And now that the vacuous and noisy luck which had dazzled him for so many years had come to an end, he had fallen in love with her, when she had no use for his love. Or rather a sort of pungent lust had been kindled in his blood, something shy and awkward as in a boy. As he followed her he found himself watching her with a sad and surly desire that astonished him. She was tall, thin, elegant, boyish, and when her long, strong legs, sturdy in relation to the slimness of her torso, moved clumsily over the uneven sand, they recalled the legs of an awkward foal. Lorenzo paid special attention to those legs on which innumerable hairs were visible through her transparent stockings – black, long hairs which looked as though they had been stuck on to the skin and were flat and lifeless. She didn't have them plucked, as many women do. When she put up her hand to arrange her hair, disordered by the wind, he seemed to make out the blackness of her armpit through the linen shirt and felt profoundly troubled.

They reached the sea. Offshore the wind was pushing up long and sonorous springtime billows, rolling one over the other; but farther out the sea was almost calm, with alternating streaks of turbid green and dark violet. For a while Lorenzo stood beside his wife, looking at the waves. He picked one out as far away as the eye could see – in fact, at its birth – and then followed it as it rose, overturned on the rump of the one ahead of it, and passed on beyond it. As the wave lingered, lost its way in the ebb and died at his feet, his glance leapt back to the sea in search of another. He didn't know why, but he wanted at least one of those innumerable masses of water breaking on the shore to overcome the rivals that held it back and the retarding impact of the backwash; to hurl itself on the shore, pass beyond him and his wife, mount the beach and wreathe with far-flung foam the barbed-wire defences and the clearing. But it was a vain wish, and he suddenly understood why he wanted it so much. As a child, on stormy days, he loved to watch the varied impetus of the waves, and now and again, when he saw a bigger and stronger one spreading quickly up the beach as far as the bathing-huts, he used to think ambitiously: 'I shall be like that wave.' He shook his head vigorously to banish the recollection and, turning to his wife, asked her: 'Do you like it?'

'The sea?' she said indifferently. 'It's not the first time I've seen it, you know.'

Lorenzo would have liked to explain his feelings – yes, to tell her about his childish fancies; but a sort of hopeless timidity prevented him from speaking. He felt a strong impulse to free himself from his preoccupation and at least seem carefree. He bent down and picked up a stone, so as to throw it as far as he possibly could. He hoped that the violence of the action would cast away his pain as well as the stone. But the stone was deceptive. It was as big as his fist, but light; it was pumice and porous with holes. It fell close to him, floated on the crest of a wave, and grounded in the sand at his feet. He felt a sensation of bitterness, as though this was reality's silent answer to all his aspirations. His suffering resembled the pumice-stone, and he hadn't the strength to cast it away; it would always come back with the jetsam and black debris that the rough sea vomited on to the shore.

He approached his wife and put his arm round her. He wanted to walk with her along the sea's edge with the health-giving wind blowing against them, in the clamorous solitude of the waves breaking on the shore. But, startled and stubborn, she pushed him off.

'What's the matter with you?'

'Don't you want us to go for a walk?'

'It's too windy.'

'I like the wind,' he said. And he took a few steps along the shore by himself. He felt his behaviour was desperate and unreasonable, like a madman's. His feeling of madness was increased by the crashing of the waves and by the wind blowing into his hair, his eyes. 'I've completely lost my head,' he thought coolly, and he started to go towards a little heap of sand which had formed round some derelict and rusty object.

'What are you doing?' he heard his wife ask angrily. 'Where are you going? There are mines about.'

'What do I care about mines,' he answered with a shrug. He would have liked to add, 'or if I'm blown up,' but was silent out of modesty. He turned to see what his wife was doing. She was still facing the sea, looking bored and undecided. Then she said: 'Don't play the hero; you know you want to live,' with a contempt which wounded him and seemed unfair. He jumped back and took her arm. 'You must believe me when I say that at this moment I don't care a fig about dying; in fact, I'd be glad.' He squeezed her round, firm arm tightly and was depressed to notice the ease with which physical contact turned his despair into desire and made him insincere in spite of himself. She glanced at him crossly: 'Leave me alone . . . It's the usual story . . . And, anyway . . . ' Then, after a pause. 'Do what you like, but I won't follow you. I haven't the slightest desire to die myself.'

Lorenzo left her and set out purposefully for the little mound. His feet sank, his shoes filled with sand. The mound was no more than fifty yards away; he reached it and discovered it was an old petrol tin. The sea had corroded and rusted it and the wind had filled it three-quarters full of sand. Beyond, the beach stretched on as far as the eye could see, swept by the grazing wind, traversed by delicate barbed-wire entanglements which in the soft whiteness of the sand looked like healed up scars. He hesitated a moment, dazzled by the reflection of the cloudy sky, and then turned back.

His wife was no longer there. Lorenzo picked his way through the narrow passage of the barbed wire to the clearing. His wife was standing by the car, one hand on the door, the other at her forehead fixing her hair. 'What are we going to do now?' she asked.

'Let's eat,' he suggested in a cheerful voice, though he felt scarcely capable of speaking, let alone being cheerful.

'Where?'

'We can go into the pine wood.' Without waiting for an answer, he took the picnic basket from the back of the car and set out in the direction of the pines. His wife followed.

They crossed the clearing towards the remains of what had once been the local restaurant. In the white, dusty light, upright stumps of half-buried ruins arose out of the convulsed ground – pale outside and coloured inside like decayed teeth. The cement stairway leading to the main hall, in which people used to eat overlooking the sea, mounted one or two steps and then suddenly stopped above a hollowed-out chaos of pieces of ceiling, twisted and rusting iron and blocks of mortar and bricks.

The other rooms inside the crumbled walls were recognizable from similar ruins agglomerated in dusty pulp. They walked round the ruins and he said: 'You remember the last time we were here?'

'No.'

'Two years ago. Things were already going badly, but I didn't want to face up to it. You had a wisp of something round your breast and another round your waist which passed between your legs. You were very brown; you had a little turban round your head. Now,' he went on in an unexpectedly strained voice, 'I realize you're very lovely, but then I didn't seem to see you. I thought about nothing but politics and let all the idiots who followed us around make love to you.'

'And so what?' she asked drily.

'Nothing.'

Behind the restaurant was a lawn and the rough, dirty grass was mixed with sand. Thick bushes and twisted trees with branches like arms grew on the edge of the lawn. The bombardment had thrown a piece of the café piano into the middle of the lawn: the keyboard with a few white notes and a great hunk of splintered wood looked exactly like an animal's jaw with a few putrefying teeth. The grass all around was scattered with felt hammers. Another part of the instrument, the frame, had been hurled into the fork of a tree. The metal strings hung from it and curled like the pendant tentacles of a grotesque creeper.

Lorenzo searched for a withdrawn spot with a blind and concentrated premeditation as though his purpose were not love but crime. His wife followed some way behind, and he felt she was looking increasingly discontented and hostile. The pine wood was full of little grassy glades unevenly bordered with bushes and undergrowth. At last he thought he had found what he was looking for. 'Let's sit down here,' he said, and slid to the ground.

She remained standing for a moment, looking around. Then slowly, stiffly, contemptuously, she sank on to her thighs and sat, swiftly pulling her dress over her knees. Lorenzo pretended he wasn't looking at her and began to take the food from the basket. There were many packets, big and small, carefully wrapped in white tissue paper of the kind used in fashion shops. And there was a bottle of wine.

'Was it you who packed the basket?'

'No. I got the maid to do it.'

He spread out a napkin on the grass and carefully arranged the eggs, the meat, the cheese and fruit. Then he uncorked the bottle and put the cork back in again.

'Would you like an egg?'

'No.'

'Meat?'

'Give me a roll with a slice of meat.'

Lorenzo took one of the rolls which had already been cut in half and buttered, put in two slices of meat, and handed it to her. She accepted it fastidiously, without thanking him, and ate unwillingly. His head still down and without glancing at her, Lorenzo took a hard-boiled egg and bit at it hungrily, then filled his mouth with buttered bread. He felt a sorry kind of hunger which seemed rather like his desire for his wife. Hunger and lust grew and prospered on his despair, he thought – as if he were only a corpse without life or will and his wants had grown on him in the way hair grows on the beards of the dead. He ate one egg, then another, then a third, hesitated, and then ate the fourth. He enjoyed biting into the elastic whites, and the feeling of the soft yolks as they crumbled between his teeth. He ate energetically and now and again put the bottle to his mouth and took long gulps. After the eggs he turned his attention to the meat; there were two kinds, a roast in large red slices, and cutlets fried with breadcrumbs. Without a glance at his wife he went on eating, and as he ate, despite his emptiness and sadness of spirit, he could feel the turgid vitality swelling in his veins. In view of his despair, this vitality seemed a useless and ironical form of wealth and he felt desolate. At last he lifted his eyes and offered her the bottle without a word. She still had her roll – she had only eaten half of it. She shook her head.

'Aren't you eating?'

'I'm not hungry.'

Lorenzo finished eating, then collected the eggshells and other remains, wrapped them in a piece of paper and threw them as far as he could. He put the half-empty bottle back in the basket. These small actions he performed with deliberate doggedness as though he were tidying up his own disturbed mind rather than the picnic. His wife, who by now had finished her roll, began touching up her face with hand-mirror and puff. 'And now,' she said, 'shall we go?'

'Where?'

'Home.'

'But it's still early.'

'You've seen the sea,' she said unkindly. 'You've had lunch. You don't want to sleep here, do you?'

Lorenzo watched her, not knowing whether to feel infuriated or humiliated by her pig-headed hostility. Then he said in a low voice:

'Listen. I've got to talk to you.'

'Talk to me? Haven't we talked enough already?'

He slid along the grass with an effort and sat beside her.

'I'd like to know what your grievance is.'

'I haven't got one. Only I don't see why we have to go on living together, that's all.'

'You no longer feel any affection for me?'

'I never did feel any, and less than ever now.'

'But at one time,' Lorenzo insisted, 'whenever I gave you a present of some money, you used to throw your arms round my neck. You used to hug and kiss me and say you loved me.'

'I liked the presents, of course,' she agreed, obviously annoyed by this reminder of her childish avarice, 'but I didn't love you.'

'It was all pretence, then?'

'No; not exactly.'

Lorenzo realized that she was being sincere. With women like her, gratitude for gifts closely resembled love: indeed, perhaps that was the only kind of love she was capable of.

'But I – ' He looked down. 'Since things have been going badly, I feel for you for the first time in my life, you see . . . I don't know how to explain . . .'

'Then for heaven's sake don't try to,' she exclaimed mockingly.

'Can't I know what you have against me?'

'Against you?' She was growing angry. 'I have the fact that I don't want to be the wife of a jail-bird.'

'I was only in prison for a few days and anyway, it was on political grounds.'

'So you say. But others say there was something else, and . . . that you might be locked up again any time.'

Lorenzo noticed a trace of uncertainty in her voice, as if she were repeating something she had heard rather than thought out for herself.

'You're talking about something you know nothing about. I bet that all these years we've been together you never even knew who I was or what I was doing.'

'Don't be absurd.'

'Well then, tell me.'

'You were . . .' She hesitated. 'Well, you were someone in control.'

'That's not enough. What was my position?'

'How do I know?' she said scornfully. 'All I know is that everyone referred to you as one of the authorities; but you were always changing; at one time you were one thing, at another time another. I had something else to think about besides your jobs.'

'Yes,' said Lorenzo gently. 'You had Rodolfo, Mario, Gianni, to think about.'

She pretended not to hear the names of her lovers – all of them as young and silly as herself. Lorenzo went on: 'At least you know what has happened since the time when I was an official? Do you?'

He saw her lift her shoulders impatiently. 'There you are. Now you're taking me for a fool. I'm much more intelligent than you think.'

'I don't doubt it in the least, but tell me what has happened.'

'The war came. Fascism came to an end. That's what happened. Now are you satisfied?'

'Fine. And why do you think I lost my career?'

'Because,' she said, unsure, 'now the government has been taken over by the enemies of Fascism.'

'And who are the enemies of Fascism?'

This time she lifted her eyes to heaven, tightened her lips, and said nothing. A kind of rage took hold of Lorenzo. Such ignorance, he thought, was far worse than any mere facile condemnation. It made even his mistakes, not to mention his few merits, fall into a void; there remained no more trace of his life than his footsteps, a little while ago, on the sand along the shore.

'What was Fascism?'

Again the same silence. Abruptly Lorenzo seized her by the arm and shook her. 'Answer, you fiend. Why don't you answer?'

'Leave me alone,' she said sullenly. 'I don't answer because I know you want to tie me up in knots and make me change what I think. I don't want to stay with you any longer, that's all.'

Lorenzo was no longer listening. The contact of that arm had once again aroused his desire. He looked at her skirt stretching tightly over her thighs as she sat; the softness and warmth and weight of her flesh seemed to communicate themselves to the material. At the sight of it, he felt his mind melting away and his breath catching. Nevertheless, he said slowly: 'Don't you realize that you're leaving me at the very time when another woman would stand by me, and for motives you don't even see clearly, for some mere whim or piece of gossip?'

'I realize that many society women don't invite me to their houses any more, or greet me in the street. I've already told Mother that I want to go back to her. That's all; I don't want to stay with you any more.' She stood up.

Lorenzo looked her up and down. She stood erect and scornful, her legs in an ungainly attitude with her overtight skirt and her high heels. He realized that it would be easy to fling her down and disarm her contempt. Those legs of hers, hampered by the tightness of her skirt, were like her character, which was hampered by her silliness. He felt a violent desire to upset her balance. With one thrust of his whole body, he threw himself at her legs and toppled her over on to the grass. She fell headlong and, startled into fury, exclaimed, 'Leave me alone. What's the matter with you?'

Lorenzo didn't answer, but threw himself on her, crushing her under his body. He said, 'I am what I am,' holding his lips

against hers as if he wanted to insert each word into her mouth.
'But you're not really any better than me; you're a silly, empty,
corrupt girl; as long as it suited you you stayed with me. Well,
then, now it doesn't suit you any more, you'll stay with me just
the same.'

He saw her look of terror and then she said again, almost in
supplication, 'Leave me alone.'

'I won't leave you,' Lorenzo said between his teeth. He knew,
because he had proved it in the past, that his wife, for all her
fury, would surrender to violence in the end. At a given moment she always seemed to be overtaken by a kind of languor
or complicity with the force she was being subjected to, and
then she yielded and became passively loving, as though all the
previous repulses had been no more than wilful coquetry. That
was another aspect of her silliness – the incapacity to carry any
feeling, whether hostile or friendly, to its conclusion. And so,
when they began struggling, she defending herself and he trying to overcome her defences, Lorenzo suddenly saw in her
little innocent eyes the tempted, passive, and languid look he
knew so well. At the same time he felt her resistance weaken.
Then she said in a low voice: 'Stop, I tell you. Someone might
see us.' And that was already an invitation to go on.

But suddenly he felt disgusted with his victory. After all,
nothing would be altered, even if she did yield. He would get
up lovelessly from the body he had enjoyed; she, scornful and
untidy, would pull down her crumpled skirt; and with the first
words she spoke their disagreement would begin again, but
with added feelings of disgust at the meaningless, mechanical
coupling. And it wasn't that that he had intended when he
brought her out for the day's trip.

With a brusque movement, he left her and drew himself
away on the grass. She sat up looking injured and deluded.
'Don't you know that violence gets you nowhere,' she said
crossly.

Lorenzo felt like bursting out laughing and answering that
on the contrary violence was perhaps the only thing that worked with her. But at the same time he couldn't help recognizing
that what she said was true; for what he really needed, violence
didn't get anywhere.

Despite this, he said cruelly: 'That doesn't alter the fact that if I'd gone on a bit longer you'd have opened your legs.'

'How vulgar you are,' she said with sincere disgust. She rose to her feet, clambered through the bushes and set out determinedly for the clearing.

Lorenzo stayed sitting on the ground with his eyes on the grass. When he thought over his wife's answers he felt as though he himself no longer knew what he had done or stood for all those years. 'She's right,' he thought. 'It was all an empty dream, a delirium; and now I've woken up.' As he looked back over the past he realized that he couldn't remember anything except his constant cordiality – cordiality to his inferiors, his superiors, his friends, his enemies, to strangers, and to his wife. He reflected that in the end his cordiality must have had a bad effect, for after so much talking and smiling he now felt incapable of either; as if his tongue had dried up and the corners of his mouth had become sore. In these conditions even an idiot like his wife found her game easy.

He jumped at the distant throb of a car; and paused a moment listening; then, suddenly suspicious, he leapt to his feet and began to run across the pine wood, leaping over the bushes and the uneven ground towards the clearing. When he arrived there, panting, it was only to find it empty. The air was still full of the dust raised by the car in which his wife had fled.

It seemed a worthy ending to the day, and he didn't even feel annoyed. He would probably be able to get a lift back on a military truck. At worst, he would have to walk a couple of miles to the main road; plenty of cars passed along it, and he could easily get a lift.

But as he set out along the path through the pine wood he felt the call of the sea, a longing to go back again to the everlasting motion, the everlasting clamour, before returning to the city. And then he wanted to do something he would never have dared to do in front of his wife, take off his shoes, roll up his trousers, and walk along the sea's edge in the shallow water of the ebb and flow of the waves.

He was aware, too, that he wanted to walk along by the edge of the sea to prove to himself that he didn't care about his wife's flight. But he knew that this wasn't true, and when he

sat in the sand to take off his shoes he noticed that his hands
were trembling.

He removed his shoes and socks, folded his trousers up to
below the knee, and picked his way through the barbed wire to
the water's edge. He set out walking in the ebbing and flowing
water, with shoes in hand, his head bowed and eyes lowered.

His attitude was that of thought but he wasn't really thinking. He liked seeing the surf pass over his feet, rise along his
legs, form a whirl of water round his ankles, then flow back
peevishly, carrying away the sand beneath his feet, tickling like
something alive. He liked, too, to keep his gaze down and see
only water to right and left, turbid, swirling, sprinkled with
white rings of foam. The sea near the shore was full of a black
sedge which each wave threw on to the sand and then carried
away again in the backwash. There were minute sticks like
ebony, oval and smooth scales, tiny wood splinters, myriads of
little black objects that the movement of the turbid sandladen
water kept in continuous turmoil. The transparent shells of
tiny dead crabs, green seaweed, and yellow roots put some splash
of colour into this carbonized chaff. When the surf ebbed the
sedge clung gluttonously to his feet, making an arabesque of
black on their shining whiteness. Here and there some flotsam
of larger bulk floated in between one wave and the next, in the
ground-glass turmoil of the foamy water. He saw something
not far away of uncertain colour and shape which made him
think of an animal; but as he drew near, overcoming the water's
pressure, he discovered that it was the wooden hoof of a woman's orthopaedic shoe. Little shells of pallid amethyst had
spread thickly over the toe, making a kind of dense tuft, while
the heel was still covered with red cloth. As he was looking
at the remains a high foamless billow passed by, rapidly bathing
him as far as the groin. He threw the shoe away and retreated
nearer to the shore.

He didn't know how long he walked along the beach on the
soft and fleeting sand with his feet in the riotous water. But as
a result of looking down at the waves which broke ceaselessly
on his legs and passed beyond towards the unseen shore, he
felt a kind of dizziness. He lifted his eyes over the sea and for
a moment he imagined he saw it tall and upright like a liquid

wall. The sky on the horizon was no more than a streak of vapour. There some sea bird was skimming the skin of the water in distant and dangerous flight which revived the thought of the drunken violence of the wind. Dazed, he nearly fell under the weight of a heavier billow. And the clamour of the waves seemed suddenly to become shriller and fiercer, as though redoubled by the hope of his collapse.

Almost fearfully he turned towards the beach, thinking to get out of the water and sit down for a moment on the dry sand. He had walked a long way. He had left the clearing and the ruins far behind. Here the sand, mounted in dunes and defences, was criss-crossed by barbed wire and stumps which looked like people holding hands with arms outstretched so as to block the way. His attention was attracted by a thick bank of black and shining seaweed underneath which the waves had hollowed out the sand. He jumped as far as this seaweed and, touching the ground with one hand, he leapt on it.

The torrent of seaweed and sand which soared into the air with a thundering echo darkened his eyes to the sky for a moment as he fell back in the whirlpool of the explosion. He thought he was falling headlong for ever in a perpetual din of cataract. But silence and immobility followed. He lay on his back in the water; the noise and movement of the sea were singularly sweet and distant under a sky again visible. The water pulled him under by the hair; head down and feet up, his body moved with the passage of a wave, and he saw a large red stain hastening towards the shore with the rings of foam and the black debris. Then another wave came and pulled him under and he closed his eyes.

THE ENGLISH OFFICER

SHE stopped in front of a shop to see if the car was following her or had merely slowed down for some other reason. It was a small, mud-covered Army vehicle with an officer alone at the wheel. When the car was alongside the shop-front it slowed down until it nearly stopped. She asked herself whether she would agree to get in if invited, and decided she wouldn't. Certainly not in that street of little hat-shops and dress-shops where she was well known. She turned her back on the car and started looking at a silk scarf in the window, one she had found out the price of several days ago because she hankered for it. She heard the car creeping along behind her against the kerb, and then she heard it move off and, completely absorbed in staring at the coveted object, she gave her shoulders a slight shrug as if to say 'Good-bye'. But after she had derived a sort of detached and fascinated pleasure from looking at the silk scarf, so desirable yet, in view of her shortage of money, so unattainable, her thoughts switched back to the car that she had so disdainfully allowed to move off. And yet it was with the scarf in mind that she had encouraged the officer with two or three distinct and meaningful smiles. Besides, she had more or less left home that day with the express intention of looking for someone who would enable her to buy the scarf. These contradictions between her intentions and her character exasperated her. Why, for once, was she not capable of being really consistent? Given that as from now on she had adopted this profession, why not make up her mind to shake off her qualms and fits of dignity for good and all?

Regretfully she stopped looking at the scarf and glanced at herself for a second in the mirror of a side window in which brocade materials were exhibited. The wind had dishevelled her hair and long, fair wisps were falling over her forehead

and into her wide-open, laughing eyes. The biting cold of the
fine winter day had stiffened her face and it was white and
bloodless beneath the colours of her make-up. Her mouth was
redder and fuller by contrast. Her head was bare and she had
on a brown coat with upturned collar and a belt tight round
the waist. Anyway, she thought, she certainly didn't look like
those horrible girls you saw in the streets arm-in-arm with
soldiers. She felt an unexpected desire – it seemed to her final
and unbreakable – not to allow herself to be led into temptation
by chance encounters. This decision restored her normal carefree and frivolous peace of mind. Thus calmed, she lingered
in front of the mirror to look at herself and tidy her hair.

The street was on an incline and sloped up to an esplanade
overlooking the city. In the centre of the esplanade there was an
obelisk. She drew away from the mirror and, looking along the
street, saw that the car had stopped underneath the obelisk so
that the officer could watch what she was doing and, if she
didn't come towards the esplanade, could turn round and continue to follow her. 'He's waiting for me. He'll buy me the
scarf,' she thought happily, lightly, as if all the time she'd been
looking in the mirror her mind had been tortured with regret
at having let her opportunity slip. Without thinking, she went
to the door of the shop, opened it, called the manageress, whom
she knew, and asked her to hold aside the scarf till the following morning. Then she set out briskly in the direction of the
obelisk.

But while walking she suddenly remembered the decision
she had taken a few moments earlier and bit her lip and shook
her head angrily. So that was what her decisions were worth.
She felt strong irritation with herself, yet she didn't think of
turning back. As justification, she assured herself that it
wouldn't have been any good; he would have caught up with
her in any case. But she decided she would pass him without
looking at him, and should he accost her she would answer
in a way that left no doubts as to her respectability.

When she reached the esplanade she walked in front of the
car with lowered eyes and went straight to the parapet from
which you could enjoy a view of the whole city. She was well
aware that to linger here and contemplate such a well-known

panorama amounted to inviting the officer to get out of his car and join her. But she thought that, taking all in all, there was no harm in that. There was a big gulf and there were infinitely subtle distinctions between letting oneself be accosted, even answering – and the other business. She rested her elbows on the parapet and fingered her hair as she gazed down.

As she had foreseen, the officer came up and leant over the parapet beside her. She watched him out of the corner of her eye. He must be very young, younger than her. He had a round, ruddy face with rather coarse features and two small deep-set eyes of soft blue. He put his hand on the balustrade and stared at length at all the rooftops below with a kind of wonderment, as if he hadn't expected to see them. She looked at him insistently, shamelessly, thinking that he might turn round and the meeting of their eyes might produce acquaintance with words. But the officer seemed unable to make up his mind to turn his head. As the minutes passed she became more and more angry with herself for making it so plain that she wanted to be accosted. The first stages of such encounters always got on her nerves, and the man's voice with its pretext for starting a conversation always made her jump angrily. But this time she felt that if she didn't take the first step nothing would ever happen. Furiously, opening her eyes wide at the impassive, silent face, she said abruptly: 'Lovely day, isn't it?'

The officer turned immediately and answered with deep conviction: 'Yes; lovely.'

He had a soft, agreeable voice. Silence fell once more. 'I won't speak to him again,' she thought, pulling a face that showed her irritation. 'I'll stay a minute longer and then be off.'

The officer was obviously struggling against his own shyness. At last, with an air of taking the bargaining usual in such cases for granted, he pointed to the car and said: 'Shall we get into the car?'

At this invitation the woman felt as if her legs might move in the direction of the car of their own accord, and her rage increased.

'Why?' she asked, gazing at him and smiling unpleasantly.

'So as to be together,' the officer answered frankly.

'But why should we be together?'

She now felt she ought to behave just like a lady who has been stopped in the street by a stranger with dubious intentions and is determined to show him his mistake. The young man looked disconcerted.

'So as to talk,' he answered, and added tactfully, 'We could go to a café.'

'But I never go to cafés.'

'Why not?'

'Merely because,' she began, dwelling on the syllables and smiling with superior respectability, 'I'm not in the habit of going to cafés.'

'Oh,' said the officer, as though the words had revealed all kinds of things. 'Let's go for a drive, then,' he proposed, pointing again to the car.

'But I'm not in the habit of going for drives with people I don't know.'

She saw that he was blushing to the roots of his hair.

'My name's Bruce,' he said, 'Gilbert Bruce. . . . And yours?'

'I've got no name to you,' she answered, preening herself on her cutting rejoinder.

There was a moment's silence.

'You think badly of me,' the officer persevered, 'but you don't know what I want of you.'

She flared. 'I know perfectly,' she said. 'You want to pay me for a couple of hours' fun, don't you?'

She noticed that he blushed again without answering.

'And I also know,' she pursued sourly, 'how much you want to give me . . . two or three thousand lire, perhaps even more . . . Aren't I right?'

The officer tried to joke: 'As you know the price so well . . .'

'Of course I know it. . . . And, by the way, your sort are usually quicker than you and mention the sum at once without so much beating about the bush.'

'My sort are not so shy as I am.'

'And then,' she went on, 'you would offer me a packet or two of cigarettes.'

'Oh, cigarettes – of course,' said the officer, attempting a smile.

'And perhaps some tins of food if I asked you?'

She saw him shake his head kindly and go on smiling. Then he held out his hand and said with an effort: 'I see I've made a mistake. Please forgive me.'

She saw that this was a farewell and suddenly felt almost terrified at being taken for the kind of woman she wasn't and then left in the lurch after so much trouble. Her pig-headedness and irritation vanished.

'No,' she said, so hurriedly that it sounded really comic to her. 'No; you haven't made a mistake.'

'I haven't made a mistake?'

'That's what I said.' She was impatient.

She saw him blush a deep red, but this time it didn't seem to be with embarrassment.

'Then shall we go?'

'Let's.'

They went to the car. The officer helped her in, leapt in beside her and started up.

'Where?'

'To where I live,' she said simply. 'I'll show you the way.'

The car circled the obelisk and moved off quickly towards the public gardens under the low branches of the trees. It was a fine day and all the avenues as far as the eye could see were crowded with strollers. As the woman passed them, she couldn't suppress a profound feeling of vanity to be overtaking all the pedestrians in a car, even a muddy Army one. She now wondered why she had treated the officer so badly in view of the fact that she had already decided to accept. She felt cross and at the same time vaguely pleased at doing yet again what she knew she shouldn't have done.

The officer, meekly following her instructions, drove the car through the gardens and then along a wide, tree-lined avenue. With the speed of the car and in the wind that filled her mouth and untidied her hair he felt the urgency of his desire that was now sure of being soon satisfied; and she felt both shame and a savage satisfaction. They had entered a poor district where the overcrowded windows of squalid blocks of flats rushed by behind the bare branches of tall plane trees.

'This way,' she said, pointing to a side road.

The officer turned skilfully on the tramlines and entered the road. Those tenements on the avenue had been merely a façade concealing a vast stretch of miserable little villas.

'This way . . . right . . . left,' the women directed as the poor streets crossed and re-crossed. Intent, the officer altered the direction of the car at each new instruction. Finally, she said, 'Here we are,' and the car stopped.

They were facing a gate covered with creepers. The garden looked crowded and narrow, hardly more than a passage round the little villa which was dull brown and undecorated, with a stumpy little tower and façade of four windows. It looked very small and very modest.

'If you like, you can leave the car in the garden.'

The officer nodded and started up again. She opened one side of the gate and then, with an effort, the other. 'I wanted him to put his car in the garden,' she was thinking, 'because I'm really rather embarrassed at the thought of it being left outside.' On one side of the high porch in front of the door was a paved space just big enough to hold the car. But on the other, near the road, between the wall of the villa and the little surrounding wall, there was a patch of grass covered with old ivy and at the bottom a small enclosure with wire-netting round it. Here the woman kept three hens and a cock. To fill in the time while the officer was manoeuvring his car into the restricted space she went to look at the hen-run. The cock was yellowy white, and his bright feathers and flaming red comb and wattles stood out against the dark dank background of decayed leaves and stunted shrubs, while the hens were black and hard to distinguish against the drab undergrowth. 'I couldn't have stayed standing beside the gate like a servant,' she was thinking. 'I might as well see to feeding the fowls now; and then he'll come and get a good impression, seeing me looking so domesticated.' She picked up a bowl of chicken food and began scattering it, slowly, so as to give the officer time. She heard the car come in with a roar that suddenly stopped. She didn't turn round. The three hens pecked greedily and she felt she presented a charming picture, well-dressed, with the bowl in her hands and the hens at her feet. She heard the creak of the gate as it closed and went on scattering the food. The cock didn't seem hungry, but stood aside, every now and again worrying his spur with his beak. The officer entered the hen-run and came up to her.

'I've shut the gate,' he said, pleased with himself.

'That's right,' she answered without looking at him. The food had just come to an end. She bent down and put the bowl on the ground.

'Do you like hens?' she asked as she straightened up.

'Well, to be quite honest, I don't,' the young man answered with a smile.

'They lay eggs,' she said portentously and with deep significance, as much as to say: 'I am poor, and in these days hens that lay are valuable.'

The cock had been standing apart; but suddenly and as if casually he approached a particularly puffed up and dignified hen and leapt on her back. The hen squatted, but made no attempt to escape. The cock gripped her comb ferociously with his beak and fluttered for a moment on top of her. Then he left her and began pecking busily at the last grains of food. The hen got up, ruffled her feathers with a shake of the body, got them straight again and then, more dignified and strutting than ever, began pecking the ground beside the cock. 'They make love too,' said the officer with a sheepish smile.

The woman thought this remark in bad taste and said nothing.

'Shall we go?' she proposed after a moment, in a detached, worldly voice.

They left the hen-run and made their way along the wall to the entrance.

The little muddy car stood in front of the porch.

'Have you come from the front?' asked the woman, indicating the car.

'Yes.'

'Are they fighting there?' she asked, smiling at him as they mounted the steps. But she felt dissatisfied with her tone; she didn't know why.

'Yes; they're fighting,' the officer answered, bored.

The woman took the key from her purse, unlocked the door and went in. The officer followed and removed his beret from his head. They were facing a dingy, cold staircase with a primitive iron banister.

'I live on the first floor; there are other people on the second,' she announced as she went ahead. The officer said nothing.

At the first landing the woman opened the door and ushered him in. Then she shut the door, locked it and left the key in the lock. She took the beret from the officer's hand and hung it up on the rack. The officer took off his cape and hung it up under the beret. The clothes-rack of shiny wood and metal was in a tiny passage with dark, dingy walls. They went into the sitting-room, a small, square room with walls the same dead colour as the passage. The furniture consisted of a divan and two armchairs placed round a glass and nickel table. In a corner a radio stood on a stool. She went to the window and pulled up the blind, but not much light came in. The windows were long with blue curtains through which could be discerned the skeleton branches of a large tree. The officer looked round, hesitating to sit down on the hard bleak divan with its cold blue cover.

'Sit down, sit down,' she said, passing with cool familiarity from 'you' to 'thou'. The officer sat, and as the woman moved within his reach, possibly encouraged by the change of pronoun, he leant forward and tried to catch one of her hands.

'No, no . . . Wait a minute,' she said and left the room.

She went to the bottom of the passage to a little house telephone and took off the receiver. Almost at once she heard the voice of her mother asking in her usual breathless way whether she was back. 'Obviously, since I'm ringing you up,' she answered unkindly. 'Don't let the child come down . . . I've got a visitor . . . I'll come up myself.' Her mother began asking further questions, but she cut her short and put down the receiver.

She now began wondering whether she cared enough for the officer to keep up her initial line of conventional contempt for venal matters. 'At least,' she thought, 'for this once I won't accept any money.' The first time she had let one of these soldiers in search of pick-ups come home with her she had done so disinterestedly, without thinking of gain. And then at the moment of parting the man had offered her money – which, with a pleasant, light, unthinking spontaneity that had astonished her, and an air of capitulation that the man must have thought calculated, but which was really the result of her surprise, she had accepted. Afterwards she had repented, when she observed, or thought she observed, a faint hint of contempt in her first lover's attitude. And she had sworn to herself, while putting the money into her purse, that this would be the first and last time. But for some unknown reason things had turned out in exactly the same way with the second, the same capitulation, the same spontaneity, both gratifying and humiliating. And similarly with the third. And in the end she had given in entirely though reluctantly to this profitable avocation. But always with a miserable feeling of shame, vented on this occasion in the rude remarks with which she had greeted the officer's advances. And now the question had come up again. Would she accept payment or no? True, she didn't like this officer any better than the others, but this youth appealed for disinterested love – he was almost a boy, certainly five or six years younger than herself. His youth was manifest, she thought, both in his shyness and his well-brought-up and respectful manners. He must be a student, she went on to reflect, and obviously a boy of good family, and it was doubtful whether he had ever had a woman before. Turning over these considerations in her mind, she went into a small, clean kitchen. She opened a cupboard, took out a bottle and two glasses, put them on a tray, and went out again.

The afternoon was now drawing to a close. The flat was steeped in murky shadows that seemed to make the figure of the officer more unreal and improbable, sitting there on the low divan, with his legs stretched out and his hands in his pockets, between the two empty armchairs and facing the empty table. She put the tray on the table, uncorked the bottle, and, leaning over so that her hair fell over her nose, making her look a trifle exhausted and somehow more attractive, she filled the two glasses.

'It's English,' she said with a smile, sitting down beside him. 'Do you like it?'

'Yes. It's excellent,' he answered with conviction. He drew a cigarette case from his pocket and offered it to her.

'Cigarettes,' she said with exaggerated vivacity. 'Thanks . . .

but I have some . . . ' and she began looking for her bag. The officer insisted with a gesture as if to say, 'But do take one of mine,' and she immediately gave up her search and with the same mortifying meekness that made her accept the money she took a cigarette. For a short while they smoked in silence. The woman had taken off her coat and was shivering in the cold room, wearing only a tight woollen pullover and a thin, narrow skirt.

'It's cold,' she said with a smile, puffing into the air to show him the white cloud caused by her breath.

'Yes; very,' he said equably.

'You English are more used to the cold than we Italians are. In your country it's always cold.'

'It's even cold in London this year,' the officer said without looking at her.

'Why?'

She saw him shrug his shoulders.

'The trains are being used for Army purposes and no one has any coal.'

'You wage war seriously . . . In England everybody does war work, even women, don't they?'

'Of course,' said the officer with profound conviction 'Every-one is in the war . . . women too . . . you're perfectly right.'

There followed a long silence. The officer looked fixedly at her with his little, deep-set eyes of intense blue, and under his gaze she felt she was becoming nervous and wandering. 'Now he'll try to kiss me,' she thought, and felt something like terror and as though in rebellion her mouth instinctively contracted into a little grimace of disgust. The imminence of the first kiss always aroused feelings of revulsion and indignation in her. She had been married and had a daughter, she had had lovers, yet when two unknown lips came near to hers, they caused her skin to creep with a kind of hysterical and virginal repugnance. However, the officer merely took her hand and, seeing the wedding-ring, asked, 'Are you married?'

'Yes.'

'And where's your husband?'

She hesitated. Must she tell the truth? That she was quite simply separated from her husband? With another officer she had taken it into her head for some unknown reason to say that her husband was a prisoner of war, and for a moment this lie had seemed a justification – for if it made her behaviour worse from one point of view, from another it made her seem pathetic – she must shift for herself in her poverty and loneliness. So 'He's a prisoner,' she said, looking him brazenly in the eyes.

The officer looked at her as before without saying anything, but she thought she could detect in his eyes a glimmer of compassion, and she clung to it.

'I've been left alone,' she said, weighing the syllables. 'My husband was earning, but now I have nothing . . .'

It seemed to her that she was telling the truth, even though she knew perfectly well that it wasn't true, that her husband wasn't a prisoner, that he sent her enough money for elementary necessities, and that the money she herself had made so far and was preparing to make again was used for buying luxuries. Yet it seemed to her she was telling the truth, and she felt upset, just as someone does when telling a truth that hurts.

'And you, are you married?' she asked.

'Engaged.' She watched him put his hand into the back pocket of his trousers, draw out a wallet and from this a photograph, which he handed to her. It was of an average girl, neither pretty nor plain, leaning on a bicycle against a background of trees. She was conscious of putting a fatuous conventional expression on her face as she looked at it, one that mixed respect and compunction. Then she handed it back.

'Pretty,' she said.

'Yes; she's very pretty,' said the officer complacently, putting the photograph back in the wallet. She suddenly felt scared lest the sight of the photograph had cooled him off, and she felt she now wanted to entice the kiss that before she had been so afraid of.

'We've hardly known one another for an hour,' she said, smiling, 'and yet it's as though we've known each other for ages, isn't it?'

As she said this, she clumsily put her hand on his, twining his fingers in hers.

It was now twilight and the shadows from the corners of the room had reached the divan and the couple seated there.

The officer squeezed the woman's hand and with the other drew her head towards him – not towards his lips, but towards his shoulder. Thus they remained in the cold, dusky shadow for some time, her head on his shoulder. She didn't quite know what to do, and she opened her eyes wide in the darkness. It wasn't the first time that she had come across this kind of sentimentality where she had expected forthright uninhibited procedure, and on each occasion she had felt acute embarrassment and irritation. At long last, after a delay that seemed to her endless, the officer made a move to kiss her. 'Wait,' she said with foresight, and with her handkerchief she removed the red from her lips. Then they kissed.

After the kiss the officer once more drew her head on to his shoulder and began caressing her with his hand, stroking the hair on her forehead, ruffling it, smoothing it and then ruffling it again. There was a kind of mute and sentimental frenzy about his caress, as if he wanted to wear her forehead away, like a wave that wears away a white pebble on the beach. She realized that she had fallen in with a man more in need of affection than physical love, of tenderness than lust, and while she let him continue she became cold and bored. Every now and again the officer broke off his caress to give her a short kiss, and then began again, pressing his hand with open fingers on her forehead a little above her eyes, and then travelling up to the very roots of her hair. His hand was both light and heavy – light because inspired by a kind of fervour, heavy because he pressed hard as if to rub the caress into her skin, as though it were a kind of ointment. Unexpectedly, in the deep silence, there came a knock at the door.

'Sorry,' she said, getting up. Through the shadow she went and unlocked the door, opening it only a little way. At first she saw nothing and then, on looking down, she saw the round face of her daughter, with her long hair tied on top with a ribbon.

'I told Granny not to send you down . . . I've visitors,' she said without opening the door.

'Granny wants to know if you'll be in to supper.'

'Yes. I'll be in. And now be off with you, and don't come back . . . I'll be coming up.'

'All right.'

The child turned away obediently. Through the door she could hear her mounting the stairs one by one with little steps, for they were too steep for her legs. Then the noise died away and she slowly shut the door. She could feel his presence as she entered the room; and without turning, with her hair still falling over her eyes, she said, 'Shall we go into my room?'

From the passage they went into the bedroom. Here too the cold dusk spread like an impalpable dust over the low bed and the two or three characterless pieces of furniture, giving an uninhabited and deserted feeling. The woman showed the officer in and closed the door. When she turned she found herself in his arms. This time his embrace was so impetuous and clumsy that they both fell in a sitting position on the bed. She managed to stretch out her hand and turn on the light on the bedside table. They broke apart almost immediately and, not knowing what to say, she asked like a child, 'What do you think of me?'

She could see he was examining her attentively. For a moment she was afraid of some facile and wounding answer that would offend her, and she regretted her question.

'I think,' he said finally, with deep sincerity and seeming humility, 'that you are very beautiful.'

She looked down with a pleased expression.

'Thanks. You're very kind.'

Then she pulled herself together and rose to her feet.

'I'm going to shut the window.'

She went to the window and lowered the blind. She was thinking, 'Now I'll have to tell him to get undressed,' and she felt renewed irritation at his inexperience that obliged her to throw all delicacy to the winds. Scarcely had this thought entered her head than she saw him calmly taking off his jacket and hanging it over a chair. Then he began unbuckling his trousers. This seemed at variance with the timidity of his first embrace.

She sat on the edge of the bed and began undoing her shoes, her teeth clenched in undefined anger. She heard the young man stretching out on the bed behind her, and suddenly the idea that he might be watching her became unbearable.

'Please,' she snapped, turning on him violently, 'turn over . . . I can't stand being watched while I'm undressing.'

She noticed that he seemed astonished by her outburst, yet he turned his head round obediently on the pillow while still lying on his back with half his chest naked outside the cover. She got up and hurriedly, shivering, took off all her clothes. But whether out of impatience or curiosity, the young man turned his head at the very moment when she was in her most awkward and ungainly position – when with one knee on the edge of the bed and one foot on the ground, leaning forward with her breasts and hair hanging, she was climbing in beside him. Her irritation increased. But she leant over him and he shut his eyes in the warm shadow of her armpit, and she put out the light on the bedside table.

Later they lay in each other's arms under the rough embroidered material that tickled their naked limbs. She felt his hand in the darkness resume the long insistent massage of her eyes and brow, sentimental as before, but with a new vibration that came from jealousy and possessiveness. Every part of her body that was not touching his was cold and yet, under the rain of his caress, she felt her mouth take on an embittered sceptical, ill-humoured line. She would have liked to stop thinking, but her mind pursued its stream of reflections independently of her will – not reflections exactly, but absurd disordered fantasies mingled with out-of-the-way memories and associations. She imagined, for instance, the young man falling in love with her and carrying her off to his own country. This fantasy begot others about the life they would lead, the people they would meet, the house they would live in, and about her daughter and her mother. Thence she passed on to others with little connexion with where she had started, and these in their turn, as if by spontaneous generation, subdivided and diverged in strange, unforeseeable directions. At a certain point she was aware that she was wondering who on earth it was who had greeted her in the street that afternoon shortly before she met the officer. These uncalled-for thoughts caused her a dull irritation, especially as at the same time, as insistent and uncomfortable as the cold down her back, the question, 'Should I or should I not get him to pay me?' nagged at her.

So they lay in the dark and silence of what was now night. At last she dozed off and after an indefinite time woke up again.

She observed that the officer had got up and was already dressed and buttoning his tunic. The light was on and revealed a room in the sort of disorder that inevitably goes with encounters of this kind.

'I'll wait for you outside,' he said, pointing towards the door; and he went out.

After he had gone she lay still in the crumpled bed, then suddenly felt afraid that the officer might escape without paying her. The fact that he had gone out in such a hurry was suspicious. She was disgusted at her fears, and while a prey to them almost hoped that the officer really had made off; in that case she would be a creditor, and not merely financially. However, she dressed quickly, unable to rid herself of her fear which was as sticky as the odour of love.

She combed her hair in the wardrobe mirror and observed that her eyes were dilated in a frenzy of greed, anger, and suspicion. As she gazed at the ignoble spectacle in the depths of the mirror, she caught sight of the folded notes lying on the bedside table. She counted them with a frown of eager curiosity. There were far more than she had hoped for. She was then gripped by the fear that the officer might really have gone, and she ran from the room.

She found him in the sitting-room, seated on the divan. He had switched on the light, poured out a glass, and had his pipe between his teeth. When he saw her he got to his feet.

She went up to him and said: 'I'm glad you gave yourself a drink . . . Give me a little too, will you?'

The officer took the bottle and filled her glass. She sat down and drank it greedily. She now dreaded the officer's departure as much as she had dreaded his first kiss. She experienced physical desolation, a feeling of separation that was insulting and harrowing. She would have liked him to stay. They could go on drinking together; they could get drunk. She wanted to drink because she thought that in their cups she would be able to tell the officer a whole lot of things that she knew some time or other she would have to tell someone.

She poured herself out a second glass and began to fill his. But she saw him refuse with a motion of the hand.

'Won't you have some more?' she asked, frightened.

'No, thank you.'

'I've got an idea,' she exclaimed, her eyes bright with sudden hope. 'Why don't you stay and have supper with me? I'll cook a meal for you. I'll make spaghetti. Do you like spaghetti?'

'Yes; I do indeed,' he answered regretfully; 'but I'm afraid I've got to go.'

'No; don't. Stay for supper, and for the night, too.'

'It's impossible.'

'You can't stand the sight of me now . . . It's all over?'

She was comforted to see his astonished shake of the head, as though she had accused him of a crime he hadn't committed.

He said simply : 'I would like to stay. Anyone in my position would like to stay. But I can't.' As he said this he rose. She was seized with panic and, leaning forward, she grasped his hand and put it to her lips.

'Don't go,' she begged. And without realizing what she was saying, added : 'I have a feeling that if you stayed I would fall in love with you.'

'I have to go for strict military reasons,' he explained. And he added with a smile, though not maliciously : 'Tomorrow you'll have someone else and forget all about me.'

She didn't dare contradict him, and she followed him wearily and sadly, fixing her hair and biting her lips. The officer put on his cape, took a torch from the pocket and went to the stairs. At the bottom of the stairs, in the darkness of the garden, the bright beam of the torch lit up the muddy side of the car.

They went down the last steps.

'Goodbye,' said the officer, holding out his hand.

'Goodbye,' she answered, shaking it. And she added : 'Get in. I'll open the gate for you.'

The officer got in and started up the car. Meanwhile, the woman ran to open the gate; she needed all her strength to throw open the two sides. The car backed into the road. Then she suddenly remembered that after she had opened the gate the first time she had gone to look at the hen-run. How swollen with dignity the hen had been before love-making! And how equally swollen with dignity she had been afterwards. And how quickly she had liberated herself of love – a ruffle of the feathers and all was over. But at the same time how false that dignity had seemed to her and how contemptible the ruffling of the feathers.

She started as she heard the car move off into the night. She shut the gate, one side after the other, and made for the front door. 'With dignity and a ruffle of the feathers,' she thought as she went in.

BITTER HONEYMOON

THEY had chosen Anacapri for their honeymoon because Giacomo had been there a few months before and wanted to go back, taking his bride with him. His previous visit had been in the spring, and he remembered the clear, crisp air and the flowers alive with the hum of thousands of insects in the golden glow of the sun. But this time, immediately upon their arrival, everything seemed very different. The sultry dog-days of mid-August were upon them and steaming humidity over-clouded the sky. Even on the heights of Anacapri, there was no trace of the crisp air, of flowers or the violet sea whose praises Giacomo had sung. The paths winding through the fields were covered with a layer of yellow dust, accumulated in the course of four months without rain, in which even gliding lizards left traces of their passage. Long before autumn was due, the leaves had begun to turn red and brown, and occasional whole trees had withered away for lack of water. Dust particles filled the motionless air and made the nostrils quiver, and the odours of meadows and sea had given way to those of scorched stones and dried dung. The water, which in the spring had taken its colour from what seemed to be banks of violets floating just below the surface, was now a grey mass reflecting the melancholy, dazzling light brought by the *scirocco* which infested the sky.

'I don't think it's the least bit beautiful,' Simona said on the day after their arrival, as they started along the path to the light-house. 'I don't like it – no, not at all.'

Giacomo, following several steps behind, did not answer. She had spoken in this plaintive and discontented tone of voice ever since they had emerged from their civil marriage in Rome, and he suspected that her prolonged ill-humour, mingled with an apparent physical repulsion, was not connected so much with the place as with his own person. She was complaining about

Anacapri because she was not aware that her fundamental dissatisfaction was with her husband. Theirs was a love match to be sure, but one based rather on the will to love than on genuine feeling. There was good reason for his presentiment of trouble when, as he slipped the ring on her finger, he had read a flicker of regret and embarrassment on her face; for on their first night at Anacapri she had begged off, on the plea of fatigue and seasickness, from giving herself to him. On this, the second day of their marriage, she was just as much of a virgin as she had been before.

As she trudged wearily along, with a bag slung over one shoulder, between the dusty hedges, Giacomo looked at her with almost sorrowful intensity, hoping to take possession of her with a single piercing glance, as he had so often done with other women. But, as he realized right away, the piercing quality was lacking; his eyes fell with analytical affection upon her, but there was in them none of the transfiguring power of real passion. Although Simona was not tall, she had childishly long legs with slender thighs, rising to an indentation, almost a cleft at either side, visible under her shorts, where they were joined to the body. The whiteness of her legs were chaste, shiny, and cold, she had a narrow waist and hips, and her only womanly feature, revealed when she turned around to speak to him, was the fullness of her low-swung breasts, which seemed like extraneous and burdensome weights, unsuited to her delicate frame. Similarly her thick, blonde hair, although it was cut short, hung heavily over her neck. All of a sudden, as if she felt that she was being watched, she wheeled around and asked: 'Why do you make me walk ahead of you?'

Giacomo saw the childishly innocent expression of her big blue eyes, her small, tilted nose and equally childishly rolled-back upper lip. Her face, too, he thought to himself, was a stranger to him, untouched by love.

'I'll go ahead, if you like,' he said with resignation.

And he went by her, deliberately brushing her breast with his elbow to test his own desire. Then they went on walking, he ahead and she behind. The path wound about the summit of Monte Solaro, running along a wall of mossy stones with no masonry to hold them together and rows of vines strung out above them. On the other side there was a sheer descent, through uninhabited stretches of vineyard and olive grove, to the mist-covered grey sea. Only a solitary pine tree, half-way down the mountain, with its green crest floating in the air, recalled the idyllic purity of the landscape in its better days. Simona walked very slowly, lagging farther behind at every step. Finally she came to a halt and asked: 'Have we far to go?'

'We've only just started,' Giacomo said lightly. 'At least an hour more.'

'I can't bear it,' she said ill-humouredly, looking at him as if she hoped he would propose giving up the walk altogether. He went back to her and put his arm around her waist.

'You can't bear the exertion or you can't bear me?'

'What do you mean, silly?' she countered with unexpected feeling. 'I can't bear to go on walking, of course.'

'Give me a kiss.'

She administered a rapid peck on his cheek.

'It's so hot . . . ' she murmured. 'I wish we could go home.'

'We must get to the lighthouse,' Giacomo answered. 'What's the point of going back? . . . We'll have a swim as soon as we arrive. It's a wonderful place, and the lighthouse is all pink and white . . . Don't you want to see it?'

'Yes; but I'd like to fly there instead of walking.'

'Let's talk,' he suggested. 'That way you won't notice the distance.'

'But I have nothing to say,' she protested, almost with tears in her voice.

Giacomo hesitated for a moment before replying:

'You know so much poetry by heart. Recite a poem, and I'll listen; then before you know it, we'll be there.'

He could see that he had hit home, for she had a truly extra-ordinary memory for verse.

'What shall I recite?' she asked with childish vanity.

'A canto from Dante.'

'Which one?'

'The third canto of the *Inferno*,' Giacomo said at random.

Somewhat consoled, Simona walked on, once more ahead of him, beginning to recite:

'Per me si va nella città dolente:
per me si va nell'eterno dolore:
per me si va tra la perduta gente . . .'

She recited mechanically and with as little expression as a
schoolgirl, breathing hard because of the double effort required
of her. As she walked doggedly along, she paused at the end
of every line, without paying any attention to syntax or meaning, like a schoolgirl endowed with zeal rather than intelligence.
Every now and then she turned appealingly around and shot
him a fleeting look, yes, exactly like a schoolgirl, with the blue-
and-white cap perched on her blonde hair. After they had gone
some way they reached a wall built all around a large villa. The
wall was covered with ivy, and leafy oak branches grew out
over it.

'E caddi, come l'uom, cui sonno piglia,' Simona said, winding up the third canto; then she turned around and asked:
'Whose place is this?'

'It belonged to Axel Munthe,' Giacomo answered; 'but he's
dead now.'

'And what sort of a fellow was he?'

'A very shrewd sort indeed,' said Giacomo. And, in order to
amuse her, he added: 'He was a doctor very fashionable in
Rome at the turn of the century. If you'd like to know more
about him, there's a story I've been told is absolutely true . . .
Would you like to hear it?'

'Yes; do tell me.'

'Once a beautiful and frivolous society woman came to him
with all sorts of imaginary ailments. Munthe listened patiently,
examined her, and when he saw that there was nothing wrong,
said: "I know a sure cure, but you must do exactly what I say
. . . Go and look out of that open window and lean your elbows
on the sill." She obeyed, and Munthe went after her and gave
her a terrific kick in the rear. Then he escorted her to the door
and said: "Three times a week, and in a few months you'll be
quite all right." '

Simona failed to laugh, and after a moment she said bitterly,
looking at the wall: 'That would be the cure for me.'

Giacomo was struck by her mournful tone of voice.

'Why do you say that?' he asked, coming up to her. 'What's come into your head?'

'It's true . . . I'm slightly mad, and you ought to treat me exactly that way.'

'What are you talking about?'

'About what happened last night,' she said with startling frankness.

'But last night you were tired and seasick.'

'That wasn't it at all. I'm never seasick, and I wasn't tired, either. I was afraid, that's all.'

'Afraid of me?'

'No; afraid of the whole idea.'

They walked on in silence. The wall curved, following the path and hanging slightly over, as if it could hardly contain the oak trees behind it. Then it came to an end, and in front of them lay a grassy plateau, below which the mountainside fell abruptly down to the arid and lonely promontories of Rio. The plateau was covered with asphodels, whose pyramidal flowers were of a dusty rose, almost grey in colour. Giacomo picked some and handed them to his wife, saying: 'Look, how beautiful . . .'

She raised them to her nose, like a young girl on her way to the altar, inhaling the fragrance of a lily. Perhaps she was conscious of her virginal air, for she pressed close to him, in something like an embrace, and whispered into one ear: 'Don't believe what I just told you . . . I wasn't afraid . . . I'll just have to get used to the idea . . . Tonight . . .'

'Tonight?' he repeated.

'You're so very dear to me,' she murmured painfully, adding a strictly conventional phrase, which she seemed to have learned for the occasion, 'Tonight I'll be yours.'

She said these last words hurriedly, as if she were afraid of the conventionality rather than the substance of them, and planted a hasty kiss on his cheek. It was the first time that she had ever told Giacomo that he was dear to her or anything like it, and he was tempted to take her in his arms. But she said in a loud voice: 'Look! What's that down there on the sea?' And at the same time she eluded his grasp.

Giacomo looked in the direction at which she was pointing

and saw a solitary sail emerging from the mist that hung over the water.

'A boat,' he said testily.

She started walking again, at a quickened pace, as if she were afraid that he might try once more to embrace her. And as he saw her escape him he had a recurrent feeling of impotence, because he could not take immediate possession of his beloved.

'You won't do that to me tonight,' he muttered between clenched teeth as he caught up with her.

And she answered, lowering her head without looking around: 'It will be different tonight . . .'

It was really hot – there was no doubt about that – and in the heavy air all round them there seemed to Giacomo to reside the same obstacle, the same impossibility that bogged down his relationship with his wife; the impossibility of a rainfall that would clear the air, the impossibility of love. He had a sensation of something like panic, when looking at her again he felt that his will to love was purely intellectual and did not involve his senses. Her figure was outlined quite precisely before him, but there was none of the halo around it in which love usually envelops the loved one's person. Impulsively he said: 'Perhaps you shouldn't have married me.'

Simona seemed to accept this statement as a basis for discussion, as if she had had the same thought without daring to come out with it.

'Why?' she asked.

Giacomo wanted to answer, 'Because we don't really love each other,' but although this was the thought in his mind, he expressed it in an entirely different manner. Simona was a Communist and had a job at Party headquarters. Giacomo was not a Communist at all; he claimed to attach no importance to his wife's political ideas, but they had a way of cropping up at the most unexpected moments as underlying motives for disagreement. And now he was astonished to hear himself say: 'Because there is too great a difference of ideas between us.'

'What sort of ideas do you mean?'

'Political ideas.'

He realized, then, why her standoffishness had caused him to bring politics into the picture; it was with the hope of arousing a reaction to a point on which he knew her to be sensitive. And indeed she answered immediately: 'That's not so. The truth is that I have certain ideas and you have none at all.'

As soon as politics came up she assumed a self-sufficient, pedantic manner, quite the opposite of childish, which always threatened to infuriate him. He asked himself in all conscience whether his irritation stemmed from some latent anti-Communist feeling within himself, but quickly set his mind at rest on this score. He had no interest in politics whatsoever, and the only thing that bothered him was the fact that his wife did have such an interest.

'Well, whether or not it's a question of ideas,' he said dryly, 'there is *something* between us.'

'What is it, then?'

'I don't know, but I can feel it.'

After a second she said in the same irritating tone of voice: 'I know quite well. It *is* a question of ideas. But I hope that some day you'll see things the way I do.'

'Never.'

'Why never?'

'I've told you so many times before . . . First, because I don't want to be involved in politics of any kind, and, second, because I'm too much of an individualist.'

Simona made no reply, but in such cases her silence was direr than spoken disapproval. Giacomo was overcome by a wave of sudden anger. He overtook her and seized her arm.

'All this is going to have very serious consequences some day,' he shouted. 'For instance, if a Communist government comes to power, and I say something against it, you'll inform on me.'

'Why should you say anything against it?' she retorted. 'You just said that you don't want to be involved in politics of any kind.'

'Anything can happen.'

'And then the Communists aren't in power . . . Why worry about a situation that doesn't exist?'

It was true then, he thought to himself, since she didn't deny it, that she would inform on him. He gripped her arm tighter, almost wishing to hurt her.

'The truth is that you don't love me,' he said.

'I wouldn't have married you except for love,' she said clearly, and she looked straight at him, with her lower lip trembling. Her voice filled Giacomo with tenderness, and he drew her to him and kissed her. Simona was visibly affected by the kiss; her nostrils stiffened and she breathed hard, and although her arms hung down at her sides, she pressed her body against his.

'My spy,' he said, drawing away and stroking her face. 'My little spy.'

'Why do you call me spy?' she asked, taking immediate offence.

'I was joking.'

They walked on, but as he followed her Giacomo wondered whether he had meant the word as a joke after all. And what about his anger? Was that a joke too? He didn't know how he could have given way to such unreasonable anger and have made such even more unreasonable accusations, and yet he dimly understood that they were justified by Simona's behaviour. Meanwhile, they had come to the other side of the mountain, and from the highest point of the path they looked down at an immense expanse of air, like a bottomless well. Five minutes later they had a view of all one side of the island, a long, green slope covered with scattered vines and prickly pears, and at the bottom, stretching out into the sea, the chalky promontory on which stood the lighthouse. The sweep of the view was tremendous, and the pink-and-white checked lighthouse, hung between sky and sea, seemed far away and no larger than a man's hand. Simona clapped her hands in delight.

'How perfectly lovely!' she exclaimed.

'I told you it was beautiful, and you wouldn't believe me.'

'Forgive me,' she said, patting his cheek. 'You always know best, and I'm very silly.'

Before he could control himself, Giacomo said : 'Does that go for politics too?'

'No; not for politics. But don't let's talk about that just now.'

He was annoyed with himself for having fallen back into an argument, but at the same time he suffered a return of the left-out and jealous feeling that overcame him every time she made a dogmatic, almost religious reference to her political ideas.

'Why shouldn't we talk about it?' he said as gently as he could. 'Perhaps if we talk about it, we might understand one another better.'

Simona did not reply, and Giacomo walked on after her, in an extremely bad humour. Now he was the one to feel the heaviness and heat of the day, while Simona, intoxicated by the sight of the distant sea, shouted: 'Let's run down the rest of the way. I can't wait to get into the water.'

With her sling bag bobbing about on her shoulder, she began to run down the path, emitting shrill cries of joy. Giacomo saw that she was throwing her legs in all directions like an untrained colt. Suddenly the thought, 'Tonight she'll be mine' floated through his head and quieted him. What could be the importance of belonging to a political party in comparison to that of the act of love, so ageless and so very human? Men had possessed women long before the existence of political parties or religions. And he was sure that in the moment when he possessed Simona he would drive out of her every allegiance except that of her love for him. Strengthened by this thought he ran after her, shouting in his turn: 'Wait for me, Simona!'

She stopped to wait, flushed, quivering, and bright-eyed. As he caught up with her he said pantingly: 'Just now I began to feel very happy. I know that we're going to love one another.'

'I know it too,' she said, looking at him out of her innocent blue eyes.

Giacomo put one arm around her waist, catching her hand in his and compelling her to throw it over his shoulders. They walking on in this fashion, but Simona's eyes remained set on the water below. Giacomo, on the other hand, could not tear his thoughts away from the body he was holding so tightly. Simona was wearing a skimpy boy's jersey with a patch in the front. And her head was boyish in outline as well, with the unruly short hair falling over her cheeks. Yet her slender waist fitted into the curve of his arm with a womanly softness which seemed to foreshadow the complete surrender promised for the coming night. Suddenly he breathed into her ear: 'You'll always be my little friend and comrade.'

Simona's mind must have been on the lighthouse, and the word 'comrade' came through to her alone, out of context, without the sentimental intonation that gave it Giacomo's intended meaning. For she answered with a smile: 'We can't be comrades . . . at least, not until you see things the way I do . . . But I'll be your wife.'

So she was still thinking of the Party, Giacomo said to himself with excusable jealousy. The word 'comrade' had for her no tender connotations, but only political significance. The Party continued to have a prior claim to her loyalty.

'I didn't mean it that way,' he said disappointedly.

'I'm sorry,' she said, hastening to correct herself. 'That's what we call each other in the Party.'

'I only meant that you'd be my lifelong companion.'

'That's true,' she said, lowering her head in embarrassment, as if she couldn't really accept the word except politically.

They dropped their arms and walked down the path with no link between them. As they proceeded, the lighthouse seemed to approach them, revealing its tower shape. The water beyond it had a metallic sheen, derived from the direct rays of the sun, while behind them the mountain seemed to grow higher, with a wall of red rock rising above the lower slope which they were now traversing. At the top was a summer-house with a railing around it, in which they could distinguish two tiny human figures enjoying the view.

'That vantage-point is called La Migliara,' Giacomo explained. 'A few years ago an Anacapri girl threw herself down the mountain from it, but first she wound her braids around her head and over her eyes so as not to see what she was doing.'

Simona tossed a look over her shoulder at the top of the mountain.

'Suicide is all wrong,' she said.

Giacomo felt jealousy sting him again.

'Why?' he asked. 'Does the Party forbid it?'

'Never mind about the Party.' She looked out over the sea and thrust her face and chest forward as if to breathe in the breeze blowing in their direction. 'Suicide's all wrong because life is beautiful and it's a joy to be alive.'

Again Giacomo didn't really want to get into a political

argument; he wanted to make a show of the serenity and detachment which he thoroughly believed were his. But again his annoyance carried him away.

'But T—' (this was the name of a Communist friend they had in common) 'committed suicide, didn't he?'

'He did wrong,' she said succinctly.

'Why so? He must have had some reason. What do you know?'

'I do know, though,' she said obstinately. 'He did wrong. It's our duty to live.'

'Our duty?'

'Yes; duty.'

'Who says so?'

'Nobody. It just is.'

'I might just as well say that it's our duty to take our life if we feel it's not worth living . . . Nobody says so. It just is.'

'That's not true,' she answered inflexibly. 'We were made to live and not die . . . Only someone that's sick or in a morbid state of mind can think that life's not worth living.'

'So you think that T— was either sick or in a morbid state of mind, do you?'

'At the moment when he killed himself, yes, I do.'

Giacomo was tempted to ask her if this was the Party line, as seemed to him evident from that stubborn note in her voice which annoyed him so greatly, but this time he managed to restrain himself. By now they had reached the bottom of the slope and were crossing a dry, flat area, covered with woodspurge and prickly pears. Then the land turned into rock and they found themselves before the lighthouse, at the end of the path, which seemed like the end of all human habitation and the beginning of a new and lonely world of colourless chalk and stone. The lighthouse soared up above them as they plunged down among the boulders towards the sea. At a bend, they suddenly came upon a basin of green water, surrounded by rocky black cliffs, eroded by salt. Simona ran down to the cement landing and exclaimed: 'Wonderful! Just what I was hoping for! Now we can swim. And we have it all to ourselves. We're quite alone.'

She had no sooner spoken these words than a man's voice

came out of the rocks: 'Simona! What a pleasant surprise.'

They turned around, and when a face followed the voice, Simona shouted: 'Livio! Hello! Are you here too? What are you doing?'

The young man who emerged from the rocks was short and powerfully built, with broad shoulders. His head contrasted with his athletic body, for it was bald, with only a fringe of hair around the neck, and his flat face had a scholarly expression. The face of a ferret, Giacomo thought, taking an instant dislike to it, not exactly intelligent, but keen and treacherous. He knew the fellow by sight and was aware that he worked in Simona's office. Now Livio came into full view, pulling up his tight, faded red trunks.

'I'm doing the same thing you are, I suppose,' he said by way of an answer.

Then Simona said something which gave Giacomo considerable satisfaction.

'That's not very likely . . . Unless you've just got yourself married . . . I'm here on my honeymoon . . . Do you know my husband?'

'Yes; we know each other,' Livio said easily, jumping down on to a big square stone and shaking Giacomo's hand so hard that the latter winced with pain as he echoed: 'Yes, we've met in Rome.' Livio then turned to Simona and added: 'I'd heard something to the effect that you were about to marry. But you should have told the comrades. They want to share your joys.'

He said all this in a colourless, businesslike voice, but one which was not necessarily devoid of feeling. Giacomo noticed that Simona was smiling and seemed to be waiting for Livio to go on, while Livio stood like a bronze statue on a stone pedestal, with his trunks pulled tightly over his voluminous pubis and all the muscles of his body standing out, and talked down to them. Giacomo felt as if he were somehow left out of their conversation, and drew away, all the while listening intently. They conversed for several minutes without moving, asking one another about various Party workers and where they had spent their vacations.

But Giacomo was struck less by what they said than by the tone in which they said it. What was this tone exactly, and why did it rub him the wrong way? There was a note of complicity in it, he concluded, a reference to some secret bond different from that of either friendship or family. For a moment he wondered if it weren't just what one would find between fellow employees in a bank or government office. But upon reflection, he realized that it was entirely different. It was . . . he searched for some time, groping for an exact definition . . . it was the tone of voice of two monks or two nuns meeting one another. And why then did it rub him the wrong way? Not because he disapproved of Livio's and Simona's political ideas; in the course of a rational discussion he might very well allow that these had some basis. No; there was nothing rational about his hostility; its cause was obscure even to himself and at times it seemed to be one with his jealousy, as if he were afraid that Simona would escape him through her Party connexions. As these thoughts ran through his mind, his face grew dark and discontented, so that when Simona joined him, all smiles, a moment later, she exclaimed in surprise: 'What's wrong? Why are you unhappy?'

'Nothing. . . . It's just the heat.'

'Let's go in the water . . . But first, where can we undress?'

'Just follow me . . . This way.'

He knew the place well, and now led Simona through a narrow passage among the rocks. Behind these rocks they stepped across some other lower ones and then went around a huge mass which sealed off a tiny beach of very fine, black sand at the foot of glistening, black rocky walls around a pool of shallow water filled with black seaweed. The effect was that of a room, with the sky for a ceiling, a watery floor and walls of stone.

'No swimming-bath can match this,' Giacomo observed, looking around him.

'At last I can shed my clothes,' said Simona with a sigh of relief.

She put her bag down on the sand and bent to take out her bathing-suit, while, leaning against the rocks, Giacomo stripped himself in a second of his shirt and trousers. The sight of him stark naked caused her to give a nervous laugh.

'This is the sort of place to go swimming with no suits on, isn't it?' she said.

'Unfortunately, one can never manage to be alone,' Giacomo replied, thinking of Livio.

He walked still naked, with bare feet, over the cold sand in her direction, but she did not see him coming because she was pulling her jersey over her head. Her nakedness, he reflected, made her seem more virginal than ever. Her low-swung, round breasts had large rosy nipples, and a look of purity about them, as if they had never been offered to a masculine caress. Indeed, her virginal quality was so overwhelming that Giacomo did not dare to press her to him as he had intended, but stood close by while she pulled her head out of the jersey. She shook back her ruffled hair and said in surprise: 'What are you doing? Why don't you put on your trunks?'

'I'd like to make love right here and now,' said Giacomo.

'On these rocks? Are you mad?'

'No, I'm not mad.'

They were facing each other now, he entirely naked and she naked down to the waist. She crossed her arms over her breasts as if to support and protect them and said entreatingly: 'Let's wait till tonight . . . And meanwhile let's go swimming . . . please . . .'

'Tonight you'll put me off again.'

'No; it will be different tonight.'

Giacomo walked silently away and proceeded to put on his trunks, while Simona, obviously relieved, hastily donned her two-piece suit. She shouted gaily; 'I'm off for a swim! If you love me, you'll follow.'

'Let's go in right here,' Giacomo suggested.

Simona paused and stuck her white foot into the green and brown seaweed that choked the black water.

'This pool is too murky . . . It's no more than a puddle. Let's go where we just came from.'

'But we shan't be alone.'

'Oh, we have plenty of time for that.'

They went back to the basin, where Livio was taking a sun-bath on the cement landing, lying as still as if he were dead. Somehow this increased Giacomo's dislike of him. Yes; he was the sort of fellow that goes in for purposeful tanning, and then wanders about showing it off, wearing skimpy trunks designed to exhibit his virility as well. When Livio heard them coming he leaped to his feet and said: 'Come on, Simona. Let's dive in and race over to that rock.'

'You'll have to give me a handicap of at least a length,' she said joyfully, forgetful of her husband.

'I'll give you three lengths, if you say so.'

There it was, Giacomo could not help thinking, the same intimate, conspiratorial, clubby, Party manner, that tone of voice in which, despite their marriage, she had never spoken to him, and perhaps never would speak either. Sitting on a flat rock, just above the landing, he watched his wife plunge awkwardly in and then swim like a dark shadow under the green water until she came out, with her blonde head dripping.

'That was a real belly-flop,' Livio shouted, making a perfect dive to join her. He too swam underwater, but for a longer distance than Simona, so that he came out further away. Giacomo wondered if this 'Party manner' weren't all a product of his imagination, and if there hadn't been in the past some more intimate personal relationship between them. And he realized that this second hypothesis was, on the whole, less disagreeable than the first. Then he said to himself that if he were to mention any such suspicion to Simona she would be outraged and brand it utterly 'bourgeois', not to say 'evil-minded and filthy'. The moment after he dismissed it as out of the question. No, they were comrades, as she had said, and nothing more. What still puzzled him was why he objected more to their being Party comrades than to their being lovers. With a wavering effort of goodwill, he said to himself that his jealousy was absurd, and he must drive it out of his mind . . . And all the while he watched the two of them race across the dazzling green water in the direction of a round rock which emerged at the far end of the basin. Livio got there first, and, hoisting himself up on a protruding spur, shouted back at Simona: 'I win! You're all washed up!'

'Speak for yourself!' Simona retorted.

This was the sort of joking insult he and Simona should have batted back and forth between them, Giacomo reflected. If they didn't joke that way on their honeymoon, when would they ever do it? He got up decisively, ran several steps along the landing and went in after them. He landed square on his stomach and was infuriated by the pain. After swimming several strokes under water he came up and started towards the rock where Livio and Simona were sitting. They were close together, talking uninterruptedly, with their legs dangling. He didn't relish the sight; in fact, it took away all the pleasure he should have felt from plunging hot and dusty into the cool water. He swam angrily ahead, arrived at the rock breathless and said, hanging on to a ledge: 'Do you know, this water's very, very cold.'

'It seemed warm to me,' said Simona, momentarily interrupting her conversation to shoot him a glance.

'I swam here in April,' Livio put in; 'it was cold then, I can tell you.'

With a curiosity that seemed to Giacomo somewhat flirtatious, Simona asked him: 'Were you all alone?'

'No. I came with Nella,' Livio answered.

Giacomo was trying to clamber up on the rock, but the only place where he could get a solid grip was the one where Livio and Simona were sitting. They seemed to be oblivious of his struggles and he preferred not to ask them to move over. Finally, he caught hold of a jutting piece of the rock studded with jagged points, one of which left a pain in the palm of his hand as if it had dug deep into the flesh. Just as he got himself into a sitting position, the other two, with a shout of 'Let's race back!' dived into the water, showering him with spray. He looked furiously after them as they raced towards the shore. Only when he had regained his self-control did he plunge in and follow. Simona and Livio were sitting in the shelter of a cliff and Simona was opening a lunch-box that she had taken out of her bag.

'Let's have something to eat,' she said to Giacomo as he approached them. 'But we must share it with Livio. He says he meant to go back up the mountain, but in this heat it would be too ridiculous.'

Without saying a word, Giacomo sat down in the rocks beside them. The contents of the lunch-box turned out to be scanty: some meat sandwiches, two hard-boiled eggs and a bottle of wine.

'Livio will have to be content with very little,' Giacomo said gruffly.

'Don't worry,' Livio answered gaily. 'I'm a very abstemious fellow.'

Simona seemed extremely happy as she sat with crossed legs, dividing the lunch. She gave a sandwich to each one of them, bit into her own, and asked Livio:

'Where did you get your tan?'

'On the Tiber,' he replied.

'Your whole group is very river-minded, isn't it, Livio?' she asked between one bite and another.

'All except Regina. She scorns the river completely; says it isn't aristocratic enough for her.'

The things they talked about were trivial and childish enough, Giacomo reflected. And yet there was a greater intimacy between them than between husband and wife.

'No matter how hard she tries, Regina will never be able to put her background behind her,' Simona observed.

'Who is Regina?' asked Giacomo.

'Someone in our outfit . . . the daughter of a wealthy landowner . . . a very fine girl, really,' Livio told him. 'But wiping out an old trade-mark is no easy matter.'

'And in this case, what trade-mark do you mean?'

'The bourgeois trade-mark.'

'If you people ever get into power,' Giacomo said impulsively, 'you'll have to wipe that trade-mark out of millions of people.'

'That's exactly what we'll do,' Livio said with complete self-confidence. 'That's our job, isn't it, Simona?'

Simona's mouth was full, but she nodded assent.

'The Italian bourgeoise will be a tough nut to crack,' Livio went on, 'but we'll crack it, even if we have to kill off a large proportion in the process.'

'There's a chance you may be killed off yourselves,' said Giacomo.

'That's the risk we have to run in our profession,' Livio retorted.

Giacomo noticed that Simona did not seem to go along with Livio's ruthlessness; at this last remark she frowned and uttered no word of approval. Livio must have been aware of this, for he brusquely changed the subject.

'Simona, you really should have told us you were getting married, you know. There are some things it's not fair to hide!'

There was a note of tenderness towards Giacomo in Simona's reply.

'We decided from one day to the next . . . Only the legal witnesses were present. Even our own parents weren't in on it.'

'You mean you didn't want them?'

'We didn't want them, and anyhow they might not have come . . .Giacomo's father and mother didn't want him to marry me.'

'Because you're too far to the left, is that it?'

'No,' Giacomo interposed. 'My people don't go in for politics at all. But my mother had her eye on a certain girl . . .'

'They may not go in for politics, as you say,' Livio said, after another mouthful, 'but there are always political implications. How could it be otherwise? Politics gets into everything these days.'

True enough, Giacomo thought to himself. Even into honeymoons and a newly-married couple's first embrace. Then, annoyed at his own train of thought, he held out the hard-boiled eggs to his companions.

'You two eat them,' he said. 'I'm not hungry.'

'Be honest now,' Livio said with a look of surprise on his face.

'Why aren't you hungry?' Simona asked him.

'That damned *scirocco*, I imagine.'

Livio looked up at the cloudy sky.

'There'll be a storm before night. I can promise you that,' he said.

Livio's conversation was made up of commonplaces and clichés, Giacomo reflected. But Simona seemed to like them. They conveyed more to her than his own attempts to express emotions that were difficult if not impossible to put into words. Meanwhile Simona, having finished her lunch, said: 'Let's lie down for a sun-bath now.'

'Will you be my pillow, Simona?' Livio asked, sliding towards her with the plain intention of putting his head on her lap.

For the first time Simona took her husband's presence into account.

'It's too hot for that, and you're too heavy.'

And she looked at Giacomo out of the corner of her eyes as if to say: From now on, I won't let anyone do that but you. Giacomo's spirits soared, and he once more felt that there was a possibility of love between them. He got up and said: 'Shall we go for a walk among the rocks?'

'Yes,' she said promptly, following his example. And she added, to Livio: 'See you later . . . We're going to explore.'

'Have a good time,' Livio threw after them.

Simona led the way through the passage which her husband had shown her before. She made straight for the black beach, sat down at the foot of a rock and said: 'Stretch out and put your head on my legs. . . . You'll be more comfortable that way.'

Overcome by joy, Giacomo threw his arms around her and drew her to him. He gave her a kiss, and Simona returned it, blowing hard through her nose, almost as if she were suffering. When they had drawn apart, she repeated: 'Stretch out, and we'll snatch a bit of sleep together.'

She leaned her back against the rock, and Giacomo, his heart overflowing with love, lay down and put his head on her lap. He closed his eyes, and Simona began to stroke his face. With a hesitant and timid motion, she passed her hand over his cheeks, under his chin and up to the top of his head, where she ran her fingers through his hair. When Giacomo opened his eyes for a split second he saw that she was looking at him with childish intentness and curiosity. Meeting his glance, she bent over, placed a quick kiss on each of his eyes and told him to go to sleep. Giacomo closed his eyes again and gave himself up to enjoyment of the light touch of her tireless little hand until finally he dozed off. He slept for an indefinable length of time and woke up feeling chilled. Simona was sitting in the same position, with his head on her lap. Looking up, he saw the reason for his feeling so cold. The sky was filled with heavy, black storm clouds.

'How long have I been asleep?' he asked her.

'About an hour.'

'And what about you?'

'I didn't sleep. I was looking at you.'

'The sun's disappeared.'

'Yes.'

'There's going to be quite a rainstorm.'

'Livio's gone,' she said by way of an answer.

'Who is that Livio, anyhow?' Giacomo asked without moving.

'A Party comrade, a friend.'

'I don't care for him.'

'I know that,' she said with a smile. 'You made it pretty plain. As he was going away he pointed to you as you lay there asleep and said: "What's the matter? Has he got it in for me?".'

'I haven't got it in for him. . . . But he has no manners. I'm on my honeymoon, and he acts as if it were his.'

'He's a good fellow.'

'You used to be in love with him. Admit it!'

She came out with a peel of innocent, silvery laughter.

'You must be crazy. I couldn't possibly fall in love with him. He doesn't appeal to me in the least.'

'But the way you talked to one another . . .'

'He's a Party comrade,' she repeated, 'and that's the way we talk.' She was silent, for a moment, and then said with unexpected bitterness: 'He's unintelligent. That's why he doesn't appeal to me.'

'He doesn't seem to me much more stupid than the next man.'

'He said a lot of foolish things,' she went on angrily. 'That we'd kill people off, for instance . . . He knows better and spoke that way just to show off . . . But such loose talk is harmful to the Party.'

'You're the one that's got it in for him now.'

'No. I haven't got it in for him; but he had no business to talk that way.' Then she added, more coolly, 'As a matter of fact, he's of value to the Party, even if he isn't too bright. He's absolutely loyal; you could ask him to do anything.'

'And what value have I?' Giacomo was bold enough to ask jokingly.

'You can't have any value, since you're not one of us.'

Giacomo was displeased by the answer. He got up and looked at the lowering sky.

'We'd better get back home before it rains. What do you say?'

'Yes. I think we had better.'

Giacomo hesitated for a moment, put his arm around her waist and asked softly: 'When we get there, will you be mine . . . at last?'

She nodded, turning her head away in order not to meet his eyes. Feeling easier in his mind, Giacomo quickly got dressed. A few steps away, Simona pulled on her shorts and jersey and started to adjust her bag over her shoulder. But with a tender protectiveness such as he had not displayed on the way down, Giacomo said: 'I'll carry that for you.'

They started off. First they crossed the flatland, where the pale green branches of the prickly pears seeemed to gleam discordantly against the dark sky. As they reached the beginning of the slope they turned around to look behind them. The pink-and-white lighthouse stood out against a majestic mass of black storm clouds rising from the horizon to invade that part of the sky which was still empty. These clouds, shaped like great rampant beasts, had smoking underbellies, and irregular fringes hung down from them over the sea, which was spottily darkening in some places, while in others it still shone like burnished lead in the sun. The fringes were gusts of rain, just beginning to comb the surface of the water. Meanwhile, a turbulent wind covered the prickly pears with yellow dust and a blinding stroke of lightning zigzagged diagonally across the sky from one point to another. After a long silence they heard the thunder – no clap, but rather a dull rumble within the clouds. Giacomo saw his wife pale and instinctively shrink towards him.

'Lightning scares me to death,' she said, looking at him.

Giacomo raised his eyes to the half-clear, half-stormy sky.

'The storm isn't here yet,' he said. 'It's still over the sea. If we hurry, we may get home without a wetting.'

'Let's hurry, then,' she said, continuing to climb up the path.

The clouds, apparently driven by an increasingly powerful wind, were spreading out over the sky with startling rapidity.

Simona quickened her pace to almost a run, and Giacomo could not help teasing her.

'Afraid of lightning? What would the comrades say to that? A good Marxist like yourself shouldn't have any such fear.'

'It's stronger than I am,' she said in a childish voice, without turning around.

There were steps, first narrow and then wide, to facilitate the ascent of the lower part of the path, and higher up it rose in wide curves through groves of olive trees. Simona was a long way ahead; Giacomo could see her striding along fifty or sixty feet in front of him. At the top they paused to catch their breath and look around. Anacapri, momentarily at their backs, stood reassuringly behind a barrier of green, looking like an Arab city, with its terraces, campanile, and grey-domed church. Giacomo pointed to the shrunken lighthouse on the promontory below, profiled against the threatening storm.

'Just think, we were right down there!' he murmured.

'I can't wait to be home,' said Simona, perhaps with the thunder and lightning in mind. Then, meeting Giacomo's eyes, she added with hesitant coquetry: 'What about you?'

'I agree,' he answered in a low voice, with emotion.

The climb was over, and all they had to do now was follow the level path to their rented house, which was well this side of Anacapri. They walked by the wall around the Munthe villa, along a meadow planted with oak trees, and there, just round a bend, was the white wall of their house and the rusty iron gate in the shade of a carob tree with pods hanging all over it. The clouds were straight above them now, and it was as dark as evening. Simona hurriedly pushed open the gate and went on ahead without waiting for her husband to follow. Giacomo walked more slowly down the marble steps among the cactus plants. As he went, there was another rumble of thunder, louder this time, like an overturned wagon-load of stones rolling down a hill. From inside the house Simona called back: 'Shut the door tight!'

The house was on a hillside, set back amongst the trees, and consisted of four roughly furnished rooms. Giacomo made his way in amid almost complete darkness. There was no electric light, but oil lamps of various shapes and colours were lined up on the hall table. He lifted the glass off one of these, lit a match, touched it to the wick, put back the glass and entered the dining-room. No one was there, but he could hear Simona moving in the room next to it. He did not wish to join her immediately, and feeling thirsty, he poured himself out a glass of white wine. Finally, he picked up the lamp and went to the bedroom door. The bedroom, too, was almost dark. The window giving on to the garden was open, and through it, in what light was left among the shadows, he could make out the terrace surrounded by lemon trees planted in big pots. Simona, in a dressing-gown, was tidying the still unmade bed. He set the lamp down on the bedside table and said: 'Are you still afraid of the lightning?'

She was leaning over the bed, with one leg slightly raised, smoothing the sheet. Pulling herself up, she answered: 'No. Now that I'm in the house I feel safer.'

'And are you afraid of me?'

'I never was afraid of you.'

Giacomo walked around the bed and took her into his arms. Standing beside the head of the bed, they exchanged a kiss. Giacomo undid the sash of Simona's dressing-gown and it slipped down over her shoulders and hips to the floor. But Simona did not interrupt the kiss; indeed she prolonged it with an awkward eagerness, betrayed by her characteristic way of blowing through her nose. With sudden decisiveness, Giacomo let her go.

'Lie down, will you?' he said, hurriedly taking off his clothes.

Simona hesitated and then lay down on the bed. Giacomo was aware of being impelled by strictly animal feelings, as if he were not in a house, but in a dark cave – yes, as if he were a primitive man, moved by carnal appetite alone. Yet it was with a certain tenderness that he lay down beside his wife. She was facing the wall, but brusquely she turned around and pressed herself against him, snuggling into his arms. For a few minutes they lay there, motionless, then Giacomo began chastely and gently to caress her. He wanted to possess her on her own virginal terms, without bringing any of his masculine experience into play. His light caresses and the words he whispered through her hair into one ear were intended to calm her fears and lead her almost insensibly to give herself to him. He was not in a hurry and it seemed to him that his new policy of consideration and patience would win for him what his haste of the previous evening had failed to obtain. And by degrees he had the impression that, in response to his words and caresses, she was yielding not only her body, but also that inward part of her which had resisted him heretofore. Simona did not speak, but her breathing grew gradually heavier. All of a sudden, almost involuntarily, he gave way to a natural impulse and attempted to take her. Under the impact of his body, Simona seemed at first to surrender, then brusquely she rebelled and struggled to free herself. With a mixture of anger and submission she whispered: 'I can't do it! I can't!'

Giamoco refused to heed her change of heart and tried to prevail over her by force. She defended herself with her feet and knees and hands, while he did everything to overcome her. In the combat their naked bodies were bathed in sticky perspiration. Finally Giacomo lost his patience, leaped out of bed, and went into the bathroom, saying: 'I'll be back in a minute.'

Guided by a furious inspiration, he groped his way to the wash basin, took the razor blade he had used for shaving that morning and plunged it into the cushion of his thumb. He felt the cold blade cut through his skin, but had no pain. Then he put the blade back on the shelf and squeezed his thumb, which gave out an abundant flow of blood. He went back to the bedroom and threw himself upon his wife, rubbing his bloody thumb on the sheet between her legs. Then he shouted angrily: 'You may not realize it, but you're no longer a virgin!'

Trembling she asked: 'How do you know?'

'Just look!'

He took the lamp from the table and threw its light upon the bed. Simona was hunched up on the pillow, with her knees against her chin and her arms crossed over breasts. She looked down at the place where Giacomo had thrown the light and saw a long streak of red blood. Batting her eyelids in disgust, she said: 'Are you sure?'

'Positive!'

But just at that moment her eyes travelled to the hand in which Giacomo was holding the lamp. Blood was streaming out of the cut in the cushion of this thumb. In a plaintive voice she cried out: 'It's not my blood. It's yours! . . . You cut yourself on purpose.'

Giacomo put the lamp back on the table and shouted in a rage: 'That's the only blood I'll see tonight or any night to come. You're still a virgin and you always will be!'

'Why do you say that? What makes you so unkind?'

'That's the way it is,' he answered. 'You'll never be mine. Some part of you is hostile to me, and hostile it will remain.'

'What part do you mean?'

'You're closer to that fool, Livio, than you are to me,' he said, coming out with his jealousy at last. 'That part of you which is close to Livio is hostile to me.'

'That's not true.'

'Yes; it is true. And it's equally true that if your Party came to power you'd inform on me . . .'

'Who says so?'

'You said so yourself this morning, on the way to the lighthouse.'

'I said nothing at all.'

'Well, what would you do, then?'

She hesitated for a moment and then said:

'Why do you bring up such things at a time like this?'

'Because they prevent you from loving me and becoming my wife.'

'I wouldn't inform on you,' she said at last. 'I'd leave you, that's all.'

'But you're supposed to inform on your enemies,' he shouted, angrier than ever. 'It's your duty.'

Still huddled up at the head of the bed, she burst into tears.

'Giacomo, why are you so unkind? . . . I'd kill myself. That's what I'd do.'

Giacomo did not have the courage to remind her that on the way to the lighthouse she had branded suicide as morbid and absolutely inadmissible. After all, this contradiction was more flattering to him than an open declaration of love. Meanwhile, still in tears, she had got down from the bed and gone over to the open window. Giacomo lay on the bed, watching. She stood straight, with her head bent to the side and one arm raised against the frame. Suddenly the room was lit up, and every object in it, her naked, white body, the garden and the potted lemon trees around the terrace. There followed a metallic crack and a violent tremor which made the window and the walls of the room tremble. Simona gave a terrified cry, left the window and threw herself sobbing into her husband's arms. Giacomo pressed her to him, and almost immediately, while, still weeping, she sought his embrace, he penetrated her body without any difficulty whatsoever. He had the feeling that a hidden flower, composed of only two petals, had opened – although still remaining invisible – to something that in the dark night of the flesh played the role of the sun. Nothing was settled, he reflected later on, but for the time being it was enough to know that she would kill herself for him.